THE CHINA EGG
AND OTHER STORIES

Brought together in one volume, these stories, both old and new, underline Gillian Tindall's acute powers of observation and her ability to take an important theme and to develop it effectively within the confines of a short story. The title story is on one level a simple one: a well-to-do British couple go to India to find a baby to adopt. But much more is going on besides. It is a story about Anglo-Indian relations, about sexual and other forms of obsession, about the inadequacy of twentieth century rationality, but first and foremost it is about a daydream: the wish for a child.

THE CHINA EGG

EGG

and other stories

Gillian Tindall

A Lythway Book

**CHIVERS PRESS
BATH**

First published 1981
by
Hodder & Stoughton Limited
This Large Print edition published by
Chivers Press
by arrangement with
Hodder & Stoughton Limited
and in the U.S.A. with Curtis Brown Ltd
1982

ISBN 0 85119 867 8

British Library Cataloguing in Publication Data

Tindall, Gillian
    The China egg and other stories.—
    Large print ed.—(A Lythway book)
    I. Title
    823'.914[F]   PR6070.I/

    ISBN 0–85119–867–8

CONTENTS

ACKNOWLEDGMENTS

Golden Girl was first published in *Women's Journal* in 1974; Bloody Bad Luck, Really in the *Jewish Chronicle* in 1974; The Thought That Counts in the *New Statesman* in 1973; Winter's Tale in *Encounter* in 1977 and The Other Railway Children in *Encounter* in 1979.

THE CHINA EGG

GOLDEN GIRL

I hadn't seen Jenny for over ten years so, as the prospect of meeting again actually came near, I began to get quite excited. Not that I'd really thought of her all that often since we'd last met in Cadogan Gardens in another decade and another phase of life. Even in the early days after she'd disappeared from Chelsea and from my world, when she did slip into my mind I'd just register fondly, Dear old Jenny; and pigeonhole her at once into a compartment comprehensively labelled *South of France* which she shared with improbably blue seas, vines and olives (rather vaguely visualised), bougainvillaeas, cicadas, and the horde of people at any one moment away, the lucky beggars. But there was this quick, warm, permanent glow round her name which, as the years clattered by, did not evaporate but grew, if anything, a little more intense and, in a small way, golden.

I had always, I used to tell myself at long intervals, been very fond of Jenny. And I suppose at these times I gave the general impression—to Madeleine, to myself, to anyone who might be around—that Jenny was the Other Girl I Might Have Married, that indispensable nostalgic accessory to any fulfilled existence.

Actually, though, around 1960, when Jenny

and I and people like Andy and Tim and Debo were lording it as the immediate descendants of the Chelsea Set, I didn't have the faintest intention of marrying anyone. I was having far too good a time, and anyway I was a lot poorer than Andy and Tim and the rest of them. Without exactly thinking the matter out in the traditional coldblooded monster fortune-hunter manner, I believe I was pretty clear in my own mind even then that, if I ever did get married, it would have to be to someone well-heeled herself if we were either of us going to be happy. (Which, of course, I have.) Jenny wasn't totally penniless, I think, but her father had been a lord who compounded his general incompetence by dying less than five years after he'd inherited the title from *his* father, so a double dose of death duties had removed most of the spare loot from that family before I ever met Jenny.

When I first got to know her she was living with her widowed ma in a flat in Cadogan Gardens just being a Girl About Town, as the press used to call it: girls could still be that, in those quaintly remote days, without having to pretend to be just about to get a job, or be training for something unsuitable and timewasting, like social work or art. But as her ma shortly took it into her head to marry a hideous American millionaire, Jenny upped and offed from Cadogan Gardens to a little flat of her own in Oakley Crescent, where she used to sit

2

making clothes for her friends out of lengths of curtain material. I used to stay there sometimes when I was without a permanent base myself, and once she made me a shirt as a birthday present. It was pretty unwearable actually—that was before men could dress up as John the Baptist without being regarded as either wet or queer—but I thought, as I still think, that that was one of the sweetest things anyone has ever done for me.

She was like that, Jenny—she had lovely ideas. She could be boring too, of course, and demanding, and she had a perfectly maddening habit—almost a neurosis—of not wanting to go on a trip that had been arranged when it came to the point. We'd have some great scheme for a day in Oxford looking up mates, with a grand eat at the Trout in the middle of it, and Jenny would say, 'Super, darling, simply super—I'm longing for it,' and her eyes really would shine, too; she wouldn't be putting it on. And then, when I turned up on the morning, after infinite sweat and borrowing a car from Tim or someone, feeling pleased with myself and keen on Jenny, there she would be not even dressed, just sitting round with whoever had wandered in, drinking coffee and playing records, and there she'd go on sitting till I almost had to force her to get ready and boot the other people out. By that time I'd be in a bad temper, feeling a fool, and then she'd go softly reproachful and

I'd feel worse, because actually people who are enjoying whatever they're doing at the moment too much to want to stop it are just much *nicer* than people like me who are always bent on getting to places on time, and making it, and various other obsessions. I, and other people, used to lecture Jenny about her indecision, telling her that when the time came she'd tell some poor devil she was longing to marry him and then fail to turn up at the church. But of course we were wrong.

The other thing I had against Jenny—really, the only other thing—is that she wasn't too choosy about whom she went to bed with. I daresay that sounds an old-fashioned complaint today. But I thought, and still think, that a lot of the people she went round with weren't good enough for her. Like many really nice people she was not much of a judge of character and, in spite of quite a sophisticated line of chat, she was endlessly gullible. She was also—like, I suppose, her defunct lordly parent—somewhat incompetent. I myself saw her through two abortions, and that was no joke in those Dark Ages when it meant canvassing your mates for an address in deathly secrecy and then a trip to some hidden crematorium in Barnet or Herne Hill. But there was absolutely no vice in Jenny; and, as I said, I was very fond of her.

*   *   *

4

In 1962, it must have been, I finally joined Tim's father's company and spent a year rotting in Frankfurt learning the trade. I was homesick and felt as if I had suddenly become invisible. I used to write to Jenny quite often—chatty, jokey letters, naturally, nothing about how really fed up I was; the pattern of our relationship had always been that she confided in me but not me, much, in her. And the funny thing was that her letters back to me used to be full of wistful Darling-Tony-I-do-wish-I-could-see-you sort of thing, even though odd scraps of information in them seemed to indicate that she was actually leading a pretty gay life much as usual. Perhaps she really did miss me; perhaps she needed me, or someone, more than I'd ever thought... I'll never know. By and by her letters tailed off. I wasn't surprised; she never had been much of a correspondent. But I *was* put out when, not having heard from her for months, I came back to London in the spring of 1963, after the worst winter in Europe for a hundred years, and heard on the grapevine that she'd actually got herself engaged while my back was turned to a lawyer in the South of France. A Frenchman, naturally. The image of Yves Montand, I bet, I thought sourly.

After a few days I got sick of nursing my injured dignity alone, and went round to look for her in Cadogan Gardens where she was apparently roosting briefly before taking off again for France and her new life; everything seemed to be happening very quickly. I wondered glumly if she were in the pudding club again and thought it served her right; she should have listened to me!

But when she opened the door to me she didn't look pregnant but just more beautiful and sparkling than ever—golden hair, blue eyes, lovely crooked smile, funny breathy voice.

'You monster,' I said crossly, but with my crossness already melting at the sight of her. 'You might have told your old Uncle Tony. You really might.'

'Oh, darling Tony,' she said, flinging her arms round my neck and looking at me tragically. 'I tried and tried and I simply *couldn't*. I kept writing letters and then tearing them up. But then when I heard from Tim that you were coming home I *did* write—didn't you get it?'

'No. You must have posted it too late. You know what you're like . . . Anyway, out with it: who is he, where did you meet him, when's the wedding—I want the whole sordid story.'

Actually there wasn't much to tell. In the worst of the winter Jenny had got pneumonia and had been sent to recover in the South of France, the one then-habitable rim of icebound Europe. There she had rapidly met, in some way I never did discover, a French lawyer with

6

what that vulgar crone her mother described as
'a Riviera practice'. She fell in love with him,
with France, with Roman Catholicism, with
everything. And that was that.

Strange as it seems now, I was both impressed
and jealous. In spite of the cosmopolitan airs I
was giving myself after my grim sojourn in
Germany, I had travelled abroad very little in
those days, never having had any money. My
image of that never-never-land known as 'the
South of France' was extremely vague,
geographically. I didn't know Cannes from
Toulon, Nice from St Tropez and merely had a
concentrated conglomerate image of a small
strip of coastline with villas half-hidden in olive
groves under an unending sun. Lucky old
Jenny, I thought ruefully: it seemed an ideal
setting for her.

Her wedding—quite a small one, the family
being excessively mean—was at the end of May
but, for some reason I now can't fully grasp, I
didn't go to it. I know that by that time the
company was sending me to New York and no
doubt that was why I said I couldn't turn up at
the Brompton Oratory, but as a reason it now
seems inadequate. I suppose I just didn't much
want to be there, really. I think I didn't want to
meet her Maître de Loubet just yet, or at least
not in that setting, being afraid of both liking
him and of not liking him. Anyway, I couldn't
stand her mother who had always disapproved

of my influence on Jenny because she thought I was 'flighty' and would 'lead her astray'—how wrong she was. So I made sure she was out when I made a quick descent on Jenny just before I went to New York, to say goodbye and to give her my wedding present. It was a lovely day which made that lugubrious Cadogan Gardens lair seem darker than usual, and Jenny came towards me through the dimness and the plush armchairs wearing a white dress and looking like a princess.

I plonked my present in her hands—it was some pot or other, I forget what; it was on the list with Harrods—and then said, 'What's all this about him being a Master, then? Master of what—apart from you? Sounds very medieval; you'd better watch it or he'll start beating you.'

She laughed and said, 'Oh, Tony, you never know anything. *Maître* is what French lawyers are called.'

Well, it sounded grandish to me, though I wouldn't let on, and I expect it did to her, too. We were both pretty young still, and neither of us really knew much about anything, except restaurants and abortionists. Certainly nothing about marriage and time passing and things being for ever. She told me how her Phillipe's family home was on a heavenly hill covered with olives just outside a little town and how everybody in the place knew his family, and I, too, thought it sounded pretty good in a feudal

8

sort of way. I could see Jenny as a châtelaine and told her so, adding that I was sure a procession of knights errant would wind their way past her tower so she'd better watch it that her Master didn't get jealous.

And she opened her eyes wide and said sincerely, 'Oh gosh, there's not going to be any of *that*.'

What a pity, I thought, already nostalgic for what had, without warning, become the past, holding her to me there in that dim, monstrous drawing room.

Suddenly, now when it was too late and she was an inaccessible princess belonging to a fierce foreigner and not Jenny sitting on the floor in Oakley Crescent in her nightdress, I wanted her very much. We had slept together a couple of times, actually, but neither occasion had been a great success. My fault, probably.

Anyway, she wrote down her address for me on the Z sheet torn off her mother's telephone pad; it stayed in my wallet for years, a reminder of her loopy writing: *Mme de Loubet, La Treille, Beaucaire, par Marseille*. I told her I would certainly be looking her up, and I meant it, having hazy but pleasant visions of future holidays in her house when I'd got used to the idea of her as Madame de Loubet.

And she said, 'Oh darling, do—I shall miss you dreadfully, all of you.' But she said it gaily, insulated from any real sense of goodbye by the idea of her brand new, shining life which enveloped her like a protective aura.

After leaving Cadogan Gardens I was miserable for an hour or two but not, I must admit, for much more. I did mind, when I thought about it, but—well, there were a lot of other things in life, including other girls. I really did mean to visit her pretty soon, but I spent the rest of that summer and autumn in the States and didn't come back to England till the following year.

For several Christmases I sent Jenny a card, and for the first two she sent one back, scribbled with love and promises to look me up next time she came to London. But after that she didn't send cards any longer, so in the end neither did I. Why should she come to London anyway? I thought. She was no doubt happy where she was and up to her old trick of not wanting to move.

$\star$ $\star$ $\star$

About ten years went by. I got older, considerably richer and married, and, though life was good, there was never quite enough time for anything any more. I was actually in the South of France several times in the years immediately after Jenny's wedding, but twice I was just passing through on my way to Italy or Greece or somewhere, and once I was at St Tropez with a girl called Leila and a descent on

10

Jenny didn't seem, in the circumstances, appropriate.

Then I got married and the next year we had Sebastian and the year after Emma and Sophie, and by that time St Trop and other similar necks of the wood seemed crowded and faintly squalid and just not our style any more. When Madeleine and I go to France now, either with or without the children and their attendants, we usually stay in friends' houses, not on the coast but up in Provence in the hills, or the Dordogne where a lot of people we know have bought property recently. All jolly nice and comfy and fabulous food and scenery, even if otherwise it is just a bit like being at home in Wiltshire.

So, one way or another, it wasn't till last summer, in June, that the opportunity I had been half-awaiting for years came, and I found myself south of Lyon with an appointment in Marseilles, but not till the following morning, and Jenny's address still tucked in my wallet like an old love letter or a never-used French one. And I knew the moment had come to pay that call. To be more exact, I had known two weeks earlier that this would probably be *the* opportunity and had scribbled a quick letter from my office in London warning her I might be coming, but until I was actually *there*, driving down the autoroute past the turn-offs for Valence and Avignon, the reality of the situation

11

didn't hit me. When it did, as I say, I began to get really excited.

By this time, my knowledge of French geography had got a good deal better than it had been in the days when the South of France had simply meant the Corniche road between Nice and Cannes. I knew, for instance, that Marseilles is the other end of the coast and that, strictly speaking, that bit isn't the Côte d'Azur at all but the Bouches du Rhône. In fact Beaucaire, when I looked it up on the map, turned out to be right in the middle of the estuary. But the implications of this didn't strike home. After all, there are several Riviera-ish places up that end: Toulon, Bandol. My fixed image of Jenny's life did not even begin to waver.

I got the bit of paper out of my wallet to check the address, though I did not really need to. La Treille: this pretty name had always conjured up for me a vineyard not as it really is, low and green and rather dull, but as I used to imagine it from the Scripture lessons at school—a paved place with vines hanging from above as in an arbour. I managed to superimpose this image on to one based slightly more on reality, in fact all those provençal and Périgordine châteaux and farmhouses owned by our friends, with their medieval pigeon-lofts and ruined towers.

Altogether, my picture of La Treille was pretty good, and as I peeled off the kilometres down the southbound lane everything else seemed pretty good too: the endless blue sky above, the songs on the radio, the rush of wind in my ears (I had the top of the Merc. off), the scent of pine forests, the stalls by the road selling olive oil and early peaches when I got off the autoroute, even the little place where I stopped for lunch, with clean paper on the tables and a bog out in the garden. When I'm with Madeleine we usually stick to caffs in the Michelin guide, but I like these little places when I'm on my own. It's as if they remind me of something I've forgotten and can't quite remember, or of something known in another life or at second hand and only seized again fleetingly and incompletely.

Beaucaire, when I finally reached it around three in the afternoon, was, I must admit, rather a shock. This elegant name—I had vaguely envisaged somewhere like Sarlat, or one of those medieval hill-towns—turned out to hide a straggling, dusty small-town-grown-slightly-larger, separated only by a sleazy-coloured channel of the Rhône from a precisely similar place on the opposite bank. In the course of a decade with Chemik Inc. I have developed a fair familiarity with the surroundings of industry, and I can therefore state one fact with depressing certainty: Beaucaire, whatever it may once have been, is today an industrial dump.

I made up my mind that La Treille must be,

as it sounded, a large property, probably several kilometres from the town itself.

The first filling station at which I stopped to get directions had never heard of it. The next said that it must be on the other side of the town since that was where all the 'nice houses' were. I didn't think this was the right track but I drove there, and eventually reached what was an obviously expanding residential suburb. There were the remains of olive groves but they were abandoned, the trees wilting greyly into the white dust, while there sprouted instead boards saying: *Lotissements* and *Terrain à Bâtir* and *Pavillons de Luxe*. There were lots of *pavillons* already there, stark little villas with bright red roofs and mock-Moorish ironwork at the windows, each in its shrivelled patch of garden, and also a few older houses cowering within rather shadier gardens as if in resentment at the new buildings. Nothing here anyway, I thought, looking round for someone I could ask about La Treille before I drove away again, though in pointless suburbs like that no one knows anything about the surrounding country anyway.

Then suddenly I saw La Treille itself. There was no mistaking it. The name was clearly marked on a board by the locked iron gates, which also bore the notice *Chien Méchant*— Beware of the Dog. It was one of the older houses—perhaps the oldest; there was no way of

14

telling. It was fairly large and looked moderately pleasant and comfortable, though dusty and rather shabby and overlooked by its neighbours. But it was not, oh not, by any stretch of the imagination, the historic, vine-hung, hill-top château in which, for the last ten years, my imagination had comfortably ensconced Jenny.

Well, what would *you* have done? Perhaps at that point you would have started up your car and gone away again, and perhaps you would have been right. But discretion has never been my strong suit and, having got this far, I wanted to find out more. So I parked the car and, after a circumspect look round for the *chien méchant*, pulled at a rusty bell-pull beside the gate. It jangled.

Straight on cue the invisible dog began to bark. The only other sound came from a mechanical digger, chuntering around a couple of hundred yards up the hill, gouging out a new road. In the now airless heat I waited. The dog went on barking but half-heartedly, as if it were really off-duty.

Presently a woman came round the corner of the house and began walking slowly down the white dust path towards me. She had short, blondish hair going straggly over her forehead with perspiration, and she walked as if the heat were getting her down and she couldn't feel much curiosity about who was at the gate. Like twenty million other Frenchwomen she wore a sort of loose, sleeveless overall and espadrilles, and while she was still walking towards me—the garden was a fairly long one—I had time to visualise in one comprehensive picture her entire bleached, airless existence in this place, her lifelong burden of respectability and caution, her unending family commitments, her fundamental loneliness—yes, I swear I am not just being wise after the event; I swear that as this unknown thirty-fiveish housewife, housekeeper or whatever she was approached me, I felt that I knew all there was to know about her and at that time that that all was, really, nothing.

It was her general bearing I was going by. Although the sun was behind my own back I couldn't see her features clearly, first because she was in shadow from the trees and then because she was screwing up her eyes and putting up a hand to shade them against the violent light. I must have been nearly invisible to her till she got up to me.

I stood waiting for her to reach the gate and rehearsing a sentence to say to her: '*Excusez-moi, Madame, mais est-ce que la famille de Loubet habite toujours ici?*'

And then if, as seemed highly probable, she said, '*Ah non, Monsieur,*' in the slightly smug tone of voice the French adopt when they cannot help you, I would attempt to ask where they had moved to.

16

She was opening the gate, tugging at it because it was stiff, just as if no one ever went in or out. I was stepping forward and saying my piece. And then, suddenly, I stopped in utter confusion. Because of course—as you will have realised long before I did—it wasn't a depressed French housekeeper or unknown new occupant in front of me at all. It was Jenny.

★   ★   ★

What stopped me short was not even recognition—that took several long seconds to come—but the fact that she recognised me first and blushed to the roots of her cropped, sun-dried hair. Because I so clearly did not realise who she was, she herself felt an agony of embarrassment. This in turn, when I finally did tumble to who she was, made me feel awful, and at last I sort of shouted—it seemed to come out absurdly loud in the oppressive afternoon— 'Jenny darling, it's you!' and plunged forward and—

No. No, I didn't after all kiss her. Instead I shook, gauchely and hard, the limp French hand she automatically extended. In all my brief imaginings, over the years, of our reunion I had certainly seen us embracing. But now that I was actually here . . . Anyway, we shook hands.

And then she went on tugging at the gate and saying—with a faintly recognisable hint of the old Jenny now—'Oh bother this *grille*, it's always sticking, the sand subsides... There. Come in.' She shut it carefully behind me. (She would never have done that in the old days, I registered, already hideously embarked full tilt on comparing the Jenny of now, this faded, ordinary woman, with the Jenny of then.) Then we looked at each other. I said desperately, 'Did you get my letter?' thinking that she must have or she would be more surprised to see me.

'Yes. Yes—I did... Did you get mine?'

I shook my head and said to her (for the second time in my life, as I afterwards realised): 'No. You must have posted it too late.' Feeling ungracious I added, 'I've been in France since Tuesday... What did it say?'

'What?'

'Your letter to me.'

'Oh... Well, just...' She hesitated, as if looking for the words in English. She seemed uneasy in the language altogether; presumably she hardly ever spoke it these days. Finally, biting her lip, she said, 'Well, actually it said don't come because my *belle-mère*—my mother-in-law—has been rather ill, you see, and needs to be absolutely quiet... But of course *do* come in now you're here.'

She seemed dreadfully ill at ease and I thought for a moment that she was actually frightened of the *belle-mère* or of the dog which was still barking on in the house in a desultory

18

way like an accessory to some sinister film. But then it dawned on me that what was making her so self-conscious was simply her appearance, because she hadn't been expecting me. She kept pulling at her overall and trying to smooth down her hair and tease out the fronds of her fringe. It's awful to catch a woman on the wrong foot like that and it made me feel low. At the same time, I thought it was pretty awful of her to have let herself go like that. She wasn't fat or anything. Just—quenched.

'I'll go away,' I said. It was stupid, I knew, since obviously it was too late for that, but I just wanted to turn tail and blot the whole disastrous encounter out of my mind.

'No, no,' she said anxiously. 'Please don't. Don't be silly! After you've—you've come so far. Come in and have some tea.'

So I followed her up the path, towards that house where every metal shutter was drawn tight against the enemy sun. I know it's merely sensible to shut everything in the middle of the day in such a climate, but I made the place look like a tomb, or like somewhere in which the inhabitants at best do not live but barely exist, creeping in felt slippers over stone floors, muting their voices to an exhausted half-tone.

'What about the dog?' I said loudly to her self-conscious back. 'Will he bite me?'

'The what?'

'The dog—the *chien méchant*.'

19

'*Ah, le chien. Mais il n'est pas vraiment méchant.* My husband—that is, we put that notice up mainly to scare off burglars.'

'And what about friends?' I was going to ask. But, of course, on reflection I didn't. Friends? Here?

Inside it was darkish and almost cool. She put me in a very French drawing room with a ticking clock and one or two nice pieces of old furniture in it. It was unnaturally tidy, and I remembered how chronically untidy Jenny had been in the old days. But perhaps this room wasn't used much—just for the occasional formal party for her husband's clients, and for odd and not particularly welcome strangers like me. Excusing herself, Jenny left me alone. The barking stopped. I sat on the edge of a hard sofa asking myself *how*—how on *earth*—this had all come about.

When she came back again she had brushed her hair and—Oh God!—changed her dress. Changed for me, who had seen her in a nightdress, in tears, in nothing, vomiting with morning sickness, in an old shirt of mine she had pinched ... But of course I was wrong to think like that. All that was long ago, just not real any more, and the only reality was now: this house, this country, this climate, our virtual strangeness to one another. I had made the simple and commonplace mistake of thinking that the past still exists somewhere. It doesn't.

20

She said she was going to make some tea. She said that her *belle-mère* was resting but would be down presently. She said that her husband might be home by and by; he often did come home in the late afternoon, she said, because he found it more pleasant to do paperwork here than in his office *en ville*. As if in a sudden spurt of apology—yes, apologising to me, to the past—she added that unfortunately it was not as nice here as it had been up to a couple of years ago 'before all these new *pavillons* were constructed'. Although I knew that she wasn't sprinkling her conversation with French words and turns of phrase from affectation but just because these were the words that came naturally to her now, I found this broken English maddening. It seemed to put a further barrier between us—a soggy, mushy one of linguistic confusion. We had spoken the same language exactly, once.

I was going to give a verbatim account of our conversation, a masochistic, blow-by-blow record in order to deal with the whole thing once and for all and then shove it out of sight. But, really, now I come to it, I find I haven't the heart—and what's the point anyway? I will just record that when she came back with a tray of tea and some very boring biscuits I began to talk with desperate determination about myself. I told her about my job with Chemik Inc. and about Madeleine and the children. It's always

21

easy to talk about your own children and you won't actually *offend* anyone by doing that; at worst you will merely bore or hurt them. I hope I didn't hurt Jenny—more than I'd already hurt her by turning up and not recognising her, I mean—but the fact is, as of course I realised once I was fairly embarked on the subject of Sebastian and Emma and Sophie, that Jenny hadn't any herself. Naturally I couldn't ask why.

The stupid thing is that though in the half-baked picture I'd always had of her in 'the South of France' I'd always seen her as happy, I had never thought to analyse what might reasonably be expected to make up this happiness. Had I bothered to think properly at all, I suppose I would have garnished her vine-hung château in due course with three or four enchanting Anglo-French kids. Most women want children eventually, and Jenny was a totally unspoilt and unexceptional woman in that sort of way: that was one of the nice things about her. But there were no children here.

It was as if my foolish dream of the golden girl, stuck for ever in an unchanging meridian landscape, had come true in a nightmare form: nothing *had* happened in her life since her marriage—no children, no change of habitat, no growth in any direction. In that shuttered villa, time had stayed still during two thousand afternoons on which nothing had happened.

And it was the gradual accumulation of all this no-change which had, over the years, wrought such a deadening change in her.

At one moment I remembered to say I had heard of her mother's death and had been sorry—the crone had succumbed to a liver condition some three years before.

'Oh well,' said Jenny with a brief, suppressed flash of her old self. 'We weren't actually terribly fond of one another, you know.' And then, as if she felt that she had betrayed a carefully concealed former identity or had ventured too close to a past with me which she did not even want to acknowledge, she went on to say how different French families were; how much more genuinely devoted to each other. I listened and thought helplessly, Oh Jenny!

*　　*　　*

As if on cue, the *belle-mère* came down. Apparently she lived with them and had always done so. Any British visions I had had of the Monster Mother-in-Law receded; she was a nice old lady in a black silk dress who seemed genuinely pleased to see me, though quite vague as to who I might be. Jenny waited on her affectionately and I found myself, after all, warming fractionally towards this very French scene, enjoying the tea-party just a little as if I were a tourist in a strange land (which I was)

23

and this was some picturesque folk ritual.

And by and by Jenny's husband came in, and part of the mystery was solved. Phillip de Loubet was a large, strikingly handsome person with a pretty taste in manners. Once introduced to me, he concealed the surprise he must surely have felt and put himself out to talk to me in a friendly way and a Maurice Chevalier accent. My original image had not been so far wrong after all; I could see only too well what his initial appeal for Jenny must have been.

He chatted pleasantly about the house and 'the region'; it was a great pity, he conceded, that this, his family home, was now encroached upon by other properties, but of course (alertly) house values in the area had gone up considerably in recent years: the Bouches du Rhône was very much of an expanding region; if I could spare the time from my business while I was in the area he was sure it would interest me to drive around a little and see for myself the type of development, and of course Marseilles was a fascinating city. Etcetera, etcetera.

A charming, friendly person, unpretentious yet cultured, with a delightful old mother to whom he was obviously absolutely devoted . . .

A pompous, conceited, small-town notary, a minor local big-wig with his absurd 'de', who had probably married Jenny (*la fille d'un milord!*) out of pure snobbery without the faintest true concept of her background or her

24

personality, and then had proceeded to subjugate her to the demands of his alien and suffocating culture.

No. No, this provincial nonentity could not have had the faintest idea who he was marrying. But, that being so, one could hardly blame *him*—or no more than one blamed Jenny herself.

At last I gauged that I might decently take my leave. At Phillipe de Loubet's polite but not particularly pressing inquiries about my plans for the evening, I lied that I had a business dinner in Marseilles. He seemed about to chaperon Jenny and me all the way to the gate, but at the last moment he apparently thought better of it and let us go down the garden alone.

I was afraid she would feel she had to make noises about how nice it had been to see me and how I must come again. But Jenny always had a lot of integrity. She just walked beside me to my car in silence. When we got there I said, knowing it was an awful thing to do but not able to stop myself: 'Jenny—what's made you stay here all these years? Why?'

She stared at me and flushed, and I thought for a moment she was going to hit me—she would certainly have been entitled to. But instead she lowered her head again and said in a dull, matter-of-fact voice: 'You forget: I'm a Catholic. I got converted when I got married.'

'Even so...' I said with feeling.

There was a pause and then she said, almost impatiently, as if the subject had no real meaning for her or none she could convey: 'Oh, I can't expect you to understand. I can't explain it myself. Goodbye, Tony. Thank you for coming.'

And then I was alone again.

As I drove in fits and starts through the clogging, homebound traffic of that fetid town, it presently occurred to me that in one fundamental respect she had not changed. Or rather that, by changing her outward appearance so utterly, she had merely remained true to herself: she had always been a bit of a chameleon. That was how, in the old days, she managed to get on with so many different sorts of people. Her glowing, exuberant personality had perhaps, after all, not been so much fired from within as reflected from external circumstances and from others around her. She glowed only in certain surroundings. Elsewhere her light was extinct, like the light of a glow-worm in the daytime. Here in Beaucaire she had not been brutally quenched by others, I decided after all. She had simply become, by a spontaneous, pliable process of her own, a suppressed bourgeois housewife.

When a relationship, or the idea of it, is spoiled, everything is spoiled. Marseilles was not too bad, but as I started back up the autoroute the following afternoon, the France I had been half in love with only the day before had gone. The blue sky seemed not heavenly but cruel and meaningless, the autoroute not an exhilarating escape but a brutal and dangerous treadmill. The sentimental French songs which I had enjoyed on the radio coming down now mocked me. And I was glad when the landscape gradually changed and the olives and vines were replaced by proper fields with ordinary, English-looking cows in them. I never did really like France all that much, anyway.

When I finally got back to London four days later Jenny's letter was waiting for me—I mean the one she had written before seeing me. Her writing had not changed at all, which now seemed poignant and inappropriate. She hadn't marked it *Personal* or anything, so of course my secretary had opened it. And read it, no doubt.

Darling Tony,
Oh gosh, it will be so super to see you again after all these years. I can hardly bear to think of it. But please, if you don't mind, don't come here to Beaucaire. Phillipe's never really understood my English friends, and anyway his mother lives with us—she keeps being ill. Anyway, I think it would be more fun for us two to meet in Marseilles. I shall say I'm going to do a day's shopping . . .

She went on to describe a prominent central

café, and wrote:

I don't know what your appointments are, so I'll wait there on the café terrace for half an hour at eleven am, at three in the afternoon and again at five, and you just roll up at whatever time suits you best and then we'll have a super time, together. All my love—always—J.

Underneath, in a different pen, she had scrawled: *Oh darling, you can't think how I am longing to see you.*

In spite of the fixed image of her I had carried inappropriately all those years, it had simply not occurred to me till I read that letter that she, also, might be harbouring an image of me—that I too might be fixed for her in an artificial golden glow which the ill-timed pressures and errors of present reality could only destroy. To be someone else's dream is to be condemned, one way or another.

BLOODY BAD LUCK, REALLY

Michael Macnamara was born and brought up a Catholic, and when he was older it wasn't so much that he lost his Faith as that he acquired other faiths in addition. From the time he left his RC private school, at sixteen (his family having run out of money), he was seldom without some deeply-felt conviction, some crusade either for or against a passionately envisaged and often geographically remote objective. His crusades gave meaning to his life, illuminating it from within as a Byzantine ikon glows with the light of its own gilding even in a dark place. Not that Michael's life was dark exactly, but it was scrappy and uncertain, marked by dramas of love or politics which promised all, but something petered away into nothing-very-much, leaving only great spaces of wet street with the pub not open yet and hardly a familiar face in sight: there were too many urban Sunday afternoons in Michael's life.

He did not think of himself as an urban creature. As a child, he had been deeply involved in the Irish countryside; as a man he felt a passionate kinship with the world's peasantry: the names of remote Siberian territories and tiny African or Indian settlements came readily to his lips. He worried dutifully (just as he still said his prayers dutifully) about arable lands being eroded into deserts, about fish in distant oceans with nitrate in their bones, about the destruction of the rainforests of the Amazon and the tigers of South-East Asia, about DDT and nuclear waste. But, though his mental landscape was thus both rural and exotic, his physical one remained circumscribed. Not only did he rarely leave

London, he seldom moved far from the few square miles that had constituted his territory ever since his days as a firefighter (and Conscientious Objector) in the Second World War. Bounded by Soho to the south, and Hampstead to the north, he was centred on Camden Town, where he had rented the same basement room for so many years that he had no accurate perception of the way the street had changed around him. He still thought of it as an entirely working-class area and took a pride in the fact. Jokes about trendy NW1 baffled him and—yes—even hurt him rather. Something had happened in the last ten or fifteen years that he did not entirely understand and preferred not to recognise. It couldn't, no, really it couldn't be true, that he, Michael Macnamara, despiser of possessions, lover of the poor, champion of underdogs, inveterate and shameless borrower of what had once been half-crowns from friends, was actually living in a fashionable area? Like decimal coinage, the fact that Joe's Café in Parkway was now called 'Le Bistrolou' seemed an indecency which was better ignored.

It was the same with the way people he'd known practically all his life had developed, in recent years, a disconcerting habit of becoming not only eminent but rich as well. The old enemies in public places had, many of them, melted away, and some of their seats had been taken by people he himself had marched with since his early teens against Mosley, for Arms of Spain, for Peace under Socialism, against Suez, for CND, against Vietnam. . . . He was, he told himself when he remembered, glad to see his old friends doing so well, their talents recognised; he was even determinedly glad when people whom he had first known as eager juniors, following where he had led, turned up a few years later in a quite different rôle. He had never been a jealous or ambitious person on his own account; the Cause—all the Causes—had always been the thing. But all the same it was a bit saddening. Like suddenly finding that all the grown-ups had moved out and their places had been taken by your own school-mates who then, mysteriously, did not seem like your contemporaries any more. In the last few years Michael had not seen many of his oldest friends. Oh, they still asked him to their parties—some of them. But he did not often go. He felt awkward in décors of conspicuous success, particularly when that success was worn so casually, as if it were quite natural. It had been more fun when he had been able to drop in and play with their children. But even the actual children had mostly grown up now, becoming tall and polite and inaccessible. He still vaguely hoped to have children himself—sometime, if he ever met the right person and managed to put his affairs in order a bit . . . Sometime? He was already over fifty. It simply did not add up to a believable fact. He brushed it away.

With the passing years, which seemed long at the time but which succeeded one another as alike as a string of unremembered parties with bottles in people's flats, Michael let some of his beliefs drop into abeyance. Never discarded utterly, for he was a faithful soul, they lay about on the floor of his mind partially covered by more recent litter. Catholicism itself silted down in this way, and so did vegetarianism (dreadfully expensive and boring in practice), and so did his early passion for D. H. Lawrence. (He still believed fervently in the holy power of sex, but somehow these days all the new magazines in newsagents' made him feel foolish, as if he had arrived at a shrine after a long barefoot journey only to find it vulgarly crowded with coach-parties). But there was one great love which never dropped out of sight, and which sustained him in many a disappointed hour: he loved Israel.

He would have liked to have been born a Jew, and had come to think of himself as an honorary one. Martyrdom was natural to him. The image of the gentle, suffering Jew on the cross had dominated his childhood: later, he envied his many Jewish friends that extra, secret dimension in their lives. Something like that, he vaguely felt, would give coherence to his own rather amorphous existence, pull it together somehow... The passion of crusading love, pity and concern that was fully awakened in him by the first reports from Auschwitz and Belsen never faded. The day in May 1948 when Israel had proclaimed her independence had been one in which he walked the streets of the West End in a dream, seeing the orient and immortal wheat that would be grown by the Children of Israel on the hills of Galilee. Five years later, after heroic financial struggles, he actually managed to see those hills, and the love-affair was consummated. He spent three months working at a recently-founded kibbutz near the Sea of Galilee, and it was the happiest time of his life. For a long while afterwards, whenever things went wrong and he could afford nothing nice to eat or to give people, and the editor of the *Jewish Chronicle* or the *New Statesman* had returned yet another batch of manuscripts to him, and no one wanted to buy his pictures, he would say the names of the people he had met Sdot Or over to himself like a protective incantation: Eli, Ytzak, Sarah, Haim, Harry, Miguel, Yehuda, Esther, Zvi... He didn't dare write to them. Something made him sheer off doing so. He was bad at writing letters anyway. But when the wars came, regular as pogroms, rekindling his love, he sent the kibbutz passionate telegrams saying thinking-of-you-all-every-hour: in 1956 he did that, and in 1967 and in 1973.

He had said, and honestly believed, when he

had left in 1953, that he would soon be back. But the years slipped by and he never had any money. By and by Israel became for him the Promised Land in a different sense: a kind of Earthly Paradise which he himself had once, for a brief summer, inhabited, and which he had had to leave not through any specific sin of his own but because that was just how life was, on earth, since the Fall. Ecstasy cannot last, he told himself: in the nature of things, we are 'all of us poor and each of us lonely'. (He had long forgotten who had said that, but it had become his favourite quotation, along with *nous sommes tous des juifs*') He still wanted very much to go back to Israel, and believed that one day he would, but felt it was no good making great practical efforts to do so. Paradise was not to be bought with an airline ticket, nor Redemption to be had just for the wanting. When it was time for him to return to Israel, to the Sea of Galilee and the Fields of Light, he would return: that was all. Of late years, a concept of Fate, in the form of an unknowable but vaguely satisfying destiny lying already formed and in wait for him in the decades to come, had played an increasing part in his personal belief-system. After all, what he could see from his present vantage-point could not be all there was to life. Could it?

The fact was, once Michael had turned forty-five, things began to go—well, not wrong exactly, since they had never in any case gone all that right for very long at a time, but an insidious change took place. Nothing was quite so much fun any more. He didn't think the change was in himself. He still felt exactly the same inside as he always had, and knew he still looked very much the same too: a slightly built and almost boyish figure with blue eyes behind glasses, wearing a worn corduroy jacket that he'd had for years and years. Unlike many of his old friends he had not become fat or bald; he had not changed his style either. His hair, once long—a permanent snook cocked at his old Headmaster—had now, just by staying the same length, become on the short side. He was vaguely aware of this, but did not see why he should change. But the fact was, a change had taken place. Certain things seemed to have got confused, and he no longer felt quite clear where he stood.

He first became strongly and uneasily aware of this in 1967, just after the Six-Day War. He had loved that war. Jerusalem had been all around him as he had run about Camden Town the day the Israeli troops had marched into the Holy City. He and other members of the Stand by Israel NW London Committee had forgathered all the week in each others' houses: it had been like one long party. But—afterwards? It was almost at once afterwards, it seemed, that people began talking about the Palestinian case at much greater length and with

35

greater intensity than they ever had before. Advertisements appeared. Articles were written. Some of his friends even stopped speaking to others. In winning the war, it now seemed, the Israelis had made a big mistake. It had cost them a lot of support. Some of Michael's oldest Jewish friends even turned anti-Zionist; it confused and disturbed him dreadfully. Even worse was when his newer friends, all a good deal younger than himself these days, began talking about the Israelis as tools of American imperialism, and implying— or even saying—that they were comparable with white South Africans and that the Palestinian Arabs were the poor blacks of the Middle East.

It was gradually and painfully borne in on Michael that he, lover of freedom, champion of the oppressed, was apparently backing the wrong horse. Or was *thought* to be doing so, which came to almost the same thing.

But he couldn't change. Perhaps he really was getting old, or perhaps (as he preferred to think) his love of Israel was so deep and seminal in his life that there was no question of forsaking it. He regretted the fact and resented it. He resented being cut off from the sort of people— radical students, and so forth—with whom he felt he naturally belonged. He felt misunderstood, unfashionable in the wrong sense. It seemed hardly fair of society to be so fickle when he himself had been so constant.

But after a while he even began to derive a kind of glum pleasure from the thought of his own blood-and-bone deep fidelity to Israel compared with others' marketable sophistry. Wasn't this, after all, a martyrdom of a kind, though not one he had ever foreseen for himself? Blood was thicker than ink. (He must remember that phrase for an article some time.) After all, what was all this clever new anti-Zionist propaganda but old-fashioned anti-Semitism disguised in the trappings of radical chic? When he'd put it to himself like that he felt better. But he still went on being sad about it. And Israel, with its sun-baked villages, its rough roads and blue hills, seemed very far.

And then, quite suddenly in 1974, he could pay all his debts and still had several hundred pounds over. The year before he had tried to hop on a bus in Camden Town, in his usual style, just as it was moving off, and his foot slipped. He was run over by the car behind. His leg would never be the same again, and still gave him quite a bit of pain. But the car driver, a Mr Jacobs from Hampstead Garden Suburb, had admitted partial liability. Since Michael secretly knew that the whole thing had been his own fault, he was overcome by his good fortune. Such money from Heaven could only be spent on one thing: he would make that return visit to Israel, his own private homecoming.

At last, after considerable hesitation for which

he himself could not define the reason, he wrote off to the Secretary of Sdot Or to ask if he could come and stay again.

He had meant, of course, 'stay and work for my keep'. Perhaps he should have spelt it out more clearly? For what he received back eventually was a letter, not from the kibbutz office itself, the shack he remembered among the cedars, but from something called in English and Hebrew: The Sdot Or Guest and Rest House, which would, it said, be pleased to reserve him a single room, with or without bath (terms as per brochure, enclosed) if he would send them the booking dates by return, as this was their busy season.

He made evasive enquiries among his friends. It seemed that, over the last twenty years— could it really be twenty?—his own unique experience of work on a kibbutz had become, well, commonplace really. So much so that the more attractive Galilean kibbutzim were now innundated with requests from would-be volunteers and scroungers, and had become blasé about them. He very much doubted, one friend said, if Sdot Or, of which he knew by reputation, would take on a middle-aged non-Jewish volunteer by letter. Of course, the friend added hastily, seeing the expression on Michael's face, once he was actually *there* and had looked up his old friends among the members, no doubt he would be able to arrange it.

So Michael ought to have been prepared. But, with the dazzling light of the past shining in his eyes, it was hard for him to see clearly. And when he actually arrived at the Sdot Or Guest and Rest House, to take up his expensive room, he could hardly believe what his actual eyes were telling him. The countryside, the blue hills through which the communal taxi from Lodd had driven him, was still the Promised Land, even if there seemed to be many more bungalows in it than he remembered and an entire estate of high-rise blocks standing above Nazareth. But the kibbutz itself... It was like getting out at the wrong stop on the Northern Line and not realising it till you reached the street. The road which had lived in his memory as white with dust, rutted with farm tractors and carts, was smoothly tarmaced. It led, not past wooden huts, but by new concrete buildings, elaborate cantilevered structures: a cinema, a museum, a kind of piazza with modern sculpture. Above that, where he knew the mountain scrub ought to begin again, was a swimming pool (with bar), tennis courts (*tennis?* Oh no—) and a fair-sized car-park. Above that, crowning a knoll on which a group of pines had stood and where he had lain beside Sarah one hot Sabbath afternoon, was a large white building with chalets standing round it in carefully land-scaped gardens. This was the

Guest House: a neon sign proclaimed it.

Michael buried his face in his hands.

Admittedly it was not all quite as bad as that in the days that followed. The kibbutz did still exist, after all, with its own separate life, covertly contemptuous of the holiday club it had spawned: you could walk down the hill to it. He even found some of his old friends and they seemed pleased to see him: the boredom of kibbutz-existence leads to unfeigned delight in visitors, where it does not lead to total withdrawal. Haim seemed to have withdrawn: Michael heard he was still in the kibbutz but never managed to meet him. Eli had become a member of the government and apparently hardly ever returned from Jerusalem even for a Sabbath; and Ytzak, dear funny Ytzak, was dead: a heart attack at only forty-three, one day working in the sun. Harry had married Sarah and both had left the kibbutz for some unexplained reason in 1960. Miguel had disappeared too; no one seemed to remember quite when: constraint surrounded these traitorous names. But jolly Yehuda, now amicably divorced from Esther, was the same as ever and welcomed Michael kindly. Zvi was there too, and was agricultural manager. Michael thought how old and dry and fussy he had got, just like an elderly schoolmaster.

In fact these three survivors all seemed dreadfully old, gnarled travesties of their former lithe selves, their skins leathered by time. Yehuda was quite bald and paunchy; Esther's sinewy legs were mapped by veins. For the first time Michael realised what a lifetime of manual work under the Middle Eastern sun really meant, and felt humbled and ignorant, with his own jaunty (though limping) step and his rain-softened London skin. But it was really rather awful, wasn't it, that they didn't seem to *mind* looking old and hideous? And if only, he thought wildly, they wouldn't go on so about their new furniture, of all middle-class preoccupations.

This kibbutz had obviously had its day: it had been a mistake to return here, he knew that now. Elsewhere, further south in the untamed land of the Negev, there must be other settlements that still kept the old pioneer feeling and ideal alive? He should have been more adventurous himself and sought out one of those. Too late.

After a fortnight of enforced guestly rest he could bear it no longer and left early. In a week's time he was due to stay with friends of friends on the coast near Tel Aviv. He filled in the week riding round Israel on buses, seeking what he had lost. Sometimes for a few moments or even an hour or more, he thought he might find it. But then it would slip away from him once more, thrust out of sight behind a Coca-Cola hoarding, lost, like the old plantations in the

41

streets of a new and glaring suburb, vanishing with the money that stall-holders and café-proprietors seemed so ready to wrest from him. Could it really have been *here*, he asked himself at this crossroads, that he and Sarah and Yehuda and Esther had been given drinks of well-water by an Arab villager? They were building a supermarket here now, but he was sure it was the same place. But what was 'same', what was 'here', if 'here' and 'same' were no longer recognisable, nor people nor emotions nor anything else?

The Israel he had cherished all these years was no doubt still there if you knew how to look for it: he clung to that thought. But it no longer offered itself readily to view—or he no longer knew how to seek it out. And now, because of this, he was in danger of losing it in memory too. Paradise was given once in a lifetime and he had had it: he should have known.

Bereft now of hope and therefore anaesthetised against further disappointment he went soberly to the resort near Tel Aviv. 'Resort' was the word: any lingering memories he may have had of empty sands and rocky waves shrivelled and dried before the Mediterranean-bijou style of the place, with its discotheques and straw-roofed beach-huts and signs in different languages. But the friends of friends were genuinely hospitable and their flat was very comfortable. He began, tentatively, to enjoy himself just a little—almost as if he hadn't been in Israel at all.

It was on his next-to-last day there that the incident happened.

'Incident' was how it was described afterwards in the world's newspapers. For the world is, by tradition, interested in such things when they happen in Israel, though of course it did not rate extensive coverage like the Kiriat Shmonah or Ma'alot massacres. And indeed, though the first reports had described Michael's assailant as an Arab terrorist, it turned out that he wasn't a real terrorist but an ex-mental patient, and the various anti-Zionist organisations disclaimed him. Not that Michael ever knew that, though he might have appreciated the irony of it if he had.

Briefly—we must be brief, now, for Michael's unresolved life is nearing its close, the last sands running out even as he himself is walking on the evening sands in a clean white shirt with rolled up sleeves—briefly, the lunatic-terrorist-New Left agent-angel of Fate (or whatever he was) had been tailing Michael all the afternoon, apparently under the impression or delusion that he was a well-known hard-line Israeli journalist. There was, in fact, a bizarre and fleeting resemblance between that man's painfully astute face and Michael's hesitantly open one. It was when Michael chose to stroll on the beach alone as the sun was doing its showy

43

disappearing act that the moment came. The assailant, from ten yards away, brought a revolver out from inside his own clean white shirt, raised it, and fired.

He did not take careful aim and Michael, though he dropped instantly with a cry of surprise and reproach, was not killed outright. He had time to know he was dying. For the first and only time in his life he perceived the fact quite clearly, and was terrified. It wasn't just the pain, bubbling and tearing at his chest, progressively choking the breath from him. It wasn't even the sickness and giddiness or the way the crowd of people, running out of nowhere to gather thicker and thicker around him, seemed at the same time to be retreating, losing form and substance. No, what terrified him for many long moments as he lay there on the sand was that he had, after all, *done* nothing. All his life seemed to have been a preparation— for what?

Then, as suddenly as the shot and the pain, the answer came, and with it a vast relief. The pain of course was still there, and the dying. But they were abruptly transfigured, glorified: the horrible spinning, reeling world resolved itself smoothly into a final pattern: it had all been building up to something after all. A phrase took hold of his mind and saved him: *I am dying for Israel.*

The boyhood image of the martyred Christ

fused itself at last with the hieroglyph of the martyred bodies beneath the bulldozers at Auschwitz: the Promised Land, at once Eden, Ireland and a yet more glorious and archetypal Israel itself, shimmered before his dimming eyes. And he, Michael Macnamara, was giving away his insignificant, abortive life, gladly and freely, that the Promised Land might live and that he himself might live in it for evermore. He wanted to tell people, he wanted to shout it aloud.

But darkness came. And everything went, even pain, retreating and retreating like a distant scream, till it was nothing but the rushing of blood in his ears and then that faded and was gone.

★   ★   ★

The papers made quite a lot of the case. It was the first time a visitor had been killed in this way, though the government had known it was bound to happen sooner or later. 'Tourist murder' the headlines called it. Everyone was very sorry. It was most unfortunate, particularly as he wasn't even a Jew, it seemed. Just one of those things. Bloody bad luck, really.

In London, when his friends met, they mentioned it to each other, regretful and affectionate, yet a little embarrassed too. Somehow, Michael had always had that effect on people.

THE THOUGHT THAT COUNTS

Minnie was making her Christmas shopping list.

She was using a piece of nice squared paper neatly ruled into columns: she had always been methodical, in fact she enjoyed making lists. Long ago, as a child, she had made lists of 'Blessings'. ('Count your blessings,' grown-ups had used to say and she took them at their word, being a literal-minded child.) Sometimes—the unhappy times—she had made lists of 'Sadnesses' too. Of course she knew that, had Archie and Fred and Roland and Katie found the lists, they would have laughed at her. Keeping lists was not the sort of thing a sister of Archie and Fred and Roland and Katie did. She kept them hidden.

She was enjoying making this list now. It was a particularly complete one. As well as being itemised vertically under separate headings— 'Person', 'Possible Present', 'Suggested Shop'— it was itemised horizontally into 'Important People', 'Less Important People' and 'Odd People'. The last section didn't mean really *odd*, of course. It just meant people like the lady from the Welfare and that little nurse who had been kind to her the last time she was in hospital and the nice young man in the greengrocers round the corner who always had a joke for everyone. People who of course wouldn't *expect* presents from her but would perhaps be pleasantly surprised if they only knew ... Minnie wasn't in the least snobbish (she always maintained) but you couldn't regard people like that as quite like your own kith and kin, could you? Your own flesh and blood? Though, come to that, talking of 'flesh and blood'—a phrase which acquired a more special, secret meaning for Minnie whenever she stopped to consider it with greater attention—that was really another category anyway.

One year, she had gone so far as to note down a select subdivision labelled 'Special People'. Into that went George, who had wanted in vain to marry her, and Jack who had actually done so but had been killed in the war, and Walter who had fallen in love with her later (and she with him) but had had an invalid wife... But the sight of these cherished names actually itemised, collectively as it were, had given her a funny turn, and subsequent years she had dropped that section from her List. Anyway you couldn't give presents to the dead, and the point of George and Walter, so to speak, had been the poignantly unspoken quality of their passion for her.

Actually, of course, Archie was dead too, in the same war as Jack. The brilliant, favourite, eldest son, the dashing young officer... But she still continued to put his name on her List, for he seemed to belong there with the other three, in the dear, remote past, as fixed as four children in the sepia sunlight of a long-past year, or as a Kate Greenaway foursome upon a china plate. There had been one like that, in her nursery.

Not but what, when the Welfare lady or anyone asked her kindly what her plans were for Christmas, she always explained at once and carefully that she was going to Spend the Day with Katie in her little house in Lee Green. Her young sister Katie, for ever, for her, the child running toward the rim of the plate in a muslin dress, but a widow now herself, poor darling. Poor little Katie, lonely in Lee Green with only her cat for company: Minnie, who had always been the stronger one, protective big sister, much enjoyed the thought of going to cheer her up.

Of course there were many names of more recent date on the List both under 'Important' and under 'Less Important'. Minnie had always had a knack of making friends, she said. Near the top of the Importants—next, indeed, to the brothers and sister—was her great and good friend Emma Daventry. Emma was a widow too, but a wealthy one. She had a beautiful home in Elstree where Minnie quite often allowed herself to spend Sundays, and some most attentive grown-up sons who occasionally took the pair of them to a show in Town. Yes, they had all been to *The Sound of Music* together. Minnie had cherished that evening, perfecting it, for many a long day.

Minnie occasionally reflected that she *could* have had sons of her very own! Perhaps a daughter too, to be solicitous. Perhaps even grandchildren... But the thought had always made her head reel, imagination itself becoming inadequate. Anyway, there had been nothing like that. Jack (even before he was killed, leading his company into the attack) had always respected her too much for anything like that.

So, no children or grandchildren. There was a price to pay for everything. But such a lot of friends! Louisa, who had been the most popular girl in the school, and Wanda who was a famous artist, and John and Sally (darlings, but feckless) who had always been so grateful for Minnie's help with their *enormous* family, and young Barbara who looked on her as a mother... And memories too. Memories of jolly ski-ing holidays in Switzerland, of shopping jaunts to Paris (that was where Wanda came in), of long-ago balls, waltzing in Jack's (or George's) arms, on and on under the chandeliers...

The young girls the Welfare lady sometimes sent to visit her always listened very politely when she told them about all her happy memories. But sometimes, well-spoken and obtuse, they asked questions she couldn't answer, and that made her cross. People meant well. But they didn't always understand.

To work! It didn't do just to sit and dream. She bent to her List, underlining different types of articles in different coloured pencils. She read it through again slowly, pondering on the practical wisdom of each choice:

Katie—Fur-lined slippers.
The poor little thing had always suffered from the cold. As a child, Minnie had used to put her own cot-quilt over Katie to keep her warm.

Fred—A pipe jar.
Fred always had something to do with pipes or pocket knives. That was his type. George— poor, dear, faithful George!—was another version of it. The brotherly sort. Dependable. Not exciting enough to marry. Or to die in battle.

Roland—A hip-flask.
Roland, the deep one, had emigrated to Canada. But he still wrote her long letters, putting into them all the affectionate and thoughtful feelings he had never been able to express face to face.

Archie—Socks.
All right, all right, she told an unseen witness,

she was perfectly well aware that Archie was dead. But every year, without fail, she knitted two pairs of warm socks in his size and sent them to a charity for indigent officers. It was her way of saying Love, of saying Remember. It's the thought that counts.

To Emma Daventry she would give a little bottle of scent. Of course on her modest pension she couldn't begin to compete with the sumptuous silk stockings, crêpe de Chine undies and peaches in brandy that dear, generous Emma lavished on her but she liked to give a little something frivolous all the same.

Louisa—The new Jean Plaidy.
Louisa loved historical novels. She was a bit of a day-dreamer, Louisa. 'Of course, you're so level-headed,' she used to say to Minnie.

Wanda—A patch-work cushion. (Just right for her studio.)

John and Sally—crystallised fruits and an oven-cloth.

Barbara—A charm bracelet.

And (Oh heavens!) she had quite forgotten John and Sally's kiddies. Johnny and Paulie and Tessie and Susie and the twins and little Minnie (named after herself) and the new baby... Her

51

pencil scratched away busily between pauses for thought, creating trains, dolls, clockwork mice and woolly toys in her large, old-fashioned but legible script. It was only as she neatly erased 'woolly toy' against the baby's name and was about to substitute '?musical box' that she began to falter, the slipping clutch of her memory engaging without warning in a different gear.

The baby was older now. Of course.

They were all older. In fact, all grown up and out in the world. Even rosy little Minnie, who had just married a missionary in China. Or something like that.

Further realisation came flooding in. Feeling a fool, she put down her pencil. How could she have forgotten so much? Particularly when she had already noted down Barbara's name and awarded her a charm bracelet. For Barbara, that independent but wayward young woman about whom Minnie often worried (her dreadful young men! Her foolishly thin underclothes!) was in fact John and Sally's own eldest daughter. She had gone on the stage, and was even doing rather well. Good little cameo parts in West End comedies. Minnie used to go to the matinées and go round afterwards to sit in Barbara's dressing room and have a snack with her before the evening performance. She tried to believe that she was a stabilising influence on the passionate, talented, highly-strung girl (for that was Barbara's label). When Sally had died so tragically she, Minnie, had pledged herself to try to take over the mother's role towards Barbara in which poor Sally had so failed. Yes—suicide. It had been dreadful, quite dreadful. How she had wept at the thought. And then John taking to drink like that—

Or no, wait a minute—hadn't something else happened since then? Hadn't he been reformed again, with equal abruptness, by another marriage? Yes, that was the latest thing, of course. A very plain, dull little woman, a clergyman's widow, *quite* different from poor, darling Sally, but such a good sort. And dear John a burnt-out case now, and quite grey, but content again at last, in a sort of way—'Calm of mind, all passion spent . . .'

She realised that she herself was feeling very tired. All these changes—all this *living*—was very tiring. And she was still not sure that she had recollected the whole thing quite clearly, right up to date. Retreating, for the moment, from John and Sally and their copious dramas and progeny, she turned for comfort to her more stable friends, but met with some confusion there also. *Was* Emma Daventry still living in Elstree or had she moved to a little service flat in Knightsbridge? And hadn't she recently, come to think of it, developed some secret, mortal ailment, bravely borne? Yes, Time had been at work there too—and with Louisa and even with dear, exotic, ageless Wanda. Time was, day by day, year by year, transforming Minnie's personal world. It was Time that was the only ultimate truth, the one she really must not forget.

Actually, she thought, laying aside her List, she was not likely to. For hadn't her awareness of passing Time and her allowances for it always been her great strength, a matter of artistic pride with her? For Minnie was a true artist. In her large, elaborate, exhaustive and lifelong structure of fantasy and invention, her sense of Time was the subtle ingredient that converted the whole thing from simple self-indulgence into something more: a disciplined creation with a logic of its own. Perfecting and refining her creation through the quiet, empty, solitary years, she had become an expert in making things real. Alone, by secret trial and error, she had learnt that the art of high-class fantasy lies in restraint, in not just making nice things happen all the time but in knowing when to add touches of grief and pain too—

Joy and sadness woven fine
(She liked to misquote herself)
A clothing for the soul divine:
And when this we rightly know,
Safely through the world we go.

Thus safely through a world judiciously peopled with carefully imagined friends, Minnie went.

But she was tired this afternoon. Oh, really tired, she decided. Too vague and low, for once, to derive any comfort even from the consoling shade of Emma Daventry. Too lacking in invention today to do anything more about the lives of Louisa and Wanda, both of whom had become a bit spectral in recent years. It was such hard work, when one was getting older, keeping up with Time, with Reality.

With a sense of faintly rueful relief she retreated instead to her own family. One's own flesh and blood. After all they were the only true reality. The shades of George, Jack and Walter were elegant but very thin beside Fred, Roland and Katie (and Archie, one mustn't forget Archie, though he of course was on a rather different plane). 'Blood is thicker than water and much nastier,' her father used to say sometimes. (It was Father's Joke—and not just a joke, for he never saw any of his relations.) And it was true. Crowding into her mind now came other images: Fred always jealous of Archie and then consumed with guilt at Archie's death, Roland locked in perpetual conflict with Father (that was why he had emigrated to Canada), Katie marrying a draper's clerk, a nice little man, but really, my dear . . . Pains, griefs, hopes unfulfilled. A Real Family.

She began to plan Christmas Day. How pleased she and Katie would be to see each other! Katie would have got in a capon, and she herself would be bringing a small Christmas pudding (already bought) and the brandy butter, made on Christmas Eve and transported in a little plastic container in the basket along with the slippers for Katie and a bunch of holly, and a bottle of port which was to be this year's Surprise Treat. Of course, public transport being scarce on Christmas Day she would have to leave herself plenty of time to get across London. Tube as far as the Elephant was her usual route, and from there a tram.

A tram? She hesitated, attempting to assess, discard, recollect. Confusion was once again intervening between herself and her creation. She felt Time slipping from her grasp, eluding her. A mental giddiness possessed her, as if she were looking over an empty space of possibilities reaching farther and deeper than she had ever before imagined.

Perhaps Katie was no longer living in Lee Green? (In point of fact the small house with the slate roof she had originally designated as 'Katie's' had been pulled down years ago, though that was irrelevant really.) Perhaps Katie was dead?

Maybe the last of all those happy Christmases had been one when she had knocked and rung in vain, standing there on the doorstep with her basket of fare, until at last she had called a neighbour to help her—strong and dependable,

he had been, another George, another Fred—
and he had broken the pantry window and got in
himself and come round to let her in, and then
they had found poor darling Katie in bed, so
peaceful she had looked in her flannel nightie,
still warm but quite dead, with the cat weaving
uneasily round the foot of the bed... The
necessary injection of grief, the transforming
touch of art. (The neighbours had given her
Christmas dinner, perhaps?')

She was very tired now. Quite drained. That
last encounter with Time had taken a lot out of
her. The giddiness was gone now, and so were
the empty spaces. That was that. She could
manage no more for the moment. As always,
when courage and imagination were temporarily
exhausted, she retreated to the oldest place of
all. The imaginary adult brothers and sisters
held no more appeal for her just now. The last,
special, private retreat from these things was the
long-ago nursery of four children. Five,
counting herself. But then she had never
counted herself, much.

Archie, Fred, Roland and Katie: they had
been her earliest companions. Her only true
ones, then and always. It had all begun with
them. They at least, as children, had been Real.

Archie had been the tallest one, the one in a
white shirt open at the throat. Fred had been
beside him. They had been the horses in the
game that was being played. Behind, holding

57

the ribbon reins, had come Roland, the darkest of the four. And tagging along at the back of her brothers, holding up her long skirt in two chubby hands, had come Katie, garlanded with flowers. Four children playing horses on a summer lawn. A Real Family.

Four children in the dress of a picturesque past of ill-defined date, running for ever, motionless, gay and soundless, across a china plate on the mantelpiece of a solitary nursery, where a child without brothers, sisters or friends made lists of dreams, and, so doing, learned habits of life and thought which were to sustain her for the next sixty years.

THE CHINA EGG

Once, a designer who was working for Tony showed us some Indian pornographic photographs.

These were not specifically Indian figures, such as those temple sculptures of little people entwined in rigid ecstasy, formalised and, in their very explicitness, devoid of sexual meaning. These were pictures of human beings, detailed, careful half-plates, still beautifully clear in spite of the three-quarters of a century or more which must have elapsed since they were taken, by a heavy, draped camera, in some

58

unimaginable shuttered room.

They were sepia-toned but presumably had always been: it was illusory to think, though I immediately did so, that their tint was due to exposure at some time to a violent, un-English sun. Perhaps it was partly this tint, usually associated with likenesses of fading great aunts, that imparted an unexpected innocence to the pictures, and this was reinforced by their presentation: they had been neatly slotted into one of those heavy, embossed albums of the period. On the back of the album in rubbed, gilt lettering was: 'A. N. Taraporvala, the Mall, Simla. High-class work, Weddings a Speciality.' I suppose the album had originally contained the public record of a British Raj coupling, until some cynical person had put it to another use.

Or was it cynical? Perhaps the two participants in the photographs would not have thought so. For the air of innocence and candour came partly, I thought, from their own faces. The leering or bovine coarseness that characterises glossy modern magazine spreads was absent from this pair. They looked cheerful but dedicated, as if jointly performing a complex acrobatic act for a handsome payment, as no doubt they had been.

Only their vulnerable heads, with the man's waxed moustache, showed what a long time ago these acrobatics must have taken place, and that both those fine, smooth bodies must now be dust. The man was tall and muscular, and had a neatly combed and oiled central parting which stayed in place throughout his exertions. The girl was much shorter, with the fat calves favoured before 1914, and hair piled in a glossy and complicated European style. But her large, lovely eyes and also her skin were too dark for a British girl. She had pronounced eyebrows and a delicate, high-bridged nose, like a princess in a Moghul miniature.

'I suppose the fact that they'd different races would have given an extra kick to the whole thing when the pictures were taken,' said Tony, trying to sound both knowledgeable and off-hand, as people like us do when we're confronted with such things.

'Depends if they were taken for the home market or for local consumption.' The proprietor of the photographs could out-do Tony at that manner. 'In India, mixed-race sex would have been the only sort on offer to most Brits, I should think, because there weren't any English tarts there—just Indian and Anglo-Indian ones. This girl might be an Anglo, with that hair-style.'

'The man looks like a guardsman, doesn't he?'

'Probably was.' He sniggered suddenly, giving himself away. 'Let's hope he got well paid for this job on the side and enjoyed himself in the process. Hey—did you see this last one of her on her own, dressed again, with her skirt up round her waist? Doesn't she look just as if she were saying, "This kind photographer has promised me a whole ten rupees if I show the gentlemen my bottom"?'

He put on a chee-chee accent to say this, but even he, degraded urban parasite that he was, had sensed the girl's frankness and gentleness.

★   ★   ★

Where else should I begin? There could be so many different, apparently inconsequential starting points, each leading inexorably and intricately to the same place.

I see now that even our most transient and little-considered actions have their long-term effect: some even live on in the bones and gestures and tones of voice of descendants we shall never see or even imagine. And even if there is a break or failure that too has its effect, repercussing through the generations, changing things for ever in ways we cannot even begin to guess. Odd to think that, until very recently, I spoke—and, I suppose, believed—in the phoney twentieth-century language of individual 'choice' and 'decision' and 'options'. I thought, you see, confident in the flat, bright landscape I had drawn myself, that everything lay within my own control. Amazingly, I did not perceive the great, battered edifice of the past standing close behind me.

These days, 'control' has no meaning. Nor does 'plan', another word Tony and I used to use a lot, one way and another. These days I think in moments, getting myself laboriously from one hour to the next, one place to the next, like a semi-paralysed person who cannot contemplate the future. Yet what preoccupies me at this moment, in my myopic and enforced absorption with present events, is where it all began.

Yet that, too, sounds as if I were still attempting to control, by analysis, to apply reason to my situation; the formula by which Tony and I lived and live no longer. Whereas, in my paralysis, my lassitude, there is somewhere out of sight something beating, a sort of shuddering that is only part distaste, an obscure, helpless excitement as when a small boat begins to move away from a dark quay. Going with it for ever—

Meanwhile I have this letter to answer. For I must of course answer it. It was forwarded to me from the BBC the other day—no, several weeks ago—and it has found its way into the envelope file I carry with me, along with other letters of equal irrelevence to the present moment. It is on blue lined paper, and though the writing is painstaking the date has been left out. It is the letter of someone who expects both everything and nothing, a paper boat of a letter.

Dear Madame,

I heard your talk on the wireless about the Indian orphans and would be most obliged if you can tell us how to adopt one. We have been married fourteen years and no luck so far, and are not prejudiced or anything so please can you tell us where to write off. I felt so very sorry hearing about them and how they dont have the proper things they need there, like you said. My husband has his own business (haulage contractor) so we have a nice home and no problems. Begging the favour of an early reply,

Yours very truly,

Brenda Taylor

PS. I forgot my husband said to tell you we would pay the babys airfare and everything. I am 41, which the lady from the Social Services said was too old, but I dont see how it can be. Please do help us.

Yes, I must certainly answer it. But how?

Dear Mrs Taylor, of course I sympathise with your problem and would be glad to help. I think you should approach one of the big international organisations like UNICEF whose address you will find in the London directory . . .

Dear Mrs Taylor, I am afraid you do have a problem. It is not that you are 41, but that you lack the education, knowledge, sophistication, ruthlessness and probably (in spite of the haulage business) the means as well, which would enable you to procure one of the poorest children on earth for yourselves . . .

Dear Mrs Taylor, I too have a problem. I used to think that adoption was a straightforward business, a matter of logic and good intentions. Later, I changed my mind. Now, I really don't know what to advise you for the best . . .

Dear Mrs Taylor, dear Mrs Taylor . . . I have gone away and left no address. But, as an afterthought, why don't you write to Dr da Souza, care of the QVJ Hospital, Bombay; tell him you want a baby quick and ask if he happens to know of one personally. You never know your luck.

When I was at Bedford College in London, about fifteen—no, seventeen—years ago, I had a friend called Teresa da Souza. [Very large numbers of Indian citizens share between them a relatively small number of surnames. It is therefore almost impossible, in writing a story set in India, to avoid giving the characters names which must be possessed by many real people. The solution I have adopted in *The China Egg* is to give the Bombay characters names *so* common in that city, that nobody has cause to feel personally maligned. There are

64

inevitably hospital doctors in Bombay called da Souza, there are many lawyers called Merchant, and no doubt there are para-medical workers called Desai. The story is, however, an invented one.] I use the phrase 'had a friend' deliberately. There were other people I knew better than Teresa and saw more of and certainly had more in common with, but I prized Teresa. I consciously liked her more than anyone else, and liked to refer to her as my friend, and I used to go barefoot down the hostel passage late at night to knock at her door with the deliberate intention of keeping our relationship (another of Tony's words) in good repair. If Teresa ever found me a nuisance, coming and sitting determinedly on her floor, she never showed it. I think that tolerance and amiability of hers, which I regarded respectfully and perhaps rightly as her 'maturity', was a large part of her attraction for me. I also now think that she, too, probably regarded me as someone with whom, as a matter of principle, she liked to be friendly, someone who was 'part of the experience of being in London' to which she used, with pleasing enthusiasm, to refer. I was considered bright, and I was untidy and badly brought up and had no noticeable family—commonplace attributes in a University Hall of Residence, but she told me once, smiling in that lovely, maternal way of hers, that she had never met anyone at all like me before, at home in

Bombay.

For Teresa was Indian. And yet not really Indian, and this ambiguity about her stirred my imagination. I did not know enough then to place her in any recognisable category, or to know that, in India's enormous population, the 'exceptions' and 'outsiders' are sufficiently numerous to form whole worlds of their own; I considered her a unique creature between two cultures, and participating desirably in both of them. We had two other Indians in the hostel, real ones (as I thought of them) with dark brown skins, one of them much older than the rest of us. They both wore glasses, and saris all the time, and they had the reputation of keeping themselves to themselves; at any rate neither of them showed any signs of wanting to be friends with me, a fact which does not now surprise me. But Teresa was quite different: a big girl with a creamy skin and short, wavy hair. She used to wear saris for seminars, and for parties, and sometimes lent one to me, draping it with maternal competence on my skinny hips, but the rest of the time she wore trousers and smocks she made herself, beautifully. Mini-skirts were coming into fashion but, she said, laughing, she couldn't really see herself in one of those, 'Not with my big bottom.' Evidently she knew what to take from each world and what to leave: she had been practising that skill ever since she was a small child. In the same way, though she came eagerly to all the parties, and danced, and sometimes accepted invitations out from boys or men who were probably attracted to her for much the same reasons that I was, she never, as she told me, 'let things go too far'. She herself ascribed this matter-of-factly to being a Roman Catholic, adding indulgently 'of course, it's quite different for *you*'; and if some aspects of my behaviour shocked her she never showed it, for which I was grateful.

Now, I do not think she was shocked, because I believe that, young as she was then, she had already formed the very Indian habit of regarding the behaviour of someone in a different group as being absolutely no concern of hers. I think she listened to my long, self-absorbed discourses (on changing sexual morality and the need to know *why* we do things) out of pure amiability, and joined in only because she, too, had a mild taste for intellectual theorising. I also believe now that her rejection of sexual experience for herself, 'until I marry, of course', owed more to her essential Indian-ness than to her religion, which she otherwise wore lightly.

I see I have twice used the term 'maternal' about her, and I suppose this indicates what she really was to me: a serene, smiling, comforting figure, interested but not involved, concerned but all-understanding, the perfect mother-who-never was. (My mother was dead by then, and had in any case been so far from perfect as to abandon me at the age of eleven to my inept and overworked father, a circumstance which, for many years, I imagined to be a piece of good fortune.)

Only once, that I remember, did Teresa show that I had annoyed her or caught her off-balance. Someone in my presence had referred to her as an Anglo-Indian. I asked her if this was right, and, if so, where the British bit of her mixed blood came from, naïvely supposing that no one was sensible and open as Teresa could object to such a question. But she frowned and moved away from me.

'No, no, we are pure Goans,' she said shortly. 'From Goa—the descendants of Portuguese settlers. I told you that before.'

I saw that I had irritated her without knowing why, and went away in wretched consternation, for in spite of my independent airs I was a great coward in those days. But the next time I plucked up courage to knock on her door, she was her old, smiling self, welcoming me into her warm room that was so much tidier than most people's and more like a home, with her Indian embroidered bed-cover and her hand-made cushions and her family photographs on display. There was her mother in a calf-length white wedding dress and a veil fixed to a low bandeau suggestive of an inter-war tennis champion. There was her father, the doctor, in an impeccable dark suit and stiff collar, and her sister and herself as schoolgirls with looped plaits. There was her oldest brother who had died before she was born, in the arms of a dark ayah, and there, too, an imposing lady in a sari with a pronounced resemblance to Teresa herself: 'My auntie. She's a head English mistress at one of our best schools.' And there, in pride of place, was the surviving brother, Nicky, now at medical school in Bombay, such a handsome young man one could not help agreeing with him, as he gazed, dark-eyed, laughing and confident from his leather frame, even though his Brylcreemed hair looked, by the 1960s, old-fashioned.

Fiddling with Teresa's photos, seeking suitable and pleasing subjects of conversation though still inexorably and covertly drawn to the subject of her family's exact position in their unknown continent, I said: 'Couldn't Nicky have come to London—to Guys or somewhere?' I reckoned this was a reasonable question, as Teresa herself sometimes made wry little jokes about Indian educational standards and the classic qualification 'Failed BA, Bombay'.

'Yes, well, we hoped he would,' she said, arranging her Kashmiri boxes on the mantelpiece. 'But there's a lot of competition, you know, for places in British medical schools, and I'm afraid poor Nicky is not very fond of studying. He is a lovely person and I'm sure he will make a good doctor; he is so good with people, everyone likes Nicky, but he didn't manage to do well enough in his first MB for his professor to recommend him to a British medical school. Daddy was rather disappointed. He had hoped to give Nicky the chance he himself missed—lack of funds, you know, Daddy's family was wealthy once but they lost their money, and as for Mummy's... But I think we've all accepted it now, and Nicky writes to me that he's working frightfully hard and has even given up going out with girls!'

Thus he remained in some corner of my mind for years, fixed as in his photograph, the desirable, laughing brother whom everyone liked (I had always wanted a brother), imbued with glamour not so much from the rather commonplace things Teresa told me about him as from the fact that he was her property, an adjunct to her warm, well-ordered life that was so different from my own scrappy, emotionally hand-to-mouth existence.

I have written about Teresa as if she were securely in the past, fixed for me as if in a photograph herself. Certainly when we were at Bedford together if I envisaged the husband she confidently and calmly predicted for herself I saw him as some Indian of her own sort, some indistinct but darkly successful man in a dark suit, another photograph to join the others. But she stayed on at College after I left, doing a post-graduate degree as if, after all, she was putting off the moment of return to Bombay—as if even in her confident equilibrium she feared that it would consume her.

Later, I received an invitation to her wedding. He was English, they were to be married in his home town of Doncaster. But I didn't go, because at that time Tony and I avoided weddings on principle, regarding anything more elaborate than a sparse Registry Office formality as a sentimental sell-out.

At intervals over the years we exchanged change-of-address cards, and Teresa used to send us Christmas cards signed 'with love from Teresa and Donald', and, later, 'with love from Teresa, Donald, Matthew, Vicky and Paulie'. Tony and I didn't send Christmas cards, except to clients, but occasionally I would write off a postcard from Czechoslovakia or Mexico or the Persian Gulf or wherever else Tony's work or our inclination took us. Tony and I travelled a lot, in those years.

Once, only a few years ago, when they were living in Leicester, and Tony's firm were doing a feasibility study for a conference centre near there concerned with the Third Airport, I visited them. Teresa seemed pleased and touched to see me though very surprised, so that I felt as if perhaps I should not have come, in spite of those cards exchanged. Perhaps I had been a figure fixed for her in a frame too. She

71

kept saying that I hadn't changed a bit, and it was difficult to know what to say in return because she had changed—not dramatically but in a way that altered her all over, turning her into just another overweight British housewife. I could see that, to a stranger, she would still seem 'a nice-looking woman', but something essential had gone. She had lost most of her haunting accent, and seemed to my ears to have picked up a Midlands intonation from her colourless, off-hand husband. What perverse and unmet need, I asked myself then, could have led her to seek out in marriage a man who seemed almost a caricature of a dreary Britisher? At least the children were appealing, dark-eyed creatures, carefully brought up. I had tea with them, that dank, sad summer evening, ham and salad followed by banana custard, laid out in the clammy lounge in my honour.

Afterwards, when Donald had stalked off to his 'workroom', she said, as if apologising implicitly for the tasteless food: 'Donald likes things awfully plain, you see, and so do the children of course, and I've got used to it now.'

Later, when the two youngest children had been bathed, a neighbour came in, a red-headed girl in jeans complaining with desperate, one-track amusingness about her own 'ghastly brats'. Teresa seemed to relax a little and become more animated herself. We switched on the electric fire, and drank Nescafé and some insidiously nasty liqueur the friend had brought as a present from a holiday in the Algarve. At one point in the noisy, intimate conversation between them the friend made some reference to the Portuguese and Teresa, and Teresa's 'marvellous English', that did not, to me, make sense; Teresa glanced at me from under her heavy lids, willing me not to speak.

When the friend had gone away, and I was trying to leave too, Teresa said suddenly, face averted, plumping cushions on the settee: 'Josie has always assumed I came from mainland Portugal. People rather do, you see, once I've told them my maiden name was da Souza, and I must admit I don't usually bother to correct them. I mean, it sounds silly to you probably, living in London, but round here on estates like this people think Indians are immigrants with dirty habits who kill chickens in their back yards . . . It's really simpler, you see.'

India is a lot to discard. I wondered then, even before I had been to India, how she had managed it, and decided ruthlessly that the answer was that she had discarded most of herself in the process. This was evidently the price she had had to pay in order to live in Donald's anaemic environment which must, to her, have been as mysteriously desirable as her unguessable habitat had once been to me.

Some people are snobs about money or qualifications, but I, being married to a man

73

who has acquired both but affects to despise them, had become a snob about places. Tony is an internationally known architect. Familiarity with a range of world-famous places had become, for me, the indication of the kind of success I want—wanted—for him and me. And his professional ability to affect and alter the very nature of places was, for both of us, the final achievement, the ultimate form of control.

As I drove uncertainly away, turning right and then left through the estate, past the usual purposeless imitations of pasture dotted with little piles of dog excrement instead of cow-pats, I thought that I would quite literally rather die than spend the rest of my life in an un-place like that. (I thought a lot about death at that period, and sometimes felt it was quite near at hand, potentially, and reassuring.)

Being a snob about places, I didn't think, 'What a pity she's married such a dull man', or yet, 'What a pity that living there with small children she doesn't have much scope.' I thought: she's abandoned her context, there's nothing left of her.

In spite of promises to return, I never went back there, of course. In any case, the climate of national prosperity changed once again and the plans for an airport and hence a conference centre in the Leicester area were abandoned, after Tony's firm had earned enormous sums of money from preliminary studies. This, I am told, is the way things work. But I suppose something of what Teresa had represented to me once still clung in the back of my mind, grown there, part of me. For I kept and kept the address she scribbled down for me on a piece of paper off her shopping-list pad, saying with tense gaiety, 'But if you and your husband do go to Bombay, as you said, you *must* look up my family. Don't laugh, but I used to write to them about you, long ago! They'd love to meet you...' For some reason I kept that bit of paper, even when the scheme for Tony to visit Bombay in an advisory capacity was put off, and he went to build a national library in Bogota instead.

*   *   *

So there, on that scrap of paper that even now is in my letters-file, is the message from the otherwise discarded past, that has led me finally, through labyrinthine ways, here, to this room, this non-place, with its ceiling fan which sometimes slows and stops as if starved of current and then, as unpredictably, creaks and wobbles into action again. I lie on the bed, in the tepid, disturbed draught, listening to the unending sounds from the street below, feeling sick with excitement and dread as well as physical causes, and waiting for the telephone beside me to ring. Knowing Teresa da Souza

75

long ago at Bedford College has finally brought me here. It is the last thing she or I would have expected.

Of course this is false reasoning really, I do know that. My excuse is that the need to ascribe an intricate, cosmic pattern to life's events is a widespread one, and near-universal here in India, where people from the richest to the poorest live in a world populated by scheming deities and elaborately intermeshing influences. I do know really that the slightest, most trivial event is also the product of a long-term chain of encounters and coincidences; *everything* is significant if one cares to see it that way, which means that nothing is therefore especially so. The rational voice of Tony that is still within me might point out, with equal truth, that it is rubbish to say that anything beyond my own control 'began' with knowing Teresa, or with keeping that bit of paper, or yet even with my coming to India to get—to get what? I thought at first I knew, but, as I told Tony repeatedly on the 'phone in that stuffy booth in the Turf Club at Poona, I was wrong, I had been wrong, we both had been wrong, and *he* was wrong to go on now insisting—Poor Tony. 'I don't think I am understanding properly,' he kept saying in his most priggish, didactic voice that (I well know) he puts on when he feels at a disadvantage and is determined to bully before he can be bullied. 'I don't think I can be getting this quite clear. I thought we'd agreed about all this.' And absurdly, I thought he was saying he couldn't hear me, and kept shouting the same thing over and over again, over all those thousands of miles to our house in London, till the old bearer who had called me to the 'phone removed himself in pointed disapproval to the other end of the hall.

No, in Tony's terms nothing begins long ago, and there are no patterns. Despite clear evidence to the contrary, he continues to believe that everything is our responsibility, and within our own power and choice. For him, we retain our lonely autonomy to the last moment of surrender. He would say the beginning of this present is located very recently indeed—not in my misspent youth or in our marriage, not in all those years when, achievers that we were, we tried again and again to achieve one further thing and again and again inexplicably failed, not in our carefully discussed decision to seek what we wanted elsewhere. The beginning of what he can only see as my appalling downfall from common sense and sophistication and concern for others including himself, lies for him in one specific place only, one where I have been and he has not and where, with all the sophistication at his command, he can never follow me: one unimaginable shuttered room.

When I first met Tony he appeared like any student of the 1960s, with hair and anorak and rucksack and carefully fudged 'neutral' accent,

77

and an equally careful air of benign tolerance. But I could see that underneath he was different—watchful and ambitious. Or rather, to be quite precise about this, on the surface I myself accepted and wanted him for what he seemed to be, but at another level I think I perceived that his student persona was only a temporary disguise, as to some extent was mine, and that what really drew us to one another were quite other characteristics that, for the moment, we both kept hidden.

It is difficult to give a coherent account of someone with whom you have been, unmarried or married, for over a dozen years. Tony has become part of me, I recognise that even now. I am not, whatever my other shortcomings and failures of moral courage (a good Tony-phrase, that), going to be drawn into the vulgar modern error of pretending that our marriage was 'a mistake' or that such a great slab of time can be discounted or somehow demoted to a level of not-quite-grade-A experience. I am aware that it may have been the most significant and characteristic part of my life, perhaps the most satisfying also. But the fact is that the major hidden preoccupation Tony and I shared was the concept of essential movement—preferably upward movement, of course, in a continual drive towards further achievement, prestige, power, money, fame, but failing that *any* movement rather than stasis. We were jointly addicted to change, to action, to journeys, to arrivals in new places and the making of new relationships, the conquering of fresh spheres. It was, I suppose, inevitable (or at any rate statistically inevitable if our progress were to be projected on some celestial graph) that this joint pressure towards change that was the dynamic that held us together should eventually turn itself upon our jointness.

But that is not actually how I see it. Nor how Tony sees it either. He thinks I have, with unwonted moral cowardice and lack of resolution, balked at the next logical step, thus letting him—us—down. (Not that Tony would ever quite voice the Public School concept of letting down the side, but that's what he thinks.) Whereas I think I have, for good or ill, suddenly pitched myself over an invisible barrier and moved out into a different place altogether. The fact that I don't much like it is irrelevant.

Tony and I used to joke to our friends that we had met on the Abortion Law Reform campaign. This wasn't strictly true, as by the time we got involved in that in a selflessly enthusiastic, envelope-licking way, we already knew each other; but I moved into his flat in Chalk Farm about that time and I suppose we both felt it becoming to have met working for a cause at once so humane and so rational, concerned yet realistic. (Later it began to seem less funny that we had met on such a campaign, and we avoided the subject, particularly between ourselves.) I call it 'selfless', but although all that mailing publicity to otherwise-occupied MPs was in itself drudge-work, my own high-minded concern for The Cause was well supported underneath by the memories of the hole-and-corner abortion I had once undergone. More than one, actually, but Tony thought it was one, so I had come to think of it that way myself.

As for Tony, I believe there was no ignoble personal motivation there—beyond, of course, his desire to show the world what a caring person he was and how sensitive to the problems of women, not some beery oaf. I'm sure he had never got a girl pregnant; he is far too well organised and cool for that.

Actually I think that ALRA campaign, with its culmination in the passing of Steel's Act, was the last time Tony ever worked hard for something that was going to bring him neither money nor personal recognition. By that time he was finished training and had his first job, with Inde Koch: he wasn't particularly happy there but, being Tony, he was busy laying the foundations for his future, getting to know useful people, careful never to seem pushy but in the right place at the right time, unassuming, ever watchful. The late 1960s were still good years for young architects on the make. Tony was lucky, as he now quite likes saying to people who admire his work: 'I admit,' he says deprecatingly, 'I was jolly lucky. To be working under Hemeister at that key time when the great re-think was going on . . .' And you're supposed to know that Hemeister only selected young architects to work on his schemes whom he considered 'exceptional'.

So Tony was well established by 1973–74 when the music came to a virtual stop, and there was no more public money forthcoming and not much private either: so well established that he was one of the small number of architects in England who hardly felt the cold (his phrase). He was moving into the international field by then, and had set up his own firm, or rather our own firm since I was a partner and worked in the office, in the big house we had bought in Camden Town. Several years later we moved the whole enterprise into an even larger one in a square just south of the river, slightly more convenient and attractive (Tony said) for visiting foreign firemen.

People think that architecture is 'a creative profession'—or at least, people who use such language at all think that. I used to think so myself, gaining enormous vicarious pleasure from seeing a building grow out of nowhere. First it was little sketches on Tony's desk pad or even on the paper tablecloth of a French restaurant we used to go to; then it appeared in progressively larger and more disciplined form on the drawing boards, then spawned a balsa-wood miniature of itself. Then, eventually, the main locale would change from our offices to some wilderness of mud which gradually, in turn, would be conquered, disciplined, formed and transformed. There are few moments more satisfying, I used to think, than the one when you stand on a solid floor well above ground level, looking down through newly-wiped glass, across newly-laid brick or terrazzo paving to a view which has only become 'a view' by virtue of the building's existence. And you feel the building beginning to breathe.

But what I have only realised lately is the amount of destruction implicit in all this creation. Unlike writing a book or painting a picture or producing a play, raising a building always means abolishing something else. In a town, this is usually another building or buildings, sometimes a whole street or a line of back gardens. The era of large-scale demolition was, of course, ending by the time Tony's star was rising: Hemeister himself was one of the leaders of the anti-high-rise, back-to-site-orientated-architecture movement. So Tony never had the heady experience of laying waste whole districts, and in that he was luckier than he realised. For Tony, if the truth were told, hates the past. Had he been in professional existence around 1960 he would have been a natural comprehensive redeveloper, destructive, implacable, inexorably high-minded, and would now in consequence be discredited. As it was, he profited, discreetly as always, by other men's mistakes. These days, anyway, most of the buildings he creates are on 'new' sites, tracts of field in the Midlands, tracts of sand or scrub in other continents. Once, in Bogota, a shanty town that had unwisely appeared on the cleared ground before the building itself began did have to be cleared; but then (Tony said) the shacks virtually fell down of their own accord, and after all it had been made absolutely clear to the occupants from the beginning that they had no right to be there, so what else could he have done? Nothing, Tony, nothing.

What he does not realise is that these non-places (as he imagines them), these bare tracts of land where he creates his living, breathing buildings, are in fact places too before he gets at them, and parts of other people's unknown lives. What about the cattle that graze the grass before he comes and abolishes it with his structure, what about the herdsmen, the nomads, the men who have been coming for ever to catch their fish at that particular bend of the river which his planning diverts and 'landscapes', what about the women who use the rocks to beat their washing? Raising buildings, particularly large public ones incorporating chunks of art in the form of murals or sculptures by local artists, is, by tradition, a moral activity; but it seems to me now that it is, at best, equivocal, at worst an unwanted and meddling activity, worldly, vainglorious and often not even particularly useful. The buildings Tony and his team design now are rarely intended for anyone to live in and raise a family. They are not often even schools or hospitals; other architects are specialising in these. Most often they are demonstration buildings, structures essentially intended to display the wealth and aspirations of the international company or government that commissions them.

Architects can't leave well alone—of necessity they can't, since if they did most building would cease. Architects play at being God, indecently, wantonly powerful. That is also why Tony, with me, I will admit, as his willing accomplice, was not content to leave our joint and very pleasant life the way it was, but wanted to add to it. That is why, when no addition appeared in the natural course of events, in spite of every encouragement, Tony was not prepared to leave well alone, leave the matter to Fate, admit failure, or any of those humble human reactions, but insisted we try another method to attain our goal.

We did not have a baby.

At first, when our 'decision' to start one produced nothing, I was surprised and slightly offended, hurt in my self-esteem but not really distressed. All around our contemporaries were, in the over-confident phrase, 'starting a family'; that had contributed in a large part to our feeling that it must be time that our own life was similarly elaborated; we might be missing out on something. I did not, in those early days, particularly want a baby for its own sake, though I managed to conceal this fact from myself, and I was wary—properly wary, I considered—of the engulfing and destructive power of parenthood. At dinner parties sometimes there were wives my own age, with chapped red hands and skirts of the wrong length, who wilted visibly in general conversation but could become garrulous in corners on the subjects of perineal stitches, mixed feeding or the difficulty of organising a rota for a playgroup. I disliked and feared them, as if they might, in an underhand, motherlike way that was belied by their feeble appearance, have some power to co-opt me into their group. And there were even the occasional husbands, though these were rarer, who seemed to have caught parenthood from their wives like an intimate disease, who wore nervous exhaustion as a transparent membrane over their features, and got into neurotic quarrels with other husbands over natural childbirth or teaching babies to read. The thought of becoming like that was, Tony and I agreed, awful, and we promised that neither of us ever would.

Only we weren't offered the chance to. At first, we wore our disappointment lightly, almost congratulating one another on having, yet another month, 'got away with it'. Only as the months accumulated into a year, and then into two, and began to assume a repetitive pattern of rising hopes that would abruptly, undramatically fall, as a line falls on a temperature chart, did we begin to get rattled.

We sought the best advice, efficiently and expensively. People like us do not take our turn at NHS clinics, sitting semi-dressed in cubicles waiting for some boy-doctor to pass: still less do we go on dumbly hoping while doing nothing about it. We were doers, tirelessly executive. The first specialist we saw was confident that 'our little trouble' was nothing that could not be put right. So was the next. So was the endocrinologist whom Tony saw, who had a new theory about the part played by male sub-fertility; and so was the surgeon who performed an elaborate operation on my fallopian tubes to try to persuade them to do their job properly. That surgeon had pictures of eggs in his consulting room, vaguely surrealistic lithographs by a well-known artist. All the treatment was the latest available, and we felt sorry for all those poor, hopeful, helpless couples in distant provincial towns who did not have such facilities available to them. It was quite exciting and interesting knowing that we were the recipients of such optimistic and revolutionary new advances. It was a complication that Tony kept flying off to Bogota and Riyadh and places like that, but I usually went with him, and we had introductions to members of the world mafia of gynaecologists, and had blood and urine tests done on the appropriate day in a dozen different consulting rooms and private hospitals. Being at the right place, together, at the right moment, gave us a sense of achievement in itself. Only we did not get pregnant.

It was my fault, it was his fault. It was nobody's fault ('Well, we don't like to use the word *fault* in these cases, Mrs Um-er-'). It was both our faults. I produced eggs on schedule, it appeared—but did they get to the right place? Within me, it seemed, among all that antiquated, Dickensian female mechanism, there was some dusty, dead-letter office where misdirected eggs accumulated, unloved and unreachable, among packing cases and lumber and old bits of string and balls of dust and forgotten teamugs. ('Let me see, Mrs Er—when did you have that D and C?... Mmm, *I* see... Well, perhaps we should send you for another little clean-out.') But Tony had his problems, too. He had plenty of sperms (he kept being assured) but unfortunately, ha, ha, they did not seem much good at swimming. Or, if they swam, they huddled together, like incompetent novices drowning in a municipal pool, or silly sheep. Once I saw a crowd of them, in a drop under a microscope, and had an urge to push them apart with my finger shouting, 'Don't bunch, you little idiots, don't *bunch*', like a netball teacher I once had at school.

But, Tony's sheep notwithstanding, I got the impression that the greater part of the problem lay with me. And this was just as well from one point of view, as by that time I had developed a craving for a baby for its own sake, and at least it meant that the problem remained, literally, within me, rather than being dumped reproachfully in Tony's lap. He, I must say—though he would not hesitate to say it himself either—behaved well about the whole thing. He co-operated in batteries of grotesque tests and even reacted with humour rather than irritation when informed by me, once again, that we had got to have intercourse first thing tomorrow morning, but preferably not before seven thirty a.m. Even when my self-confidence, continually sapped by the insidious poison of hope deferred, at last failed, and I wept that it must be that abortion I had once had that had damaged my tubes, he was calm about it, and said, 'What rubbish'. It was more likely, he insisted, that I'd been trying too hard and had got tense, like Dr Thingummy had said. He was wrong of course—at least I thought so at the time—but it was nice to hear him say that, and I thought then how awful it would have been to be childless and married to a husband who was reproachful about it. I was safe on that account with Tony. Harking back to the past, reproachfully or otherwise, is not part of his make-up. In Tony's view, the idea that you pay for everything, one way or another, is just a piece of lumber from an out-dated moral system. For him the past, any past, is dead: to ascribe power to it is against his deepest instincts.

We did not 'go blabbing' (Tony's phrase) to our friends about our unique and central failure. Most of them seemed to assume that we were childless on purpose: our life of movement and action made this plausible. We did not mix with the kind of people who would have had the innocent impertinence to ask, though once or twice some friend did say something to us, respectfully or with jokey resentment, about 'taking the world population problem to heart'. I was struck dumb, literally unable to speak, but Tony passed such leading remarks off with ease, managing to create a diffused impression of understated concern and deep background thought. He was my ally, and I appreciated it. Regardless of the subject, we had the desirable marital habit of presenting a united front. Not for us the unseemly public wrangles, the 'humorous' but barbed back-chat at dinner tables, the individual whining to third parties in pubs or lunchtime restaurants. We were too successful a couple for that.

The only time I ever saw Tony lose his composure, all those time-charted years we were trying to have a baby, was with the gynaecologist who asked us: 'Have you ever thought of adoption?' It was evident to me that she herself was not thinking at all as she said this. She had simply reached the stage in a long-familiar procedure at which she made a practice of introducing that remark, in a special sympathetic voice. I now feel Tony was unnecessarily rude: after all, her concern was with people's bodies, not with the contents of their heads. Her pretence otherwise was just one of the extras of private medicine; but at the time, I thought she deserved it when he said:

'That's a damned silly question. Do you really suppose that people like us would *not* have thought of adoption? Do you imagine we might not have heard of it?'

Walking back to the car afterwards, he said levelly: 'You don't really want to adopt, do you? I mean—it sounds difficult these days, and not very satisfactory.'

'I know.'

'There was that telly programme last month ... all those depressing couples in the studio telling how long they'd been in the queue, and that social worker or whatever she was saying that her adoption society had closed its lists

90

now, and making it sound as if couples should be grateful for absolutely anything that was offered . . . I mean, I don't know about you, but any thought I might have had . . . It put me right off.'

'Yes. I know. It put me off too.' The programme, which we had not discussed at the time, had indeed haunted me unpleasantly, quenching hopes which I had only vaguely formed, aborting day-dreams. Couples like us have standards in children as in everything else. The idea of taking on someone else's handicapped baby, or an elder child that had been through a string of institutions (these had been two of the recommendations of the odiously smug social worker on the programme) was ridiculous.

If that attitude may be thought callous and worldly, it might at least be said to show self-knowledge. I intimated this to Tony. He was uncommunicative as we drove back to the office.

Presently he said, 'I wouldn't be set against *any* adoption, you understand. But it would have to be the right one. And I'm damned if I'm going to be grateful to anyone.'

Tony is such a secret operator that I don't know if he already had something in mind at that point. It is just possible he had been talking to William and Angela beforehand.

William and Angela are, I suppose, our oldest

friends. Angela and Tony were at the RIBA together, and then she married William who is a lawyer. They both come from enormously but quietly wealthy families, which is just as well; though they are both extremely nice, they are a slightly soft couple and I feel that, without all that money, they might have sunk without trace into an unenterprising existence. As it is, they have been able to inhabit without effort the kind of world which Tony and I have only attained by exertion and sharpness of view. William and Angela have not needed to become sharp, or calculating or ruthless. Even William's law is something grand and recondite to do with the Treasury. They live in Kensington and are very hospitable. Angela has never practised as an architect, and they have four children. 'Angela' has always seemed to me an orange-gold name— overtones of angels with Burne-Jones hair, perhaps—and when I say her name to myself I see her sitting in their drawing room, which does have a lot of pinky-orange colours in it as well as a Paul Klée, leaping to her stockinged feet to greet us, saying 'How *nice* to see you' in the way she always does as if she really meant it.

Come to think of it, I feel about Angela rather as I once did about Teresa da Souza. I do not really have a great deal in common with her, but I am drawn to her and like thinking of her as a friend.

We were at their house one evening for what

Angela, with undue modesty, described as 'a snack' before going to Covent Garden. William was making Bucks Fizz, which is their regular party drink and has also contributed, I imagine, to my impression of a warm goldenness enveloping their house. William, though occasionally loquacious, rarely introduces a new topic of conversation, but this evening Angela said to him almost as if she were prompting him: 'Darling, did you tell them about the Loewes?'

The Loewes are a couple we only know through the Rowans. She is an actress who was successful for a while about fifteen years ago. He deals in pictures and rather grand antiques. I have no idea where *their* money comes from. Angela and William see a lot of them, I believe, but have never thrust us together much. They tend to keep their friends separate, except at their big New Year parties, and I expect that, with their habitual tact, they have picked up that we don't care for the Loewes much.

But now Angela said, 'Did you tell them about the Loewes? I'm sure they'd be interested.'

And William, having finished easing off a champagne cork without making a fuss of it, said heartily: 'Good Lord no, I didn't. Yes, great goings on there, I'm afraid. They seemed to have put the Home Office's back up quite a bit, and I must say I'm not surprised. It's a sensitive subject these days.'

'William, you're talking absolute Greek to us,' I said, amused. '*What* subject? Why the Home Office?'

'Oh, sorry, I thought Angela had put you in the picture already... Angie?... Oh. Oh, well, *anyway*. You know that Paul Loewe has an interest in Indian art and has been importing a certain amount of stuff?'

'Don't tell me,' I said. 'He's fallen foul of Customs and Excise?' That, if the truth were told, was just the fate I should have predicted for Paul Loewe, a man whose weak, good-looking face was of exactly the sort that adorns newspaper stories about corruption, fraud or homosexuality among the well-to-do.

'Well, in a way, but not quite as I think you mean it! No, it wasn't a picture or a carving that he and Trish tried to bring in without the proper papers. It was a baby.'

'Good Lord,' said Tony—just a shade too quickly.

'An Indian orphan,' said Angela, taking over the subject. 'At least, they swear it's an orphan, and I'm sure it must be. I mean—how else could they have got it?'

'With money, my dearest innocent,' said William fondly.

'Let us suppose for the moment it is an orphan,' cut in Tony, evidently wanting to get the story narrated clearly.

'Yes, well, Trisha and Paul were in Delhi,'

Angela continued warmly. 'And they met someone who was telling them all about the number of unwanted children there are in India—over a million, Trisha said—and that got her thinking. I mean, she and Paul have never had any children—'

'She had a daughter by her first husband,' put in William.

'Yes, but she's nearly grown up now, and in America anyway with her father. And Trisha said she just found herself thinking and thinking how wonderful it would be to be able to take a child—even just one child—out of that awful environment, all that poverty and so forth, and bring it up here with everthing it could want. She told me she felt, all at once, that if they could only do that, they—she—would have *done* something with her life.'

'I can understand that,' put in Tony, a remark which sounded kind but which, as I could tell, wasn't really intended to be. Trisha wears great fluffy coats, and fluffy hair framing a little, pinched, old-doll's face, and rather a lot of very, very expensive scent reminiscent of the interior of a Greek church. You should think of hidden sensuality, but instead you think of cobwebs.

'So they did just that,' said William succintly, measuring orange juice. Angela had fallen momentarily silent, side-tracked, I thought, on to the moral question her description had raised.

'But how, William?' I asked. 'What's the procedure?'

'Ah, that's just it. There is, as I now know, having had a session at the Home Office myself the other day, a proper procedure for these things. Paul rang me up in a panic, understandably, when the baby was taken away from them at Heathrow and put into care. As I told him, this sort of case isn't my field at all, but I naturally did what I could before passing him on to someone else. Elliot Mead, actually.'

'You mean they took the baby away at Heathrow because it was an illegal immigrant?' I asked, chilled by the mental picture. Silly Trisha, I thought, did not quite deserve that.

'That's what I thought at first too,' said Angela. 'And I thought how *monstrous*, when it had a home ready for it and everything . . . but apparently it was really because the Loewes had no health-clearance papers for it. Well, they had no papers, full-stop. William and I can't understand how they got it on to the 'plane at Delhi in the first place.'

'Once again, I suspect the answer may be money,' put in William, man-of-the-world.

'Well anyway they did, and they arrived in London. But the baby wasn't allowed to leave the airport with them. Local authority social workers were called, and there was the most terrific kerfuffle—nightmarish, Trisha said, particularly on top of a twelve-hour flight. She thought at one point they were going to have to turn round and go straight back to India. But finally they said the baby could stay for the moment if it was admitted to hospital. They thought it might have TB or something. And then Trisha and Paul stuck out for Great Ormond Street rather than the local place. So that's where it went, but it turned out not to have TB anyway, just worms and things like that. I don't know what you're laughing for, Tony, children *do* get worms, even in polite society! You wait till you have one... Anyway, it's been discharged now, but there's a supervision order on it and poor Trisha and Paul don't even know if they'll be allowed to keep it. Oh, just imagine looking after a baby you didn't know if you were going to be able to keep.' There were tears now in Angela's eyes. She added after a moment: 'I don't know why I keep calling the poor little thing "it". It's a boy; about a year old, but awfully tiny. I've seen it— him. Quite light-skinned for an Indian, but with great, dark eyes. I can see why Trisha fell in love—'

'But why,' I said, needing to get this absolutely clear. 'Why might the Home Office not let it—him—stay?'

'Well, not because of race apparently—at least, that's their story. Trisha says she doesn't believe it: she's got very emotional on the subject, and I don't wonder. But they told

97

William—didn't they, darling?—that it would have been just the same whatever country the baby'd come from. Apparently it's the *parents* who have to be approved by the local Children's Department before the baby is even brought in—the adoptive parents, I mean. And Trisha says there's this awful social worker who's taken against her and Paul, and she thinks that the Home Office have instructed this woman to find fault with them and their home to pay them out for not going through the proper channels... Oh, I know, Trisha is a bit paranoid and may be exaggerating, but it does seem so frightfully unfair and stupid when the baby is *here* and you think what they can offer him compared with what he would get—or rather not get—in his own country. Why there he would very likely just have starved slowly to death, Trisha said. He might still, if he's sent back. How *can* the Home Office be so awful?'

'Steady on, darling,' said William. 'I agree the situation as it has turned out may seem a stupid one, but in principle the Home Office are right, you know. All that vetting of the adoptive parents before the adoption can go through is, in general terms, in the child's own interest, that's what the legislation is there for. After all, couples aren't allowed to adopt a baby within the United Kingdom without showing evidence that they're suitable and seriously intentioned and so forth, so there's no reason to vary the rules because the child in question comes from outside. If literally anybody could fly home from a trip to India or anywhere else with a baby under their arm, then—literally anybody might. Psychopaths. Perverts. People like the Moors murderers. Think of that.'

Angela thought, looking stricken, and said no more for the moment.

Tony said, 'But William, there's no suggestion, surely, that the Loewes could conceivably come into this category? I will admit that Trisha's always seemed to me rather a silly woman. But silliness has never been a bar to motherhood.'

'No, no, of course not.' William frowned, and I felt him thinking that he was perhaps being indiscreet and should not have been drawn so far into this discussion. But after a moment he said: 'No, it's just that Trisha and Paul are both over forty—she's older than he is—and apparently these days a couple of that age aren't usually considered for adoption. Also, it appears, Trisha did have a fairly substantial breakdown after her first marriage ended. But I'm inclined to agree with you and Angie that these things do not, in the circumstances, strike one as all that important, if the alternative is sending the baby back to a life of destitution . . . No, I'm afraid it's still more complicated than this. It comes back to this business of their not having got any clearance papers from the Indian

99

end. They should have got a lawyer to act for them there, and got some sort of signed or verified statement from the baby's legal guardian to the effect that he or she consented to let the baby go. It isn't just the Home Office being stroppy off their own bat: the Indian High Commission's a bit miffed too, apparently, and one can see why.'

'I think the High Commission have a nerve to act so concerned now,' said Angela, coming to life again. 'The baby was living on the street. Just like that, naked, on the bare pavement, Trisha told me.'

'Yes, but it wasn't living there alone, was it?' said William the lawyer. 'It wasn't lying abandoned, and even if it had seemed to be ... I know Trisha's over-emotional, but you're not suggesting, surely Angie, that she just picked up the baby and walked off with it—stole it, in fact?'

'No,' said Angela after a pause. 'She met the grandmother. She told me. The grandmother *wanted* her to have the baby. She said they couldn't feed it. Surely that should count?'

'Well, it might have, if the Loewes had had the sense to get the woman to a lawyer to make a statement. After all, Delhi is hardly the African bush ... But unfortunately there now seems to be trouble in that quarter as well. The High Commission say they've received a message from Delhi that the baby's uncle, I think it is, some male relative anyway—says his permission was never asked and he wants the baby returned.'

'You didn't tell me that,' said Angela, jerking upright and looking distressed again.

'No, I'm sorry, I meant to. Elliot Mead rang me this morning. I've had a busy day and it slipped my mind.'

The longish pause that followed, in which we all sipped orange juice and champagne and pursued our separate moral preoccupations, was broken by Tony. In his best putting-the-situation-in-perspective manner, he said: 'Well. The message seems to be that if you want to do the right thing—and I'm sure the Loewes *were* doing the right thing in wanting to give the chance of a decent life on earth to the poor little bastard—you have to go about it in the right way, or at any rate the legally approved way. Poor Paul and Trisha. Rotten for them. Let's hope it works out for them in the end.'

I could hear, and rather hoped no one else could hear, the note of faint smugness beneath his air of sympathetic concern. He was congratulating himself that *he* would never behave in that feckless, self-defeating way in an attempt to get what he wanted. Tony is the prototype of the man in the New Testament who stood praying away from the crowd, saying 'Lord, I thank thee that I am not as other men are.' I suppose I always had a certain amount of fellow-feeling with that man myself. Tony had not found the story of the Loewes' fiasco disturbing and discouraging. On the contrary, he had learnt useful things from it and had begun to form constructive plans. Again, the same was true of me.

It was *Figaro* that night at Covent Garden. As the houselights died, Tony, in a gesture that was not typical of him, took my hand and squeezed it. I squeezed back.

The overture began, those disturbing introductory bars to an opera which, however lovely, never quite seems to fulfil some thrilling promise made right at its beginning. But at the start you feel that you are embarking on a passionate journey which is familiar because you have made it before, yet never the same twice, a carefree excursion towards delight and yet also a voyage of unimaginable potential importance, like the insouciant beginning of a momentous relationship.

*   *   *

Five months later, Tony and I got on a 'plane to Bombay. Ostensibly, the purpose of the journey was for Tony to meet one of India's leading architects and to view a building in course of construction which was supposed to be an interesting example of the use of something or other, and then to go and advise on another site in Bangalore and a university in Sri Lanka. In fact, we had gone to India to look for a baby. Our baby.

It occurred to me when I was packing, folding new silk and newly-ironed cotton in layers of tissue paper while a cold rain beat the bare trees in the square, that long ago women like me used to go to India not to seek children but to seek husbands. Unmarried Victorian girls, who were felt to have exhausted the circumscribed possibilities of their own social circle, used to be shipped off to Bombay by P & O with steamer trunks full of calico drawers and tropical-weight corsets. I remembered William, whose family is of the kind that provided governor-generals for the British Raj, talking amusingly about it once, saying that the girls, who arrived at the beginning of the cool season, were known to young subalterns as 'the Fishing Fleet'. Those who, by the end of a strenuous season, had still not succeeded in catching themselves husbands or even a whiff of a possible fiancé, sailed again for home as the thermometer began to climb in March. They were known as the 'Returned Empties'. When I had first heard this, I had thought it funny. Now, with my sensitivity morbidly aroused by the impending journey and its secret aim, the anecdote struck me as horribly poignant. Poor, poor girls, I thought. How awful to be such defenceless losers in a callous social system, and how infinitely preferable to be me with the world, literally, my oyster to be opened in quest of a pearl. Sensations of power and independence which, over the last three years or so of gradually accruing disappointment, had ebbed from me, leaving me uncertain and dispirited, had returned now. I felt that Tony and I were in control of our own destiny once again. More importantly and literally, we were in control of someone else's also.

You may, I suppose, wonder why we perceived getting a baby from India as such a different matter from adopting one at home. Now, the distinction does indeed seem to be arbitrary and unrealistic. But I can only tell you that, at the time, the two courses of action seemed poles apart. If conventional adoption appeared to us a dreary second best—if not a fourth or fifth best—importing an obviously exotic child from the other side of the world struck us as daring, imaginative and, in some ill-defined but pleasant way, a constructive gesture towards world harmony and racial integration. Repelled as we were by the image of ourselves as a couple of biological losers waiting cravenly in a queue for someone to decide our fate for us, we could not fail to be attracted by an alternative demanding initiative, personal decision and (it was evident) a degree of know-how. We saw the project as a challenge, and tackled it accordingly. We also thought, rightly or wrongly, that in a country like India, where people can die of hunger through no fault of their own and babies are given up through sheer necessity, the chances of our getting a child of desirable intelligence and temperament were considerably higher than they were now at home. As Tony put it, 'What sort of dumb slob in Britain today fails to have an abortion *and* fails to cope with the aid of the Welfare State once the baby has arrived. Do we want the child of someone like that?'

Much of this reasoning now strikes me as suspiciously defensive and self-regarding and, indeed, too rational. There is in the impulse towards parenthood, I now believe, a core of essential irrationality, a need that defies analysis. Neither the vague and faintly priggish reasons people commonly advance for having children (want to be a real family, want to perpetuate our line) nor the equally priggish or fatuously trivial ones they advance for voluntary childlessness (world population problem, desire to go on going to expensive restaurants) touch the heart of the matter, the mystery.

But I have to put on record, however embarrassing or chilling it may be in retrospect, that at the time we believed we knew what our feelings were and what we were doing.

William and Angela were the only people to whom we had so far divulged our plans: we knew that they would be pleased and interested, would not tell anyone else, and would never mention the matter again if we failed. They were an absorbent couple. Like many fundamentally conservative people, they tended to live experiences vicariously, through their friends, and perhaps also to be drawn to friends who could indeed provide that experience. Or, as Angela flatteringly put it:

'I do think it's awfully courageous of you, and I do think you're absolutely right. It makes me want to do it myself, in a way, but, you know, when you've got four of your own you get sort of spoilt and cowardly... Perhaps if we were younger, or if I didn't *know* without even discussing it that William's family would be against it. Not to mention mine, though I think Mummy might understand... But I have an awful feeling that one day I may regret never having taken the plunge. Our family's complete now and growing up. Lovely children, but—oh, I do envy you! I really do.'

Later she said, with shining eyes: 'It must be so *exciting* to know that your baby is already there, perhaps, on the other side of the world, waiting for you to find him! I don't know how you can bear it so calmly. But you and Tony have always been so self-controlled, haven't you?'

No doubt she was right, because, although what she said unnerved me a little I did not show it. It unnerved me because, amazing as it

106

may seem, up to that moment I really do not think I had considered the baby as an autonomous being with a life of its own which would continue (supposing it did not die of starvation or cholera) whether we swept in and adopted it or not. It was as if, at one level, I had thought that our decision to adopt would somehow call into being a child which would not have been there otherwise.

To cover my unease, I said to Angela: 'You sound as if you believe in predestination.'

'I think I do, sort of,' she said after a moment. 'Don't you, at all?'

'I don't think so, no.' The idea did not appeal to me. I thought, but did not say: that is the sort of thing Indians believe in. *Karma*, or whatever it is.

After another pause, Angela said uncertainly: 'I didn't really mean what I said like that, though. I meant just... Well, your baby probably is there already, isn't he—or she? The baby that your contact will have found for you, I mean. It's up to you, of course, whether you take it or not, but if you don't take it, if you don't feel it's the right child for you or something, then that won't make it disappear. It'll just mean—oh, I'm sorry, I don't know why I'm saying this, I got mixed up. I'm not sure what I *do* mean.'

I said carefully, not at all liking the vista of negative responsibility she had suddenly opened

before me: 'In a sense, Angie, surely it'll only be
"our child" when we've made it ours by
bringing it back to England and looking after
it?'

'Oh, of course,' she said. 'I was just being
silly. I'm sorry. I do know really that the future
isn't there till it happens.' But she still did not
look quite happy. Presently she said: 'By the
way, Elliot Mead has been pulling strings and it
looks as if the Loewes *are* going to be able to
keep their baby after all. Isn't that *good*.'

'Very good,' I said, not entirely sincerely. It
wasn't that I wished them any actual harm, and
in the last resort I did not like to think of their
child being sent back. But I did not want to
belong to the same club as the Loewes. To know
that people like them were also bringing up a
child from India would, I felt, diminish very
slightly our own pleasure and satisfaction in
doing so.

'They've decided to call him Jeremy, which I
must say I do find a little funny. I mean, I
wouldn't expect them to call him Jamshed or
anything, but I would have thought some
simple, more international name like Jimmy or
Paul or something would have been better. It's
not as if he's ever going to *look* English.'

'Didn't he have a name when they got him?'

'Trisha says she doesn't know what it was, if
he did ... She doesn't seem to want to be able
to tell him anything about India when he's

older; she says she couldn't ever bear to go back there and doesn't want even to think about it. I think that's rather a mistake, myself.'

'Yes, so do I. I thought you were supposed to talk to adopted children about their origins.' We intended to cultivate such Indian acquaintances as we possessed in London, dredging through our address books for hitherto little-regarded names on the outer-rim of party giving. I had vaguely envisaged taking the child—our child— back to India on a trip when he was big enough. *Look darling, this is your heritage. Look at the elephant, darling, and that carved temple. You have all the Western world—and this too, you lucky little thing.*

'Trisha seems to think that environment is everything,' said Angela, knitting her pretty forehead. 'Do you know, she actually told me the other day that his—Jeremy's—skin is getting lighter now that he's in England. That *can't* be true, can it?'

'I shouldn't think so!'

'Of course,' said Angela quickly; and I recognised now that she was treading carefully with me, 'I do think, we both think, that upbringing is frightfully important, and I suppose you and Tony must too or you wouldn't be embarking on this, but—well, people do inherit things as well, don't they?'

'Tony would certainly agree with you there,' I said, masking the faint irritation I felt at her naïve remark. 'That's why he's keen to go somewhere where there's—well—a good choice of child.' I was aware as I said it that there was something slightly awful about this remark, however honest: perhaps it was, indeed, too honest for the timid present-day convention of decency in these matters. Angela looked as if she thought so too.

She said, almost coldly for her: 'Well, but surely you won't find yourselves with six babies lined up to choose from? Like puppies or kittens?'

'Heavens no, I shouldn't think so,' I said hastily. Not having been to India as yet, I could not envisage the details of our quest clearly, and indeed had avoided doing so. Perhaps I squeamishly wanted the actual mechanisms, like those of conception, to be hidden, but on reflection that was obviously not possible. 'No, I imagine our doctor-contact will pick one out. We've said we don't mind which sex it is, but we'd like something known, if possible, about its parents.' Put like that, the enterprise sounded vague and unsatisfactory. I hoped Angela did not think so too.

'Where did you get this doctor from?' she asked.

'He's the brother of someone I knew well at college, Teresa da Souza.' Saying the name gave me courage. 'You don't know her—she lives out of London. I knew that her brother practised in

110

Bombay, and I contacted her on the off-chance that he might be able to help. And it turned out that he's just the person to approach, because he has some sort of interest in an orphanage and has actually helped to place a couple of babies for adoption already—in Holland, I think Teresa said. She's written to him to expect us.'

'And you say,' said Angela, smiling at me with affectionate forgiveness after all, 'that you don't believe in predestination!'

I mistrust that sort of belief, as I have said. Fundamentally it seemed to me—seems even now—a kind of sentimentality disguised as something more honourable. But the desire after all to infuse our consciously hard-headed approach with some external, transforming magic was irresistible to me also. I succumbed, and smiled back at her.

★　　★　　★

I have landed at a number of airports in the Third World by now: I ought to know what to expect. The jet-plane descends and descends, baked earth and scrub and rock rise to meet it till you are convinced that the pilot has, with his Western-trained judgment, made some terrible error, and that this wilderness taking shape beneath you has only been created to be your grave, the holocaust of all that technological hubris. Some kind of lichen-crustation becomes

111

visible on the hillside now slanting beneath the 'plane's wheeling turn, but it is not lichen but a colony of insects or rodents, and then not rodents but human beings, living in shanties clinging to the hillside only a few hundred feet below, with no more connection with the deafening monster above them than if they were on another planet. You crane your neck in dread to see a battered toy lorry unloading metal pipes, a tiny oblivious woman carrying water, a child squatting by a chain-link fence, an old man scurrying from destruction as the very grasses within the 'plane's widening shadow begin to shiver and bend—and then, suddenly, with a bump like Alice landing on dry sticks at the bottom of the rabbit hole, you are down on the tarmac, taxiing in the engine's decelerating roar, the vision and the dread are gone and you are part of this other world yourself and must come to terms with it.

Third World airports smite you with their debilitating heat as soon as the 'plane's doors are open. As if you have abruptly changed class, you reach the terminal in chipped and rattling buses. Inside, there are ceiling fans and several different untidy queues which must be joined before you have obtained enough bits of paper from enough preoccupied officials to be allowed to penetrate the disorder of the Customs shed. The airports were always built before the days of jumbo-jets and their meagre resources always appear to be strained to breaking point. You wait interminably for your luggage, sweating and becoming neurotic, while people wrangle and wail in the quest for their own. I should know all this by now. It was unreasonable of me to become agonised at Bombay airport because *this* was India, a momentous place of destiny for us, and I felt it was eluding me, perhaps even fatally so. Our twentieth-century magic carpet that was to carry us on the way towards our hearts' desire had brought us only here, here to this confined place of twentieth-century nightmare, the décor of a banal bad dream about anxiety, claustrophobia and the loss of property and identity.

I became agonised silently, on my own, while Tony argued loudly with a series of officials about the need to bring in three cameras. Against the glass doors beyond the officials' desks, the only way out from this travellers' prison, the shapes of people were pressed, as if the Indian population problem were living up to its myth and the entire sub-continent were now full up to standing room only. Each time an escaping traveller finally reached the doors and the guard standing there pushed them open, the bodies surged forward clamouring, hands outstretched, surrounding the traveller, swallowing him up—and then the doors banged shut again. They were, of course, beggars. I had known in theory that they would be there.

113

Faced with the reality, I was appalled.

But one of Tony's professional contacts had sent his car to meet us. The elderly driver fended the beggars off, shepherded us with old-world courtesy to an old-fashioned looking car, and placed our copious luggage in what he charmed Tony by referring to as 'the dickey'. I wasn't listening, as my attention was distracted by a small, left-over, beggar child hopefully touching my elbow. Then the driver noticed him and shooed him away too.

Rich man, poor man, beggarman, thief ... whose child will be ours?

The car joined a narrow motorway: we passed palm trees, creeks, a paddy field or two, outcrops of modern cement apartment blocks, stained and crumbling already in that ruthless climate. Hoardings advertised Air-India, biscuits, family planning. Film stars, as huge, highly coloured and uncaring as Hindu gods, stared out from vast posters, oblivious of the ramshackle huts clustered in the hoardings' shadows. Similar hovels ran in a fetid ribbon along the road's very verge, and occupied a scrap of waste land beneath another monstrous exhortation which advised irrelevantly: 'Make a Friend of Your Taxman—Trust and Confide in Him.'

What did you expect, I scolded myself? You've seen poverty before, in other places. And you knew that Indian poverty is famous for

114

being in a class by itself. You were surely prepared. This, after all, is the basic reason why you are here. You do not seek a child in a rich land.

Usually arrival in a new country elates me, and I am more readily captivated by it than Tony is. Tony sees places more selectively than I do, as potential environments for transforming architecture, and gets irritated more quickly than I do by inefficiency or failures in communication. As we drove into Bombay, however, he seemed cheerful, well in control of the situation and therefore ready to be pleased with what he saw. He talked to the driver about the way the city was spreading, even produced a street map he must have obtained in London, and pointed out to me some sky-scraper overlooking a blue bay which had apparently made architectural history. As for me, although I suppose I must have known that Bombay was a port—all those unmarried British girls landing there long ago with their tropical-weight corsets and their suffocating, unmentionable hopes—I had not even realised till now that it was a seaside town as well. We passed by what appeared to be a south coast pier: the driver said it was a mosque. People seemed to be walking to it across the water.

'Are you a Moslem yourself?' Tony asked him. India had evidently gone to his head.

With reserve, the man answered: 'No, sar. I

am Christian. I was educated at Scottish Mission School. I am always working for British in old days, sar.' I thought he was rather offended, but Tony didn't seem to notice.

★   ★   ★

That mosque, or mausoleum rather, which is called Hadji Ali and has a causeway to it across a beach that emits a putrid stench at low tide, is about the only first impression I can recall. Now that I have got to know Bombay so much better—better even, in some ways, I now feel, than I shall ever know another city, including London—it is hard to think myself back into the state of mind of my first few days there. It is as if my depression that first afternoon driving in, which Tony sensibly ascribed to jet-lag and culture shock, was in fact the beginning of everything starting to change. It was the sign; though of course I did not recognise it immediately, and indeed managed to thrust it aside.

In our air-conditioned hotel room on the fourteenth floor I slept deeply but woke again to fear, asking myself in panic Which country? Which year?—as the telephone rang and rang again on the bedside table. It was the owner of the car, inviting us out to dinner.

We were invited out to dinner nearly every evening that first week, in expensively furnished flats placed to get the night breezes, or in restaurants and clubs too grand to be bothered by the permit rules on alcohol. Tony believes in what he calls 'setting up the scene' in advance in foreign countries, since he is always in a hurry. He was due to leave Bombay at the end of the week. I would remain to pursue what he referred to, to me, as 'our private venture', while he journeyed south to Bangalore, Sri Lanka, and then finally to give a lecture in Calcutta.

He lectured in Bombay also, and in the daytime he was mostly busy. There was somewhere called 'New Bombay' which people seemed very keen that he should examine. Meanwhile I walked round an older Bombay on my own, admiring the huge Gothic buildings the British had left behind, the fairy palaces of railway builders and tax collectors. The wives of the architects and business tycoons with whom we dined made ritualistic offers to take me shopping, but I did not want to shop for silk or jewellery or shawls or Kashmiri boxes or ivory or glass-paintings or brass. My acquisitiveness lay in another direction.

On the face of it, the next step I had to take was simple. 'When are you going to 'phone da Souza?' Tony asked on our second morning. 'I hope he bloody well can help us after all this.' He was restive, because Nicky da Souza hadn't written to us before we had left England. He,

Tony, had efficiently been to see someone at the Home Office, only to be told, as I had already ascertained from William, that we had to find a specific baby before negotiations could be started.

'Thought they didn't like it when the Loewes did just that,' Tony grumbled.

'First we find the baby. Then we go home and apply to the Home Office and all the DHSS bit grinds into action. *Then*, when that's all been passed, we come back to get the baby.'

'Well, you'll have to do that, love; I can't keep coming out here... Expensive hobby, isn't it? They don't make it easy, I must say.'

'Of course they don't. That's the point.' We contemplated the fact with a shadow of satisfaction.

But now, in Bombay, I found myself prevaricating.

'When *are* we going to see this da Souza?' Tony asked on the third day. 'Time's short, you know.'

'Your time's always short, Tony, there's nothing new in that. And, yes, I did ring him today at his hospital.'

'Did you get him?'

'No, I left a message.'

'He ring back?'

'Not yet.'

The next day, disliking and distrusting the telephone and the indifferent English of the hospital switchboard operators, I went to the hospital in person.

The Queen Victoria Jubilee Hospital must, I suppose, have been on the outskirts of the city when it was established, among thatched bungalows and coconut palms, but Bombay has long since engulfed it. The mill chimneys came, in glazed ochre brick that might have been exported from Huddersfield or Glasgow and probably was, and then the bazaars came to sell all the cottons made in the mills and the tenements to shelter all the people who came to work in them. Then, eventually, the Municipality came, and drove a few straight roads with the names of British governors through the unmappable lanes of the bazaars, and lined these roads with tall stone buildings— but ignored the gullies between them, which silted up with the unspeakable layered rubbish and slime of one of the most over-populated cities the world has ever known. The sea breezes never reach this part of Bombay now, and the rich have gone to live by newer reclaimed shores, but this is still where the money of Bombay is made and where the heart lies, here among the gold and silver markets, among the scrap metal, among the furniture and timber and jute and cloth, and in one of the biggest diamond markets on earth.

Not, of course, that I knew or could see one-tenth of this the first time I went to QVJ

119

Hospital. I was aware mainly of the volume of traffic which, with its incessant, futile hooting, created the same effect in sound as was created visually by the streets' multifarious signs. Words in four scripts and probably twice as many languages assailed my eyes, urgent and clamouring, as if the buildings themselves depended on all this writing to hold them up. At the crossroads opposite the hospital a huge sign, dwarfing the shop beneath it, read: 'Sex and VD Clinic. Dr N. M. Shah. Specialist in Incurable Ailments.' Moslem women shrouded in black burkhas wandered past without a glance at it, as if intent on some dreary inner vista. Nor did they look at the small girl in a ragged dress who, with an ice-cream cone in one hand and the other supporting the naked baby asleep on her rickety hip, came skipping and hobbling across their path and dangerously between the lorries and handcarts, making a beeline for the taxi in which she had spotted me, a white woman there to be begged from. The taxi moved on again before she reached it.

Inside its dusty compound, and then within its labyrinthine Victorian buildings, the hospital was cleaner than the brawling city outside, but only relatively so: I had a feeling that it was in a state of endemic siege, perpetually managing, but only just managing, to hold the fetid, poverty-stricken outer world of its patients at bay. It was, of course, a public hospital. There

120

are private hospitals in Bombay, and I had been in one already that had been designed by someone we had dined with, a great glass cube that might have been in London or New York. But the QVJ reminded me of something I had never personally known but recognised as soon as I saw it: the Poor Law hospitals of nineteenth-century London, their long tiled corridors populated with ragged, under-nourished people who would wait all day and all the next day and the next, clutching bits of paper and hoping without certainty that the doctor would see them.

There were splashes on the tiles and on the floors that looked like dried blood. They were not really, I knew that even then: they were the marks of spat-out betel juice that the ordinary people of India leave wherever they go, but they looked like blood all the same.

After considerable difficulty and several false scents, I located not only 'da Souza' but the right Dr N. da Souza's name on the door of a small office near one of the general medical wards. The door was ajar, and the opening covered by a dirty green curtain that blew in the breeze from the fan which had been left on. An elderly, barefoot man in khaki was squatting by the office and gave me to understand that the doctor was on his rounds. I loitered, like an Indian, attempting to suppress my European prejudices: I had left a message that I would be

121

here at this time but perhaps Teresa's brother had not received it, or I had picked the wrong moment. Time seeped by, a nurse appeared in a short white dress, listened impatiently to me and went again: a young, dark doctor came, listened again, smiled as if he had not really heard what I was saying, and then sent the old man in khaki to fetch me a cup of sweet tea in a dubiously cloudy glass.

Then, suddenly and brusquely, Teresa's brother was there, and I found myself jerked from my careful patience and passivity to face his—yes—his almost hostile presence.

I should not have recognised him. The handsome, laughing, assured boy in the photograph in Teresa's room at Bedford College had become a slightly paunchy man of forty with receding hair and a vague but pervasive air of discontent. He was heavily built, evidently intended by nature for physical exertion: I noticed even on that first meeting the odd detail that he stood with his fists clenched and his shoulders very slightly hunched, as if perpetually ready for some aggressive action which, in practice, he was not called upon to make.

His skin was pasty, and pale as a European's; his eyes were black, and they seemed to me angry. I suppose that was what gave me the feeling of his hostility, for what he actually said to me, though off-hand, was not positively rude.

I had been prepared for possible effusive unreliability: instead I found myself faced with what seemed a deliberate simulacrum of British reserve and refusal to be pushed around.

Yes, yes, he said, waving his head impatiently—and the Indian gesture immediately looked odd in so un-Indian a figure—he had received our letter. And Teresa's, yes. He did not seem to want to talk about Teresa, whom he referred to not by name but as 'my sister'; fulsome remarks I had prepared about my visit to her and her children faded on my tongue. His own rather deep, abrupt voice sounded faintly strangulated, as if he had not quite surmounted some childhood speech impediment or perhaps avoided certain sounds because of it. His accent was slight by Indian standards: he sounded Welsh.

'So you want to visit our orphanage,' he said resignedly. He stood looming over me, with his hands in the pockets of his white coat, which was stained and not, I thought, with betel juice. He had not sat down nor asked me to.

'If—if you think that's the best way.' I heard an intimidating echo of Angela saying, '*Surely you won't find yourselves with six babies lined up to choose from, like puppies or kittens?*'

He dropped into his desk chair, shooting me a glance under his lids as he did so which I thought might be one of contempt or amusement or both. I felt myself getting angry, and told myself I must not, must not, because this—this seedy looking hospital doctor in his bloody coat was, for me, a power figure; perhaps, incredibly, the most powerful figure in terms of my own life that I would ever meet.

He said, 'On the contrary, it's up to *you*. You are the one who has come to me. It is up to me to provide you with what you want.' The phrase was obliging; the tone was not.

I clenched my fists in what I presently realised was unconscious imitation of him: 'Dr da Souza—' I had thought of him for years as 'Teresa's brother Nicky', but he was here and now unmistakably Dr da Souza—'we are in your hands. If you think the best plan is for us to visit an orphanage with you, that is fine by us. But you must realise that inevitably we rely on *you* to organise things as you think best. We can only follow where you lead—' I was about to say more, I think: to say 'please don't try to bully or tease me', to say 'I'm sorry if for some reason you hate me', to say 'please try to understand' ... I don't know exactly what I might have said, had he let me go on, but something in my tone or in what I had already said made him relent. He said 'Good', dismissively, and took out a pocket diary. 'I could manage next Tuesday in the later afternoon.'

'Next—? Oh ... It's just that my husband, Tony, will have left Bombay by then.'

'But you will still be here?'

'Oh yes.'

'Well, then—shall we make it next Tuesday? You come here, please, at—let's say four thirty.'

I wanted to protest, to say 'But Tony and I had hoped to do this together.' I didn't, though. I just said, 'Thank you, Dr da Souza. It's very good of you to spare the time.'

As if rewarding me for my formal, submissive tone, he said in the most friendly voice he had so far used: 'The orphanage is at Borovili, on the outskirts of Bombay. I called it "our" orphanage: in fact it is run by a Christian mission, but I and a colleague here take an interest in it. We have already placed several babies from there in European families.' This was the first and only time during this brief encounter that the word 'baby' was mentioned.

★   ★   ★

When I told Tony what I had managed to arrange, he was understandably annoyed.

'Well, I must admit I had envisaged actually having *something* to do with this procedure myself, initially. Can't da Souza fit in anything for us this week?'

'Tony, I couldn't ask him. I got the impression he was extremely busy. After all doctors are, aren't they?'

'Hell, I'm busy too, as you may conceivably have noticed.'

'Don't act up like that, Tony, because there's nothing whatsoever I can do about it. Da Souza's our contact, and if we want him to do this favour—because after all that's what it is— we've got to play it his way, I can feel it. I've met him and you haven't. And honestly, you know, we can't expect to breeze into Bombay from outer space and have everyone running around to do what we want right away at our convenience.'

But of course Tony had expected that, because he is, or has become, that sort of person, and because in his own field that is indeed what happens. He continued to look annoyed.

'I'm not quite so sure as all that about us being the ones on the receiving end of a favour—' he began in his most priggish, abstract-argument tone. But I wasn't going to be drawn, not just then—and not at all if I could help it. I went and had a shower.

★   ★   ★

After Tony had left Bombay on a flight to Bangalore I began to discover a number of things.

One of them was about my own variable visibility. If I walked about on the sea front near our hotel, or along the main road past the store that had once been the Bombay branch of the

126

Army and Navy, I was continually followed by beggars. Many of them were young children, who attempted to lay their small and surprisingly cool hands on me, like spirit hands. Ghost children, Might-have-beens... I was afraid to look into their limpid eyes. But if I went elsewhere in Bombay, into the bazaars or near the QVJ or round the vegetable markets, no one bothered me. They all assumed, I suppose, that the only explanation for my presence in such places was that I had business there. So I did. But I did not yet know what. It was as if I was listening or looking for something.

I saw few people, in the social sense of the term. Evidently, with Tony's departure, I had become abruptly invisible also to many of the people who had put themselves out to be hospitable to us when we were together. I did not really blame them. Wives on their own are a nuisance, and anyway I had been uncommunicative about my own plans in Bombay, because I did not want to tell anyone the real reason I had stayed on. If I felt lonely it was my own fault.

The buses of Bombay are battered London transport ones, red double-deckers that might turn out to be taking you to Piccadilly, Waterloo or Golders Green. On the Sunday morning I got on one at random. It did not go to Golders Green, but it did take me to an equivalent, its terminus at a place called Sewri. Here, I followed small groups of people in respectable clothes who all seemed to be going in the same direction. Some were carrying bunches of flowers, others stopped at stalls to buy them: sudden poignant whiffs of flower-scent, damp and fragile, cut across the thicker, constant Indian-city smell of roasting peanuts in charcoal braziers, hot dust, spice and urine. The street, which was lined with large old bungalows interspersed with 1920s villas in modernistic cement, seemed to have been invaded at some more recent date by another order of life. It was this life that animated the market, invaded the old houses' back gardens in tangles of huts, even climbed the rocky hill that reared abruptly out of the townscape. In among the rocks people, and ever more people, were living, with their chickens and dogs and goats and washing. They had built themselves little walls of mud and roofed them with tin, plastic and rag. Filthy water ran down the contours of the hill in black rivulets. Under a moulting palm tree at the foot an old man was working a treadle sewing machine, an antique Singer, and boys were playing cricket with bits of wood and a round pebble.

'These people,' I told myself, 'are some of the poorest in the world.' But the meaning of the phrase evaded me, would not become real. The people themselves did not seem to know that any world significance was to be attached to their position. They looked humdrum, preoccupied with their own domestic affairs, almost cheerful.

The one place they had not penetrated was the big cemetery, which was where the families in Sunday clothes and carrying flowers turned out to be going. The huts did not spread in there behind the ornate iron railings and gnarled trees, only because the place was guarded by two skinny old soldiers in long British Army shorts, puttees, bush shirts and berets. They saluted politely as I passed them.

For want of anything else to do, I began to look round the graves. Almost at once I came upon a whole row of da Souzas, like a town district in itself. Some of the stones were old and eroded, others bright new marble in opulent bad taste, white and pink and green, with photos of the well-fed occupants when in life. Evidently that name in Bombay was even commoner than I had realised; at any rate the clan seemed to be prolific. There were da Cunhas too, and da Silvas and de Almeidas, Morenas and Afonsos and a horde of Fernandez: a whole world within a world. I remembered Teresa tacitly offended at being taken for a mixture of Indian and British, insisting 'We are Goans—the descendants of Portuguese settlers.' Was it really so? I watched some of my companions from the bus, now scattered among the newer graves to lay their

129

flowers. Some of them were pale, like Teresa and Nicky da Souza, but some were dark-skinned with curly, almost Negro hair. I wished I had bothered to read more about the history of Bombay before I had come here. Everyone has a past, everyone comes from somewhere, even 'one of the poorest people in the world'.

Nicky da Souza had said the orphanage he was going to take me to was run by a Christian mission. Presumably that meant Roman Catholic in his terms. I wondered if many of the babies there would have dark skins and woolly hair. If ours did, I wondered if it would feel at home with me. Or I with it.

Wandering further, among older and more ornate graves with urns, broken pillars and the occasional weeping angel, I realised that of course this Christian cemetery was also the old British one. I seemed to be in the Anglican alleys now, surrounded by dead compatriots with names like Fawcett and Wilson and Ferguson and Rivers. What would they think of me and Tony and our plan?

They would be shocked and disapproving, almost every one of them. They had come out here a hundred years ago to rule and keep their distance, to 'respect the native' maybe, if he was an honourable man and good at his job, but not to attempt to make him one of their own. And the women who followed them out, hopeful or resigned, intrepid as I was intrepid, placing, like me, a high value on being sensible—they had come not in the interests of racial harmony but of racial separation: they were encouraged on to all those P & O liners by a government at home who wanted the white sahibs of the Raj to have all-white progeny, and who deplored the unfortunate mixing of blood that had taken place in the bad old days, when India was a long way off and life was brief under the sun and moral judgments few. If Tony and I felt our own attitude to be self-evidently logical and moral, so, no doubt, had they.

Even the missionaries of the nineteenth century had been content to leave the earthly lives of the Indians where they were: it was their immortal souls they were after. Conversely, if you snatched up an Indian child and carried it away to a cool, damp sky on the other side of the world, and brought it up there as a brown-skinned upper-middle-class Englishman, did you steal its immortal soul too? Or did that remain Indian, a lost spirit perpetually seeking its own place. . . ? Always supposing that you believed in souls. Tony and I never had.

As I made my way back to the bus station, I passed a very tiny baby girl, naked as a worm, asleep on a bit of sacking on the ground in the glare of the sun. I told myself that whoever she belonged to could not be far off, and that anyone—particularly any European—who picked up such a baby and made off with it would almost instantly be surrounded out of nowhere by a shouting, gesticulating crowd. I told myself that only hysterical idiots like Trisha Loewe would even imagine doing such an awful and dotty thing. But, as if affected by some emotion below the level of conscious thought, my heart beat hard in my chest as I passed by; as a person who does not know with his waking mind that he is attracted by suicide feels an odd tightening of the chest or an inexplicable vertigo as he looks down over a sheer drop.

*　　*　　*

When I arrived in Nicky da Souza's room at the QVJ the following Tuesday he seemed, to my relief, to be expecting me. There was someone else there too.

'This is Dr Miss Desai—Shanti Desai. She is the colleague I mentioned to you. She is coming with us, if you don't mind.'

I said 'Of course not', though in fact, in my state of nervous tension, I would have preferred if she had not been there. Dr Miss Desai—I couldn't help finding this standard Indian appellation ridiculous—was a small, plain Indian woman of about my own age, with glasses, and a cotton sari wrapped firmly round her shoulders as if she were cold. In fact an unseasonable shower of rain had billowed over the surprised city that morning, but the sky had since cleared and the humid heat returned. Dr Miss Desai reminded me of those earnest Indians at Bedford who had never seemed to want to be friendly. But she turned out to have a lovely smile, and it was she who maintained most of the intermittent conversation, in her rather poor English, as we travelled first in a taxi to the station, and then in a slow, jolting, stopping train through Bombay's endless northern suburbs.

'I expect that when I told you the orphanage was in Borovili you thought that we would go by car,' Nicky da Souza remarked to me at one point, in a tone of supercilious irony that I hoped might have been intended as a wry apology.

'Not at all,' I said firmly. 'I haven't been on a train till now. It's very interesting for me.' In fact, after being among Tony's contacts during our first week, I had expected without really thinking about it that a doctor would have a car. I wondered what he might earn, attached to a public hospital: perhaps not much? My attempts to pay my own fare were, however, rejected.

From the suburban station to the orphanage gates we took a bus. The buildings out here were small and low and there were trees, and motor rickshaws, and mountains on the skyline surprising and beautiful, and the air smelt fresher than it did in Bombay.

'We are near the National Park here,' said Shanti Desai. 'And the Kennari caves. You have heard perhaps of Kennari caves? Rock temple carvings—very nice. Most interesting. You should see them.'

'Not today though,' said Nicky da Souza shortly.

'No, of course not today, Nicky, don't be foolish,' said Shanti Desai, showing for the first time some spirit, which I appreciated more than her polite attempts to entertain me. 'I mean, some other day. You are being here in Bombay for some days still, I think? You will perhaps have time for some touristic visits?'

'Her mind isn't on tourism, Shanti, it's on St Anthony's Home,' said Nicky da Souza lightly, but not unkindly this time, and I liked him better also. For the first time I caught a hint of the young man whom Teresa had said 'everyone always likes', behind his present unprepossessing manner. Perhaps, indeed, he had not had to try as a young man in order to please people, and that fact had had a damaging effect on both his personality and his career.

'When are you leaving, by the way?' he asked me.

'In another week—at least, that's what I've arranged. I'm flying to Calcutta to meet Tony and we're both flying home from there. Of course I could stay on longer if there's any need . . .'

134

'There won't be. You've got a lawyer, I understand?... N. M. Merchant? Yes, I know him. *Of* him, I should say. I could have recommended you to someone else, but I suppose you'd better go to him if you've already been in touch with him.'

'He was recommended to us in London,' I said humbly. 'Through legal friends. But of course if there's somebody else you'd rather we used...'

'No, no,' said Nicky da Souza impatiently. 'No doubt Merchant will do.' I could tell that something further had displeased him. After a moment he said: 'But one word of warning. This N. M. Merchant takes himself for a great man and may ask all sorts of questions. My advice to you is to keep everything formal. And if anything he asks bothers you—just refer him to me.'

'You mean, if he asks personal questions about Tony and me...? But you don't know us, Dr da Souza. You haven't even met Tony.'

'Yes, but he is not to know that, is he? Anyway, that wasn't what I meant.'

I could not think, then, what he was hinting about, and felt irritated in my turn. 'Dr da Souza,' I said, adopting a tone of deliberate, rhetorical reproach that sounded foreign in my own ears, 'you are talking about lawyers and awkward questions but you haven't even shown me a baby yet. I hope you actually have one for me?'

He stopped short—we were just then passing through the orphanage gates, into a tree-hung compound—and he looked into my face. I thought he seemed disconcerted and also rather amused, but I could not read his opaque black eyes.

'There is a baby inside here now,' he said quietly. 'A baby girl—about five months old. She was found abandoned in a church and there is no trace of her parents. Sister Santa Maria is waiting to show her to you... And here *is* Sister Santa Maria coming down the steps towards us.'

★   ★   ★

Black hair. Black eyes. Of course. A delicate biscuit-coloured skin like an exotic doll. Swaddled tightly in a sheet, she seemed indeed too tiny and weightless in my arms to be anything but a doll, the kind of present other little girls had but never me, because I had never, if the truth were told, much liked dolls. I had preferred teddy bears, and then china horses.

'She's awfully sweet,' I said truthfully. It seemed a ludicrously inadequate statement about a baby that might be—would be? must be?—my own, but the portly Mother Superior in her white sari didn't seem to think so. She

136

beamed as if satisfied:

'Cute little baby, isn't she? I'm so glad you like her'—and then took her from me and handed her to another Sister, who tucked her back in her cot in the large, shabby, airy room she shared with forty or fifty others. They lay with propped-up bottles and sucked or wailed in the low sunlight of the declining day, while half a dozen of the orphanage's bigger girls in blue dresses moved lethargically among them.

'Are the babies all girls?' I asked helplessly; not liking to ask—because it seemed to open intolerable vistas of choice and hesitation—why this one was being offered to us rather than any of the others.

No, the orphanage took boys as well, up to the age of five. But the majority of the foundlings and abandoned waifs (the Sister used these old-fashioned words unselfconsciously) were girls.

'Boys are considered more desirable, you see,' put in Nicky da Souza sardonically. 'A very poor family may give up a baby girl where they will make greater efforts to hang on to a boy.'

We had said in so many words that we did not mind which sex we got. It seemed foolishly ungrateful to say now, what I had only just realised, that I had secretly hoped for a boy. I did not say it. I tried instead to think of an exquisite, light-footed Indian daughter, sweet tempered and docile, good at cooking and dancing . . .

But I stopped, confused. Of course she was intended to be our child, *ours*, using our voices, picking up our faults and our strengths, not an exotic stranger.

Nicky da Souza was saying something to Shanti Desai, who was lingering by the baby looking at it in a preoccupied way. Then he said to me with the air of a man who regards a deal as settled: 'Good. OK then. Shanti will come out here another day, and do an assessment.'

'An assessment?'

'Yes. Shanti's a psychologist—didn't I explain that? I've already examined the baby physically: she was a poor little specimen when she arrived here, wasn't she, Sister? They've been feeding her up, and medically she's in the clear, but I wouldn't like to let you take her without an IQ test. To make sure she isn't retarded, you see.'

'I see,' I said helplessly. I looked down again, almost reluctantly, at the tiny doll's face. She was sucking a bottle now with her black eyes shut. How on earth could you tell if such a rudimentary little creature were retarded or not? Much less if she would be sweet-tempered and good at cooking and dancing . . . This whole enterprise was an act of faith and hope and nothing else. Of course it must be. How had Tony and I failed to perceive that before?

As if she sensed my distress but not the real

cause of it, Shanti laid her small hand on my arm: 'Don't worry,' she said warmly. 'An assessment is just a precaution. I am sure that everything will be all right.' And she looked down at the baby with her broad, loving smile.

I didn't really want to see over the rest of the orphanage. I sensed that the more of this alien place I carried away in my memory the harder it would be for me to divorce the baby—our daughter—from it in my imagination. And my companions had obviously been there many times. But Sister Santa Maria was determined to show the foreign guest round, and even Nicky da Souza acquiesced docilely. We followed her out into the compound, where the swift tropical dusk was falling—or was the sky prematurely darkened by returning rain? I was not sure. The orphanage's walled vegetable gardens, its own segregated world, stretched away behind the old-fashioned buildings. It must have rained hard out here this morning: there were puddles in one or two low-lying places and a vague but pervasive smell of sewage. Girls passed us, carrying school books, hair plaited and neatly looped. 'Good evening, Sister,' they droned politely. 'Good evening, doctor, good evening, auntiees...' I wondered where they would have been and what their lives would have been like had they not been here. And the baby's mother: what was her life like? I did not feel I could, now, remind Nicky da Souza that we had said we would prefer a child whose antecedents were known. Perhaps this was not possible. Where, in what squalid shanty or pavement slum encampment was that mother now? Or was she in a respectable family, secure, oppressed, her awful secret admitted to no one, her past tightly closed behind her?

The sound of a hymn sung to a harmonium came through an open window: I could not distinguish words, but the tune was familiar, a whiff from my own forgotten childhood, a hint of boarding school in a damp green landscape.

Sister Santa Maria said comfortably: 'Our children are always so interested in foreign visitors. There's a little boy in the Toddler's House now who is due to go and live in Germany soon. You remember him, Dr da Souza? Our little Paul. I am so pleased for him.'

'Do many of your children go to be adopted abroad?' I asked.

She shook her head firmly. 'Oh, no—just the occasional one. To someone such as yourself. Most of them, in any case, are not for adoption, you know. You see them here and you think "poor little orphans" but in fact many—most— have a parent somewhere, or an uncle perhaps or an elder brother or sister who may take them again when they are bigger. Families—even poor families—do not necessarily give up a child easily.'

'I didn't realise,' I said, digesting this fact.

'You see,' said the Sister kindly but didactically, evidently determined to spell a lesson out to me, 'people—some people that is, some foreigners, they come thinking that because India is such a poor country they can have a child from here just for the asking. But *we* care about our children—we in this Home, even if no one else does. And we are very careful about who we let them go to.' She looked me in the eye and smiled deliberately, a plump, beige sphinx. 'I am always so pleased,' she said, 'when I know that one of our little ones will be going to a home such as you can provide. You will be able to tell her, when she is bigger, how St Anthony found her and entrusted her to *you*.'

At the gates of the orphanage Shanti Desai parted from us. She lived in a nearby suburb, it appeared: she would get a bus going in the opposite direction. I was sorry in a way because I liked her. But as soon as she had gone I was able to ask Nicky da Souza: 'Did you tell Sister Santa Maria we were Roman Catholics? You did, didn't you?'

'I didn't in so many words. I said you were at school with my sister. She must have drawn her own conclusions.'

'You knew she would, then.'

'Of course.'

'But—it isn't true. We're not Catholics. In fact we're not even Christians.'

He turned wearily to face me. His shirt was

141

sticking to his chest in sweaty patches. I noticed for the first time a thin gold chain round his neck which must end in a cross.

'Look, do you want a baby or don't you?'

'Yes. Yes, of course we do. But—'

'But *nothing*. If Sister Santa Maria wants to believe you're Catholics then let her.'

'But it's a lie,' I said childishly.

'So what? It will be me that goes to hell for it, not you.' I couldn't see his expression in the fading light to know how far, if at all, he was joking. 'Look,' he said astutely. 'If you are, as you say, not even believers, then you surely cannot regard it as blasphemous to make a religious claim that is not genuine? For you, all that can just be regarded as a formality—one of the many that have to be gone through in a good cause.'

'You mean, the end justifies the means, in your view?'

He shrugged as if he thought I was being pretentious. 'If you like to put it that way. Personally I'm sick of Sister Santa Maria hanging on to perfectly good babies that could be placed with families just because of religion. I don't care *what* religion adopting couples are— Hindu, Parsee, anything—provided that other things are all right.' As if to terminate the topic he abruptly hailed a rickshaw. 'Come on, let's get this to the station. I'm tired.'

Two people only just fit into a rickshaw,

particularly if one is rather broad. Jolting past the lighted stalls of the small local bazaar, not insulated from the life around as one is in a car, it struck me that though I still did not like Nicky da Souza much, we seemed somehow to have got on to terms of mental intimacy.

I did not want this fragile entente to be broken. Courage and confidence had ebbed out of me that afternoon. I discovered that I, who had always looked down on the sort of wife who can't manage without her husband, did not want to be alone.

After casting round in my mind for a while, I said: 'I came across some of your relatives the other day. Dead ones, I mean—in Sewri cemetery.'

'What on earth did you go there for?' he asked in his rude way. I was beginning to think he did it on purpose, so as to disassociate himself from the Indian politeness of people like Shanti Desai.

In the same, British tone I replied: 'I didn't go there. I found myself in Sewri by accident. It's a dump of a place now, isn't it? Apart from the cemetery, I mean.'

'Awful. I remember when it was quite a nice area, too.'

'When was that?'

'Oh, when I was a child. An aunt of ours had a house out there. She's in the cemetery herself now, poor old Auntie... I thought you might

143

have been looking up the graves of ancestors. Sometimes British people do that when they come to Bombay.'

'I haven't any ancestors in Bombay, as far as I know. Or anywhere in India, come to that.'

'I thought you might,' he said, glancing at me. 'I mean—it seemed likely. Since you thought of coming here for a child.'

I didn't feel like going into all that, so I remained silent. In a way, of course, he was right. Although I could not, unlike William Rowan, point to specific grandfathers and great-grandfathers in the Indian Civil Service, I had discovered in myself recently a proprietary feeling about India, a generalised sense of class kinship with all those Empire builders of a hundred years ago. Because of the kind of family I came from, one subtly different from Tony's provincial one, I did feel that I had some kind of inherited stake in India. Perhaps that was why all those ladies in tropical-weight corsets kept haunting me.

'Whereabouts do you live?' I asked Nicky da Souza, remembering too late that the Indian idiom is not 'live' but 'stay', as if implying that any abode of an English-speaker is impermanent, a temporary posting from home.

'I stay in Mazagon. It's a very old Portuguese area in central Bombay. Near the docks. You don't know it.'

This was true, but—

144

'How do you *know* I don't know it?' I said, annoyed. 'I've been all over Bombay in the last few days.'

'People have been taking you around, have they? Good.'

'No, they haven't. I've been taking myself around. Do you imagine I'm the sort of tourist who can't move a yard outside her hotel without someone else's wife coming and taking her shopping? I walk around because my husband is an architect, and I work in his office and I am interested in buildings, and also—'

And also, I had been going to say, I want to understand the world our baby comes from. But we had reached the station. Nicky da Souza paid off the driver and walked into the booking hall with hardly a backward glance to see that I was following him. I did, though I was still annoyed, and stood beside him in the ticket queue. He said then, not turning round properly: 'I'll take you to look at Mazagon some time. It's quite an interesting old area—if you're interested in these things.'

A train came in, packed to its dangerously open doors, and emptied itself on to the platform. When the crowd had gone, a woman still sat slumped on the floor of the coach nearest to us, sleeping, a baby at her exposed breast.

'We get in,' he said. 'This one turns round and goes back to Bombay.'

'What about her?' I gestured nervously.

145

'Nothing about her. She'll go back to Bombay too. Unless the guard comes along and disturbs her. But I don't suppose he will.'

'But suppose she wanted to get out here?'

He shrugged. 'Well—she'll find her way back here eventually. Why bother her? In any case, I doubt it. People like her—they climb on the trains just for a ride, you know, or to have a rest out of the sun. You must have noticed how easy it is to get on without a ticket.'

'She looks very poor,' I said carefully.

'She looks doped to me,' he retorted, not looking at her. 'People like that often spend what they have on drugs, or liquor, and do you blame them?'

'But what about the baby?'

'The baby will live or it will die. In either case there is nothing you can do. Leave them alone.'

The train started. We said nothing for a while. Then I said, no doubt sententiously, but I was pursuing a line of thought: 'It must be difficult to bring a child up as a Christian here.'

He glared at me. 'Why do you say that? You who are not Christian anyway.'

'Well, I suppose I have a Christian ethic.'

'I see. And in your Christian way you think I ought to be doing something about that woman and child. Being a good Samaritan, I suppose, just because I am a doctor. What do you suggest? Why don't you do something yourself—knot some money in her sari if you're

146

really so concerned. You Westerners criticise our society, but you understand nothing.'

I felt myself beginning to tremble. My emotions had been too near the surface for too many hours, indeed days, ever since I had arrived in Bombay. His recurrent, inexplicable enmity was intolerable to me. I was afraid of bursting into tears.

'If you don't like Westerners,' I heard myself say, 'why did you agree to help me?'

'My sister wrote and asked me to. You know that.'

'Yes, but I—we—aren't the first foreign couple you've helped to adopt. Are we?'

He opened his mouth as if to answer and then shut it again. A depressed look replaced the angry one. After a minute or so, he said in a sulky but placating voice: 'Of course I know what you mean about a Christian ethic in an Indian society. But it is not easy, you know.'

'That's what I was *saying*.'

'One compartmentalises—I do. We all do. I try to help my patients and my relatives and St Anthony's Orphanage and—one or two other people. But that is all. It has to be. How can I or anyone take on the poverty of India? I find one baby—one in a million destitute children in India today—a good home with you. That act is sufficient unto itself. I can't take on this baby lying in a railway carriage and that one lying in the gutter. I do what I can.'

147

To someone who goes to such lengths in answering an accusation that has not been made there is no answer. Hoping to turn the conversation, I said by and by: 'A lot of people in the West now are interested in Indian religion, actually.'

'I know,' he said shortly. A pause. 'That interest you?'

'Not in the least.'

'Good. Nor me either.'

'I mean—I think it repels me slightly,' I said. 'Those figures of gods. Shiva and Vishnu and whoever they are. They have eyes that don't look at you, like birds or lunatics.' I had been wanting to say that to somebody since I had noticed it. 'At least saints in Christian churches look at the people who are praying to them.'

He laughed, to my relief. 'You're a Christian really, aren't you?' he said. 'You can't get away from it. When you come to Mazagon I'll show you where the oldest Christian church in Bombay used to stand. They've knocked it down now. Typical.' Of whom, he did not say.

After that he sat and yawned. He was getting out at Dadar, the junction station.

'You'll be all right to Churchgate, won't you?' he said, transparently not wanting to delay his own home-going.

'I'll be perfectly all right... When can I come and see Mazagon?'

He looked as if he now regretted making the

148

offer.

'Well—maybe you could come to our house. I'll have to see when would suit my mother... You're seeing N. M. Merchant?'

'Yes, Friday.'

'Hmm. OK. Remember what I told you. I'll call you.'

He got out and went away without turning round. I thought he won't call me, and then: But I'll have to have some sort of further contact with him about the baby before I leave Bombay. Won't I?

Rather to my surprise, however, he telephoned me on Friday evening to find out if the interview with the lawyer had gone off all right, and to invite me to tea at his home on Sunday. He lived, he explained, with his widowed mother and an unmarried sister.

'You won't be able to find the house—I'll come to your hotel and fetch you.'

'You needn't.'

'I needn't, but I will. Then we can ride around and look at some things. I'll come about half past three. *Ciao*.' He sounded brisk today and pleased with himself. I wondered if he had a car available after all.

Oh, what is the use? I could describe, stage by stage, how he fetched me, where we went, what we saw, both then and on subsequent occasions, how I felt, how he seemed, what we spoke about... But hindsight casts its peculiar deforming light over everything, imbuing details with significance, obscuring what, at the time, seemed important. I no longer really know how Nicky da Souza seemed to me that Sunday, when he turned up late in a too-tight, American-style check shirt and jeans, riding a heavy, shiny motorbike that, unlike most things in India, looked new. In retrospect, everything from that time on was leading slowly and inevitably to one place, one shuttered room in Kamathipura—perhaps had been leading there already from the moment I walked into QVJ Hospital, or even on that day of inexplicable dread when I first landed in Bombay.

Scraps remain from that afternoon, like clips of film, mainly because I played them over in my mind so often when I was back in England—and, for that same reason, they have lost meaning for me and have become separate from myself. I watch them from somewhere outside, seeing myself standing there in a flowered voile dress.

'You can ride side-saddle if you like,' he said, glancing at me.

'Can I really? That isn't allowed in England.'

'I know,' he said with satisfaction. Of course we had no crash helmets either. I thought fleetingly that Tony would be cross with me, if he knew. Tony invariably wears his seat-belt in the car.

From a little park on top of one of those

sudden, rocky hillocks that rise from the humming streets and mills and tenements of Bombay we could look right over the dockyards. They are enormous.

'I didn't realise,' I said.

'Bombay is one of the major ports of the world. That's why the city is here.'

'I suppose I knew that in theory. I just didn't realise the port took up so much space.'

'They built British ships here that were used in the Battle of Waterloo. Bombay ship-builders were that good. The sea came in closer in those days. Over there was just Mazagon town and the sea all round. That's reclaimed land, that down below.'

I looked down over a waste of railway sidings and an electrical installation.

'Really? The sea came up to this hill?'

'Yes. Somewhere near where we're standing there was a beautiful house called the Belvidere. A lady called Eliza Draper eloped from it one night by letting a length of sheet from her window and climbing down it into a small boat where her lover was waiting for her.'

'What a lot of history you know.'

'Just what I learnt at school,' he said, but he looked extremely gratified. After a while he said 'I had this British history teacher—pucka British, a Mr Wandle. He made it very interesting.'

'When did Eliza Draper live?'

He hesitated: 'Oh—about a hundred years ago . . . Of course you know the British weren't the first people to build a harbour at Bombay, don't you? We—the Portuguese—were here before you. Mazagon was a Portuguese town.'

I discovered later that Eliza Draper lived at the Belvidere over two hundred years ago. Nicky tended to be impatient with details.

His home was a big, dilapidated old house with a carved wooden gallery running round the upper floor and fretworked eaves. It had lost its garden to a row of shanty-shops on one side and a petrol station on the other, and it shook faintly all the time as the heavy traffic went past. I thought it beautiful, and said so.

'My grandfather built it. He was a wealthy man, a ship's chandler, if you know what that is, although he lost his money later, speculating. When the house was built it was the country round here then—coconut and rice paddies.'

That wasn't quite true either, I discovered afterwards, but I could believe his grandfather had been well-to-do, for there were nineteenth-century carved blackwood chairs in the family sitting room and an elaborate glass chandelier. There was also a modern couch with an orange cover that looked as if it was slept on rather a lot, and a travel poster of Portugal and one of Goa pinned up on the wall. There was a crucifix; and also a cocktail cabinet with a rising sun decorating the glass and, on top, silver-framed family photographs.

I had not known whether 'tea' might mean a small snack or the main evening meal. Social predictions can be hard to make in England, and in Bombay they defeated me. When a silver teapot appeared on a lace tablecloth, followed by cucumber sandwiches, I wondered if this was their usual Sunday afternoon fare or whether it was in my honour? The sandwiches were followed by a great many small and delicious spicy objects and coconut cakeş, which the servant kept bringing in relays. I ate greedily, hoping my hosts would be gratified. The humid heat of Bombay had been suppressing my appetite, but the ride on the motor bike had revived it.

Nicky did not drink tea but beer. He lounged restlessly by the window, though his mother several times said to him, persistently though without hope: 'Sit down, Nicky. Don't stand over us like that.'

I think I had expected his mother to be a matriarchal version of Teresa, but she was a skinny, elderly little woman, quite brown, with tightly permed grey hair. Nicky's older sister, Lina, took after her. Presumably Teresa's looks, and Nicky's own before his face had developed its present bleariness, had come from their father, whose photograph on the cocktail cabinet I recognised now from Teresa's room in Bedford College. Like her mother, Lina wore

Western dress, in her case a too-short skirt with stockings and high-heeled shoes. This attire was, I thought, unsuitable for the climate and did nothing for her high-shouldered, ill-coordinated body. Though she was friendly to me, even effusive, her manner was not that of a woman who was used to being liked; indeed, if Nicky's boorish behaviour towards her were anything to go by she was all too accustomed and even hardened to arousing a vague contempt in others. She worked as personal secretary to some local government official, and told me about it, rather lengthily, when I asked. Her accent was much more marked than Nicky's, and though English was evidently the language of their household, Lina made habitual, slight, Indian mistakes in it.

A da Souza uncle who lived in a flat of his own somewhere in the house came in to tea. He wore slippers, but also a tie. Perhaps that too was in my honour.

'Nicky tells me you've seen my sister's grave at Sewri,' he said to me when he had perseveringly eaten his fill.

'I didn't say that, Uncle,' said Nicky wearily. 'I just told her Auntie used to have a property at Sewri.'

'My poor sister was a schoolmistress,' he said mournfully, turning his large eyes to me. 'She was head of her department—might have been head of the school if she had been spared. There she is on the cabinet. What a fine woman! Cancer. We none of us knew till it was too late.'

It was the lady in the sari whom I also recalled from Bedford College. I wondered why Mrs da Souza did not wear a sari.

'They've built flats where her house used to be,' he went on. 'Flats. Fourteen storeys. Bombay is being ruined.'

'The day someone builds flats on the site of this house,' said Lina avidly, 'you'll benefit from the proceeds as much as any of us. So don't pretend you won't, Uncle.'

As if this were a signal the four of them instantly launched into a round argument which, I got the impression, had become habitual to them each time the subject of house property came up—indeed, I was to hear it again in different forms on several other visits to the house. The gist of it was that land prices were going up and up in Bombay, and that if they were to sell the old house for its site they would have enough to buy several modern flats elsewhere. Conversely, by keeping the house, they were liable for an annual tax on its value and also for endless repair bills. Each of them had therefore taken up a set, almost ritualistic stance, which effectively ensured, I came to realise, that no course of action could ever be agreed upon. Lina was clamorous in her desire to 'pull the wretched old place down—it's a perfect nuisance'. Her mother supported her, but with reservations: if she had to shift from the house she had come to as a bride, she said, she wanted another flat on the same place: why could they not rebuild on the site themselves rather than selling it to 'some nasty property company'?

'—Who will put up a fourteen-storey block,' repeated the uncle lugubriously.

'I've *told* you, Ma,' said Nicky in a tone of weary exasperation. 'If we retain the site, and whatever goes on it, then we're still stuck with the tax. And if we're stuck with that, then I'd rather keep the old place.'

'Filthy old wreck,' put in Lina, with consciously feminine squeamishness.

'"Old wreck", indeed,' sneered her brother. 'Shows how much about value you know, you little fool. You think something must be better just because it is new. Bombay *will* be ruined, like Uncle says, if it's left to greedy, stupid people like you to decide what happens to it.'

'Nicky, don't call your sister greedy and stupid,' said his mother, casting an anxious glance at me. No one took any notice of her.

'Have they pulled down all the good old houses in London too, Mrs Er—?' the uncle asked me mournfully. He seemed so fatalistic that I couldn't believe that, in spite of his feelings, he would be much use to a preservation campaign. I made some attempt to explain to them about the conservation movement in

Britain, the revival of interest in the past and the enormous change in received architectural opinion since the 1950s, but felt unequal to this considerable task. 'You see, the social situation in England is so different,' I ended feebly. None of them, except intermittently Nicky, were really listening anyway. 'Do you *have* a preservation society in Bombay?' I asked him, feeling that he ought to be a member of it.

'We do. I went to a meeting once. It's useless.'

'What do they do?' asked his sister with interest, quarrel momentarily forgotten. 'I never heard of them.'

'They sit and talk all at once and argue and don't listen to each other. Like Indians everywhere.' He stared at us threateningly, and then burst out laughing. Everyone joined in.

The conversation shifted by rapid degrees to Indians living in England, their behaviour, the kind of people they were, their possibly dubious motivations in going there and the Immigration Acts. Old Mr da Souza, it turned out, thought Britain had made a great mistake in letting in immigrants at all. They should have stood firm, he said, in 1947, against the flood.

'Actually,' I said weakly, 'I don't think many immigrants started coming till the mid-1950s.'

'Whenever it was. It makes no difference. People like that are ruining your culture—your British heritage. Your Mr Powell is right. You

157

will be swamped—swamped, I say.' His sincerity was unmistakable. It was a pity, though, that he pronounced the word 'swammped', to rhyme with 'camped'.

'May I remind you, Uncle,' drawled Nicky—and I got the impression that this too was an old bone of contention for the family—'May I remind you that a good many of our friends and relatives are now settled in the UK, including Teresa.'

'I don't mean people like us, you know I don't. I mean all those low-caste *badmashes* they have let in as well. *Goondas*. People with no possible claim on the place.'

'That's quite righⲧ, Nicky,' insisted Lina, unrepressed and masochistic as ever. 'Of course Britain was right to give people like us the chance of going home, that's quite different.'

'"Home",' he sneered. '"Home". Where were *you* born, Lina? And where were your mother and father and grandmothers and grandfathers born? Don't give me that Anglo-Indian shit.'

'It isn't—what you say—and don't use dirty American words in front of Ma. We *are* Anglo-Indians. Domiciled Europeans, anyway.'

He glared at her, fists clenched, and for a moment I thought he really might hit her. 'We are not Anglo-Indians. We are Goans—Portuguese, if you prefer.'

'Same thing.'

'Bloody well isn't.'

'Is.'

'*Isn't.*' I realised now that they were quarrelling not as grown-ups but as children, in the way they must have quarrelled incessantly, relentlessly, since babyhood. It seemed as if any minute he might pull her hair, and she would wail 'it's not fa-ir!'

'Children, children—we do have a guest.'

Nicky swung round to me, in an elaborate parody of courtesy.

'I am most extremely sorry. Even, I would say, exceedingly sorry.' I was not sure if the pronounced Indian accent in which he said this was entirely assumed or not. His own accent had slipped quite a bit while quarrelling with his sister. It occurred to me now that the slightly strangulated way in which he had spoken on our first meeting at the hospital was the voice he used when he was trying to speak like an Englishman. Like, perhaps, his history teacher, Mr Wandle.

'Does it amuse you to hear my sister and I arguing about whether we are mixed race or not?' he asked me sarcastically. His mother shifted uneasily on the couch and clicked her tongue.

'Actually it does,' I said truthfully. 'But I don't think it amuses anyone else.'

'My sister has always laboured under an unsuitable desire to be an English lady. God

159

knows why.'

I couldn't, at that moment, see why myself, contrasting her physical and mental gaucheness with Shanti Desai's self-effacing charm. There was a brief silence—though not, I felt, due so much to awkwardness as to the fact that everyone had momentarily expended their energies. The uncle belched quietly. Suddenly Nicky lunged forward from the window where he had been standing.

'Come on, we'd better go if we're going,' he said to me.

'Where?' I nervously put down my tea-cup. I had not quite finished.

'To look at the rest of Mazagon. Come *on*, it'll be dark soon.'

★   ★   ★

It was dark. Or am I confusing it with another time? Was it on the evening when he met me after work, and we went to wander round the rubble of a recently-demolished mansion, that he said to me with an apparent effort:

'I ought to explain to you about my family.'

'It was—awfully kind of your mother to invite me to tea.'

'Don't worry, she loved the idea of having a *real British lady* to the house,' he said relentlessly. 'That's where my sister gets it from—her damn-fool pretence about being part-

British, I mean. Ma's father belonged to the same community as Daddy—Goan—so that's what we are, substantially, but Ma's mother was a Miss Evans, a Protestant. That's how we come to talk English together, mostly, rather than Portuguese.' He added quickly: 'We speak Portuguese as well, of course.'

'So she would be—Anglo-Indian? Your mother's mother, I mean.'

'I suppose so; I don't know. I hardly remember the old lady. Look, don't get the idea *I* care twopence about all this. We're all Indians these days anyway, God help us. But it seems to me that if you belong to a community like ours—and we've a very old one in these parts, as I told you—then you might as well belong to it and not pretend you belong to a different one. Especially not pretend you're an Anglo-Indian, for God's sake. *Everyone* looks down on Anglo-Indians, really, even low-caste Christian Indians do, but my sister's too goddamn stupid to realise that. She's never been out of India. I have, I've been to Canada and the UK. Would you credit it, she really believes she fools people into thinking she might be British? Jesus, does she get on my nerves!'

I remembered, and understood for the first time, Teresa's uncharacteristic touchiness on the subject. If one sister felt that status lay in claiming to be 'pure Goan' and the other that it lay in claiming to be of part-British descent, it was just as well, I thought, that they were now on opposite sides of the world. There seemed a certain irony, though, in the fact that Teresa had landed up in Britain, whereas Lina was the one left in an India from which the real British had now gone.

'There's no future in being Anglo-Indian in India today,' said Nicky, with obsessive emphasis. 'None whatsoever. You have to be as dumb as Lina not to grasp that... Dumb! I wish she *was* dumb. She goes on and on, I sometimes think she does it just to annoy me and work me up.'

I'm sure she does, I thought. Aloud I said: 'I'm sorry for her, though.'

'Oh *sure*.' He pounced on the word. 'We're all *sorry* for her, poor cow, that's been a family tradition for years, being *sorry* for Lina. And does she trade on it! She knows being a failure in life is her rôle, and she milks it for all she's worth. That's very Anglo-Indian in itself—self-pity, I mean. "Since the British pulled out, deserting us, we've never had a fair chance, there's nothing left for us to be", and so on and so forth. And Uncle's just as bad in his own way.' He brooded for a bit and then said, apparently unaware of a contradiction here: 'Come to that, I've hardly been a great success in life myself. I don't exactly have a flourishing private practice like Daddy did. And Ma and Lina don't let me forget it. The only brother I

162

had died before I was born: Ma likes to think he was an infant prodigy. Really Terry—Teresa— is the only one of us who's made it, and she got out.'

'Made it?'

'Oh, *you* know.' Impatiently. 'Married to a successful company-man in the UK and so on. I mean, the company think well enough of him to move him around the country, don't they? And in the last lot of snaps she sent their house looked pretty good and they've got a big car and so forth. I'd be pretty pleased with myself if I could afford a house and a car like that.'

I said nothing. If he wanted to see Teresa as the family success story, it wasn't for me to disillusion him with a lecture on relative status in the British Isles.

'Lina was really sick when Terry wrote to us she was going to marry in England,' he said with malicious amusement. 'Poor old Lina'd been angling to marry a Britisher for years! There were still quite a few working for firms in Bombay then for her to set her sights on.'

'Yes, it's a pity she isn't married.' And you, I thought, and you. Why aren't you married at your age? You like women all right, I can tell.

'She has a boyfriend of sorts at the moment,' he said moodily. 'He's a fat Parsee who works in her department. Do you know about Parsees? . . . Well, it doesn't matter. They're Persian really. A sort of displaced community

163

too, like us... Homi, he's called. I don't suppose he'll ever come up to scratch, as Ma puts it. I think he's a pansy anyway; a lot of the Parsees are. Half of them never seem to get round to marrying—not that I can talk.'

★   ★   ★

No, it's no use. Try as I will, I cannot remember the actual sequence, the precise occasion and the conversational links that led up to the moment that dominates my memory. In that moment he stood with his back to the kerosene lamps in the windows of a tenement block and his face to an expanse of dark railway lines, and he glared down at me with such sudden, ferocious anger, just as he had on the train coming back from Borovili, that I moved away as if threatened physically.

He said, 'Godamn bloody British Raj. Can we ever get it out of our lives? And they say the Raj is fashionable again now in Britain, *fashionable* if you please, with people getting prizes for writing books about it, and some damn-fool film being made about it up at Poona that half the Bombay film-world is trying to get it on. Yes, *and* people like you—come over here, trying to get our kids, all high and mighty and disapproving of the way India can't manage things. You have the gall to suppose you're *rescuing* the children from the misfortune of being Indian, when really you're robbing them of their birthright. You talk about the 'problem of poverty' in India and you understand nothing, you Westerners. You're just as conceited as you always were. You think your money can buy everything, including a child—and the worst of it is, you're right. It can.'

Perhaps he had been going to say even more. But at that moment a train came trundling and clanking past, an intolerable cacophony. Innumerable people were silhouetted in the open doorways, holding on with one hand. People are always falling from trains in Bombay. No one seems to care. Or perhaps they care about everything so much that one more bloody accident, more or less, means nothing.

In the time it took that train to pass I realised that he had been going to ask us to pay for our baby, perhaps to pay quite a lot, perhaps the price of another shiny motorbike or its equivalent, and that his cryptic warnings about being careful what I said to the lawyer referred to this.

Perhaps he was still going to make us pay—for that baby girl in Borovili who was not his to sell. Bombay, after all, has always been one of the central markets of the world. But I had a feeling he would not ask me to pay, now.

The reason is that his angry outburst had come a few minutes *after* we had crossed the dark railway lines together to look at the place where the oldest Roman Catholic church in Bombay had once stood, on the far side, before the harbour railway had come.

'Don't be frightened,' he said, 'a train won't run us over.'

'In England,' I said, 'you're not allowed to wander around on main railway lines in the middle of cities.'

'I dare say not,' he said smugly, 'but this isn't England. I used to play on these lines when I was a little kid—we all did. Cricket, even we played here! I had all sorts of friends then: Indian Christians, Hindus, Moslems, the lot. Some of them are still living round here, but now that we're grown up we never see each other. Prejudice sets in, you see—that's typical, isn't it?'

'Yes, I expect it is. But really, Nicky, I wouldn't know. This is your world, not mine.'

'I used to be nicer in those days myself,' he said suddenly as we reached the other side. 'You know—the sort of cheerful, confiding little kid that everyone likes. I know I'm bloody to people now sometimes—to Ma, to Lina, to Shanti Desai—but Christ, so would you be, in my place.' Then, without warning, he pulled me to a stop beside him, groaned, put his arms round me, and kissed me as if there were really nothing else left to do with me that evening, as perhaps there was not.

It was after that that he lost his temper.

166

And after that I began to cry, because, although I did not think it a sensible way of dealing with his murderous attacks, I really could not help it, what with that baby girl lying out at Borovili. As I wept, and realised about the money, the train clattered past, and I turned my face from its flickering squares of light, and he put his arms round me again and said, quite gently now, that he was sorry, sorry for everything, that he really wanted to help me, that he talked too much and that I shouldn't pay attention to it all. Even at the time I think I sensed that in making me cry he had somehow achieved a victory in whatever obscure battle he was fighting and that his sudden transition to kindness was because of this. He said I was not some stupid, stuck-up European, that he knew that really, and that that was why he was here with me tonight, trying to show me things, instead of touching up some nurse in a movie house. He said he was my friend, and that he would do anything I wanted for nothing, and he went on hugging me to him till I felt it was true.

Via Calcutta, via Delhi, via Abu Dhabi with the dawn from which we were flying glinting gold on the rim of the desert (and mutton chops on a plastic tray), via a fleeting view of the Euphrates and the cradle of humankind, via green Cyprus and greener Rome where there fell what seemed a soft, English rain, via the lumpy bolsters of the Alps (with chicken sandwiches)

167

and finally down through a greyer and greyer opacity into the cold, quaint strangeness of West London, Tony and I returned to what we had been accustomed to regard as real life. I did not feel at home in it.

*   *   *

'You do look well,' said Angela. We were having lunch together at Fortnums (her suggestion) before going to see a film at the ICA Galleries. That morning Tony and I had had a satisfactory interview at the Home Office, and I was taking the rest of the day off work in private celebration.

'I feel well, thanks.'

'No tummy trouble? Most people seem to come back from India with that.'

'Not me. Tony did pick up something for a day or two in Calcutta, he said, but I've got cast-iron guts.'

'You are lucky. I'd be hopeless in India. I only have to go as far as France to need Entero-Vioform, as you may remember, and places like Greece lay me out.'

'You need your own setting,' I said, and meant it. 'You're like one of those esoteric wines that don't travel well. Me, I'm one of nature's travellers. Resourceful, insensitive—you know.'

'Oh rubbish!' she said politely, laughing. 'I mean, I'm sure you're resourceful and you're

168

obviously frightfully good at learning your way round new places and all that—I'd be much too cowardly to wander round Bombay the way you did—but you can't be insensitive or you wouldn't have been so interested in everything or learnt so much.'

'Oh, well,' I said quickly, 'I think I was a bit insensitive when we set off there. But I feel that perhaps being there has—oh, I don't know: changed the mixture inside me a bit . . .'

'You and Tony must come over one evening and tell William all you've just been telling me about the orphanage and all the poor little beggar children and so on. He'd be awfully interested. Did you take any photographs?'

'Tony must have, though not of beggar children, I shouldn't think. He always takes buildings.' He doesn't like people in front of them. William won't be interested in orphanages and beggar children, even in the expurgated, arranged-for-the-concerned-Westerner-complete-with-WHO-statistics-form that I told it to Angela. William is comfortably uninterested in things like that. But he'll think it his duty to act interested, all a part of his generally supportive attitude towards our worthy cause.

'We'd love to come over,' I said.

'Tell you what, why don't I invite Gillian Forbes-Wright and her husband over the same evening? You know, she and I were at school

169

together and she's a producer on Woman's Hour now. I'm sure she'd be interested and she might want you to do a radio talk about it! Wouldn't that be a good idea?'

'Lovely. Yes, do.' If I proceed in a calm and logical way, sticking to what we've decided, things may still—must—work out all right. It's like Tony said the other night, when I tried to tell him that, actually, as a matter of fact, I wasn't one hundred per cent sure...

... He said, 'Now love, you're bound to feel the odd moment of panic. This is such a big step it's bound to make anyone feel a bit uncertain. I bet people do when they're pregnant too, only one just doesn't hear about it. It's like getting married or something, and don't tell me you never had the faintest qualm about that because I certainly did! But things do seem to be going through smoothly. You and I have never failed to make a go of something that we've really put our minds to, so there's no reason why this shouldn't work out too. I expect that this time next year we'll be wondering how on earth we lived for so many years without a child.'

It was a good way to put it, sensible, sensitive even—but I know he is speaking on a theory, a principle, rather than out of his heart. He doesn't *feel* this is a big step: he is just repeating the accepted view. I know that, because I know Tony. You can't be married to someone for all those years and fail to perceive certain things about them, even when you'd rather not. Tony has a defective imagination; that is one of his strengths. He hasn't really envisaged what it will be like to bring up a child at all, much less what it will be like to bring up that strange little girl who is lying in that cot now, *now* in Borovili, with a hot wind rustling the leaves of the brab trees and the scent of tainted dust in her tiny nostrils, a child without a past and without a future in this, her present life.

Hindus believe in re-incarnation, don't they? If that baby girl were to die now, *now* at this moment in her cot of some violent Indian dysentery, that would hardly be a more decisive end to her present existence than will occur when—if—I fly with her on the great 'plane through space and time, down down through thickening shadow and into the cold strangeness of London. Reincarnating her as a little English girl with a funny-coloured skin.

'*You get our kids and rob them of their birthright,*' Nicky said.

Some birthright. At best, a confined, deprived childhood behind the orphanage walls, with a nun as a mother and Our Lord as a father, and His love having to be shared out between several hundred little girls. At best, surviving the smell of sewage to grow up and then having to go out into an uncaring world without a family, in a land where the family is everything, becoming a servant if she is lucky, a

171

hospital nurse if she is even luckier, with the giddy possibility of being taken to the movies and touched up by a doctor because nurses in India are no-caste and fair game. And, if not so lucky, what? A provider of casual labour in a market or mill, taking what she can get, a prostitute—a beggar?—an unmarried mother abandoning a baby in her turn?

No. You are only guessing. You don't know. You cannot begin to measure the true value and extent of that birthright of which you will rob her, any more than one can possibly evaluate the worth of 'all that a couple like you can give a child', that glib, comfortable phrase with which the nice Home Office man rounded off this morning's interview, flatteringly giving us to understand that naturally with a couple like *us* they didn't anticipate any problems. Of course, he had explained smoothly, the majority of the applications they receive to adopt children from India come from couples who are themselves of immigrant origin, and often the child in question is related to them. There, of course, certain other considerations come into play: one has to consider in some cases whether or not an abuse of the Immigration Act is involved . . .

Of course, of course. Quite so. We don't need it spelt out. We are used to pussyfooting on this subject, aren't we?

Old Mr da Souza thinks Britain should never have let in immigrants anyway. Nicky da Souza thinks that Westerners are fools who understand nothing. Both of these are honest, forthright views—

—Nicky da Souza! You really trust his judgment? A man out-of-condition physically and mentally, self-pitying, neurotic, strung up in chains between two—or is it three?—cultures. A rude, self-opinionated, randy fellow, not above making money out of people in a way that is both illegal and immoral, and probably capable of violence as well, if you only knew. Men like that beat their wives.

Tony would never raise a hand to me. The idea would not be so much repugnant to him as unthinkable. There are a lot of things Tony does not, and will not, think about.

The Satyajit Ray film Angela and I saw is about a little boy in a lower middle class Indian family who has dreams and apparent memories of a quite other existence. He is taken by two petty crooks on a wild goose chase in search of his former life. It is, to my surprise, a funny film. We laugh.

When we come out of the cinema, Angela suddenly says, 'You used to smoke, didn't you? I'm sure I remember you smoking in cinemas before.'

'Yes. I've given it up.'

'Since India?'

'Since India. I didn't seem to need it there. It was so hot, and all that spicy food . . . I didn't plan to stop. I just stopped.'

'How funny. Well you did say India had changed you.'

'Did I?' I know I did.

'You said it had sort of "changed the mixture inside you". I know you did because I was listening particularly hard. Is it—is it the baby? Oh, don't answer if you don't want. I shouldn't ask really. I just know that, with me, even the *thought* of a new baby is enough to make me go sort of soft inside. Broody, William calls it. He gets rather fierce about it.'

'Perhaps it *is* that,' I said, thinking. After all, people stop smoking when they're pregnant. Perhaps I was having a phantom pregnancy? Like Bloody Mary. Oh, ha, ha.

'You've hardly talked about the baby at all,' said Angela with one of her sudden fits of perspicacity, 'Just about babies and children in India in general. Oh, don't worry, I'm not going to nag to know more. I'm *longing* to see it— her—but I'll keep that to myself. Perhaps it's too important for you actually to talk about it?'

'Yes, perhaps it is,' I said gratefully.

A little later, as if she had been pursuing the subject in her own mind and on the same lines as I had, she said: 'I had a friend—I don't think you've ever met her, she was at school with Gillie Forbes-Wright and me and she lives in Edinburgh now—anyway, she was married for years and years and they never had a baby and

174

finally adopted one, and *then*, almost immediately afterwards, they had one of their own.'

'How disconcerting.'

'Well, yes, I suppose so—but sort of magical too, don't you think? As if having a real baby to care for had set some vital chemical in action. Lovely, really.'

'I'm not so sure about lovely,' I said, with a deep foreboding I did not analyse. 'Did she then still like the adopted child? Or did she go off it?'

'Oh, I'm sure she still liked it—loved it,' said Angela, looking vaguely shocked.

'I think that's rather an immoral story anyway,' I said unkindly.

'But it's quite true.'

'I know, but it's still immoral. Truth can be, you know. I wouldn't tell that story to any other childless couples, Angie. Just think if they then went off and adopted a baby not because they really wanted it for its own sake but because they hoped it might get some magic juice working.'

'Oh dear, I hadn't thought of that... Like putting a china egg in a chicken's nesting box, you mean?'

'Yes, that's exactly what I mean,' I said, rather surprised. 'Though I didn't know one did that with chickens?'

'Oh yes, we always used to, when I was a child, in the country.' Naturally, though

Angela's father was a merchant banker, she had been brought up in the country. 'And I remember Mummy used to give us the china eggs for obstacle races at our birthday parties.'

'Were they different colours, like those alabaster eggs people have on mantelpieces?'

'No-o. Just white china, I think. I mean, we weren't encouraging the chickens to lay pink or green eggs!'

'Well, ours is black,' I said. 'She's a black china egg.'

Angela said nothing. She was shocked.

★ ★ ★

If it's all a form of sympathetic magic in the mind, will the thought alone do the trick?

Most of the time I did not think of our black china egg at all. Not consciously, that is. Only at odd moments, in lifts, or when I was going to sleep at night, did her image present itself to me, perfect and fleeting like a picture on the retina.

Tightly swaddled in a sheet, arms and legs tucked inwards, she seemed to fit the form of an egg. Or that of an unborn baby in the womb.

My egg. My life.

One night I dreamed of broken egg shell lying at my feet. I tried frantically to gather the pieces up, but in vain. Some of the bits had been crushed to powder, but I did not know if I had done it or someone else.

I was very distressed. My throat ached with dream-tears. Then someone said reassuringly to me, 'It's all right really. It's just the shell that is left behind. The soul flies off, you see.'

I asked the person who spoke if they were Catholic. They said yes. I thought, but was not sure, that the person was Teresa da Souza.

The next day I had 'flu.

*   *   *

By the time I had recovered, the India-feeling had left me. After a month or so I even began to smoke again. I also began wandering round babies' and children's departments in big stores looking at cots and towelling suits and expensive little embroidered dresses. I didn't buy anything yet. But I looked.

I also got an out-of-work young architect, who had been papering the hall and stairways for us with perfectionist slowness, to re-do the small spare room with an extremely expensive hand-blocked French paper patterned with fruit, flowers and glossy birds, the whole thing a canopy of twining branches: an exotic nest for an exotic egg. The room did not really need re-doing: it had been freshly painted in pale green eighteen months before. But Tony, normally critical and very slightly mean about our own domestic décor, tolerantly said, 'Jolly nice, love'—and barely looked at it. He was busier than ever, just then. India had, as he put it dismissively, come to nothing: the government there had changed yet again, or the policy on overseas advisors had changed—anyway, Tony was off again elsewhere.

★   ★   ★

Four and a half months after I had first landed in Bombay, I landed there again, alone. This time, there was no car to meet me, no well-trained driver to shepherd me through the airport touts and beggars, but, except for the practical irritation of it, I did not really mind. I had decided not to involve myself in Bombay this time. I had come for one thing only. I was going to get it—her—and leave again as soon as possible. I took a taxi from the airport, and shut the windows beside me to keep out the predatory, begging hands. Through the glass, as we drove into the city, everything looked a little as if it were on film and a print I had seen many times before: highly 'realistic', so that you can't help admiring such verisimilitude, but odourless, muted, two-dimensional.

I had not booked at the same great glass hotel, but at a smaller, more central one, nearer to the QVJ Hospital. Both my room and its bathroom had a pervasive, familiar smell, which I traced to little caches of mothballs lying in every

178

cupboard, and even in the wastehole of the old-fashioned bath, as if in dotty obeisance to a misunderstood Western goddess of hygiene. I collected all I could find and shut them in one drawer. Then I opened all the windows on to the warm, noisy dark which was rapidly falling: the quick coming of the tropical night seemed just a natural continuance of the accelerated time-scale of jet-travel. I was stuffed full, after several aeroplane meals at unnaturally short intervals, and felt that in only a few more hours it might well be the middle of tomorrow, if not the day after. A taciturn bearer brought me stewed tea in a heavy silver pot, and soon afterwards I fell asleep.

I woke to a brilliant glare and suffocating heat. I had neglected to leave on either fan or the rattling electrical air-cooler jammed into the old window. It had been November in Bombay before, the 'cool season'. Now it was nearly April; I had not properly realised what this, in terms of heat, would mean. I lay on my bed as if at the bottom of a fetid swimming bath and closed my eyes again. My head ached, and I could still hear the aeroplane in my ears.

Presently I became aware that, against the inner 'plane noise and the background blare of the street below, there was another sound near at hand, smaller and more intimate. An intermittent scritting sound, like pins being picked up or a cat playing with a ball of stiff

179

paper. I heaved open my eyes again. A Bombay raven was in the room, having evidently hopped in through the open window. Black and sleek, as glossy as one of the birds on my expensive French wallpaper in London and, with its predatory curved beak, not dissimilar, it strutted about the floor and eyed me with a bright, yellow, pitiless eye, the eye of a god who cares about nothing at all.

The ravens are the best-fed and healthiest-looking creatures in Bombay. Thieves and flesh-eaters, they thrive on offal and decay, on the leavings of the vultures who eat the dead Parsees in the Towers of Silence, on the eyes of dying puppies and kittens cast on to the city's rubbish heaps, on the piles of human excrement littering the beaches, on dead babies lying on the blackened marge of polluted creeks... Whatever other people do not want, things rejected and cast out even by the poorest, belong to the plump, arrogant ravens. I suddenly hated that raven, as I leapt clumsily from my bed to send it flapping off. I also hated Bombay and everything to do with it. The journey was over and the film had ended. I was back, caught in a nerve-racking reality.

Care, I found as I slowly dressed myself, dreading to go out and face those cruel streets, is not divisible. If you care enough to offer your own love to a child (however poor and dubious a thing that love may be) then you care enough to hate and fear and dread as well. How could I ever have imagined, yesterday, that I could manage this time not to get emotionally involved with Bombay? On the contrary, the place would be loaded now with a fearful significance for me to my life's end.

★   ★   ★

'You did right to shoo the raven away,' said Shanti Desai. 'Sometimes one is coming like that and hops on to a table and steals jewellery. Yes, really! Such things are well known.'

She wasn't, I could tell, particularly interested in ravens, a phenomenon she had known all her life, but she was pleased that I was. She was searching round in her mind for suitable topics of conversation between us. With my senses morbidly sharp, I had a feeling that she did in fact have something to say to me, but was putting it off, possibly till Nicky da Souza arrived in her office, where we were at present sitting with the door open. Her sari was pale blue today, with a blue and yellow border, and she had a small yellow blouse under it, a gold chain round her neck and tiny gold rings in her ears. Her black hair was neatly knotted behind her head. Her brown skin was matt and healthy. Women like Shanti Desai, I thought, do not age gawkily into travesties of their youthful selves, like Western women do, like Lina da Souza is doing. They change little; only a patina of time gradually settles on to them as on to an old tree. If I were a man, I thought, I would rather marry an Indian woman.

'Here he is,' she said, with evident relief in her voice. Turning from where I sat, I saw Nicky coming up the stairs. As he bounded up, women waiting there clutched at his arms, and an old man in a ragged dhoti even thrust a tiny, emaciated child under his nose, but he pushed them all impatiently aside. 'Nurse told you, no one else today,' he said loudly, and repeated what was presumably the same thing in other tongues.

He banged the door shut behind him, and then, leaning against it, smiled in a forced way at both of us.

'Did you tell her?' he said to Shanti, sitting down and beginning to fiddle with some blocks and pictures, part of an intelligence test, I supposed, that were lying on her desk.

'No, I didn't, yet.'

'Why not?' He glared at her.

'I was waiting for you, Nicky.' Mournfully.

He swung round to me and made a visible effort to pull himself together.

'I'm sorry. I've had a hell of a morning. Did you—was your journey all right?'

'Fine thanks.'

'Husband OK?'

'Husband OK,' I said firmly. It occurred to

182

me that if Tony had met Nicky da Souza in the first place this whole business might have gone rather differently. I was not sure if I was glad or sorry they had not met.

'What,' I said, 'were you going to tell me?' I had no idea what it could be and for some reason no foreboding warned me. It even crossed my mind, absurdly on the face of it, that Nicky da Souza might be engaged to be married and that that was the news both were hesitating to impart.

Nicky leaned back, put his clenched fists on the desk and tapped them infuriatingly. Not looking at me, he said:

'That baby girl I showed you at Borovili . . . She's not normal.'

'Not—?' I did not take in his meaning.

'Not normal. Retarded. At least, we think so. Shanti thinks so.'

As if released on cue, Shanti began to talk, gently, persuasively, sensibly. Babies, she said, were difficult to test formally: you couldn't ask them to build up blocks or do jigsaws. Assessment had to be done, really, by informal observation, which meant that if you caught the baby in a cross or sleepy mood you could make a mistake. In addition there was the problem with an orphanage baby, and a foundling at that, that it had probably never received the attention and stimulation that a baby brought up in a family did. Even very poor families, she said, played with their babies and taught them to do things: it was necessary for the babies' survival that they should learn and learn quickly—

'Yes, to crawl around and snatch bits of whatever's going,' put in Nicky sardonically.

But an orphanage child, particularly a docile, undemanding one, got left lying in its cot all day, Shanti continued. The girls who did most of the practical work for the babies, changing and feeding them and so on, were very young, of course, and tended to treat the babies like dolls: she herself had spoken once to Sister Santa Maria about this, but it was the system, the girls were supposed to learn by doing—she hadn't liked to say too much. As a result, orphanage standards of development were not high.

'So what you are telling me,' I interrupted nervously, 'is that perhaps she is just a bit backward because she's been neglected? But surely one could make up—later—for lost time?'

Shanti frowned and bit her lip. That was evidently not quite what she had meant to say: in explaining her own uncertainty, she had become deflected from the point she really wanted to make. Or perhaps the word 'retarded'—an ambiguous and deceptive one, I now realised—had confused the issue for us.

'This is what Sister Santa Maria is saying,' she said. 'She says, "Baby will be all right when it is in a good home." But I am thinking this is not

184

so, in this case. Again I have been going to the orphanage, to see the baby first thing in the morning when perhaps she is more lively. But, you see, she does not sit, she does not put things from one hand to another . . . she does not turn over even. Also she does not try to make different sounds—babble, like we say. I am thinking this is something functional. I wonder is she deaf? But no, she hears a bell. She smiles. She holds your finger. But that is all.'

'Shanti's really been working at this case,' put in Nicky. 'She went there four separate times altogether.'

'Should they do all those other things—at five months?' I asked, feeling desperate in my own ignorance. I realised that I, too, had assumed that the baby would, at any rate at first, lie in her cot swathed in whiteness, like a precious stone in a beautiful box—a beautiful basket-work crib such as I had seen in an antique shop in North London and been tempted to buy.

'She isn't five months now, she's nearer to ten, as far as we can judge,' said Nicky shortly. 'Many children crawl at that age. Some even walk by the time they are a year old.'

Time had gone by. Of course. I had known that really. Real babies—real children—exist in time, not in a vacuum of love and dreams.

'Could it be just physical weakness?' I said humbly, after a long pause. 'Could it be that her brain is perfectly all right but that she's just—

185

just a very late developer? After all, you said she was very undernourished when she came into the Home.'

'So she was,' said Nicky, playing with the blocks again. 'But acute underfeeding in the first few months doesn't just affect the physical development. There is a theory it affects the brain as well. In any case with a young child you can't really separate physical milestones from mental ones...'

'And is that why she is like this, do you think?' I said at last.

He and Shanti looked at each other. He gave a kind of shrug. It was clearly not a question that could be answered.

'Don't forget,' he said by and by, gently for him, 'we know nothing, but nothing, about the circumstances of her birth or the first few months of her life. She could be the child of a mother who was herself subnormal. Or she could have been delivered in some room or hut somewhere with no assistance, perhaps not even a midwife or another woman there. The brain can be damaged at birth through oxygen starvation. Or beforehand, during pregnancy. Or after... In this case, we cannot possibly know. All I can tell you is that, in our opinion, this baby is too severely retarded at present for us to hold out reasonable hope that she will grow up to be like other people. She *might*. But, as things stand, you would be crazy to take on such

186

a child, whatever Sister Santa Maria says. I cannot take the responsibility of letting you.'

★   ★   ★

He had gone again, hurriedly, suddenly consulting his expensive gold watch—too expensive for the rest of his clothes, I thought. He had some X-rays to look at, and another doctor to catch before 1 p.m. He would be back, he said, distractedly: would I please wait for him? He had something else to suggest to me.

'We will go out for a cold drink,' offered Shanti to me. 'You would like some fruit juice, isn't it? There is a nice tea-shop near the hospital.'

On the ground floor of the tea-shop, which faced the advertisement of the practitioner who specialised in incurable diseases, old men in crocheted Moslem caps were slurping their tea at marble tables. Shanti looked through them and led me firmly through to the stairs.

'Upstairs is better for ladies. More expected, you see.'

She ordered us fresh orange juice. Then, evidently feeling she could ignore no longer my streaming eyes, she laid a hand on mine and tutted sympathetically. I said it was the hot wind blowing dust in the street outside that had made my eyes sting and water so. I think I half-believed this myself: tears can rise from a source

187

so deep that they take the conscious self, literally, by surprise. I kept repeating that I would be all right in a minute. With her own face full of concern, Shanti wiped mine for me with the end of her clean sari, as if I had been a child.

'Nicky has another idea,' she said softly. 'He was telling me... Everything will be all right in the end, you will see. Nicky wants it very much for you, I know. He will find you another child.'

'But *this* child,' I managed to say. 'I feel as if she had suddenly died.'

She smiles. She holds your finger. But that is all.

'I know. Is very sad. I too am sad. I try very hard with that little girl, and I keep thinking "perhaps she is not too bad". But no... It is perhaps for the best in some way we cannot tell. Is destiny, we think, in our culture. Drink some juice.'

By and by she reverted to the subject of Nicky. He was such a good doctor, she said: very caring—not like some of them. I said nothing, but I did not think this could be true. I had noticed how impatient he was of detail. I had also seen him that morning coming up the stairs arrogantly thrusting waiting people out of his way, which may be excusable for survival in an Indian hospital but hardly accorded with my notions of caring.

However, Shanti went on, as if sensing my dissent: 'Nicky may seem not a nice person sometimes, I know. He has many problems. But there is very much of love in Nicky. It does not find a proper outlet.'

I had heard other Indians say 'much of' where correct English just says 'much' or 'a lot'. 'Very much of money' ... 'too much of love' ... On Shanti's lips it struck me as intensely touching. Only later did I realise what echo it evoked for me: *Too much of water hath thou, poor Ophelia*... It was pure seventeenth-century English, preserved in Indian speech like a marker of the unregarded past: like 'gunny bag' and 'dickey' and 'waif'; like the names of the Portuguese families who sailed to India in search of spices and Christian souls even before the British came.

*   *   *

Nicky was waiting for me when I returned, going through reports with his houseman. He sent the boy away when I came.

'He's from the south,' he said. 'His English is awful. Almost as bad as his Hindi. The patients don't understand him.'

'I thought people didn't speak Hindi in Bombay anyway.'

'A lot of our patients speak Urdu. Same thing as bazaar-Hindi—more or less. But that boy doesn't seem to speak anything properly except his damned Telegu or whatever. Still, any

189

language comes in useful here, sooner or later. I'm always wasting time explaining some important point to a patient and then finding the fellow hasn't understood a word because he only speaks his own tongue. Bombay's like that. Full of people who are only a quarter taking in what each other is saying. I speak five languages, after a fashion: it still isn't enough here. It's Babel— Babylon, rather. Full of people uprooted from somewhere else. A madhouse.'

In another mood, I might have countered this overcharged and indeed old-fashioned view of the nature of metropolitan life by pointing out that all big cities have always been composed of people from elsewhere: what else indeed can they be composed of? But that morning, made stupid with spent emotion, I said mindlessly: '*By the waters of Babylon we have lain down and wept. Yeah, we have wept when we remember Sion . . .*'

'We've got Sion here too,' he said with a certain triumph. I have noticed that whenever an inhabitant of a great city is extolling its horror, a note of pride soon creeps into his voice.

'Have you really?'

'It's a ruined British fort near Thana creek. I don't know why it's called Sion. Spooky place. I used to do my courting there when I was about sixteen.'

That's quite enough of you, I thought, rousing

myself to be angry. This morning you have broken—well, not my life, no, that I won't pretend; my life is tougher than that. But you have broken and thrown away something on which I was counting and had flown thousands of miles to find, something I thought was mine: my china egg.

Perhaps he saw the way I looked at him. Anyway his manner suddenly changed: 'Look,' he said, stretching out his hand to me across the desk, palm upwards. 'I really am most awfully sorry.'

'It's not your fault.' I made my voice deliberately remote and excluding.

'Of course it isn't,' he said sharply—evidently I was not to be allowed to get away with anything either. 'How could it be my fault, or anyone else's? But that doesn't stop me being *sorry*, sorry that you're sad, sorry that it's gone wrong like this. And I still want to help you. I want to very much. Will you trust me?'

'Yes. All right, I trust you.' And oddly enough I did; although I no longer felt close to him as an equal, here in his own hospital, as I had done when we had stood together by the dark railway lines.

'Well, then. Listen. There is another baby I have in mind. A little older and also a girl. And this one *is* all right, do not worry. No, I haven't seen her myself, but a cousin of mine who is also a doctor has. She says this baby comes of good stock and is very lively, pulling herself up on everything, beginning to take steps—no problem there. Just one or two things—'

'Yes. Go on. I'm listening.'

'Well. One is, she is rather dark. Dark-skinned, I mean. Much more than the other one, who I thought was particularly suitable to be sent abroad because she was rather pale...'

Ignoring, in pain, the 'was', I said, 'Really, that's quite irrelevant, you know. She didn't look particularly pale to me but it didn't matter. You forget, in England any Indian child looks different.'

'My cousin says this one is a lovely little thing. Curly hair, very happy child—'

'Oh, stop trying to *sell* her to me,' I exploded.

As if he had taken a point sharper than the one I had at that moment intended, he covered his eyes for a moment with his hand and pinched the bridge of his nose.

After a moment I said stiffly: 'I'm sorry, I didn't mean that ... You said there was something else, some other point?'

'Yes. Yes, well it's this. I think we can use the same papers for her that your lawyer has already drawn up for the other one. It will save time, and—anyway, why not? No one in the UK will be any the wiser. But the only problem is, this baby isn't in Bombay.'

'Where is she?' I said, relentlessly. I was prepared to travel to Katmandu now, if necessary. Like Tony, I am not accustomed to being beaten.

'She is in Poona. In a state-run orphanage there. You've heard of Poona? Yes, of course, all the British have. It is a hill-station. Very nice place, if you like that sort of thing. About a hundred and twenty miles from Bombay. You can fly or go by train.'

'So, if I do that—?'

'Then, if you like the look of her, I will have to see how I can get her transferred to Bombay. In order to use the papers we already have, I mean. My cousin will help. Perhaps she—I mean the baby—could have some indeterminate suspected illness. Then I could admit her to this hospital, temporarily ...' He thought, drumming his fists.

'Why don't you get her transferred to St Anthony's, to be on the safe side?' I may not be Indian, but I too can show nerve, and a ruthless disregard for correct procedure.

'Yes, that would be the best. Unfortunately ...'

'Unfortunately what?'

'Unfortunately Shanti and Sister Santa Maria had an argument over your—over the other baby. Shanti may look soft and weak but she can be very firm when she wants to. And of course Sister Santa Maria never changes her mind about anything. She—Sister—had made up her mind that baby was going for adoption, and

193

Shanti had made up her mind just as much that it was not suitable. Shanti knows her own mind, but people think I influence her because I talk all the time and she doesn't. So at the moment I am in Sister Santa Maria's bad books. She is threatening—well, never mind what she is threatening. I dare say she'll come round to me again next time she wants anything done with the health authorities. But till then I'm keeping out of her way.'

'I'm sorry,' I said weakly.

'It's not your fault,' he said, smiling his charming smile. 'We said that before, didn't we? *I'm* sorry too.'

'Oh dear . . . So the next thing is for me to go to Poona.'

'Yes. Now it happens—these things, as Shanti would say, are meant!—that I myself am going to Poona the weekend after next, to a wedding in my cousin's family. In nine days time. Can you wait that long?'

'I—yes, I must, mustn't I?' After all, what are nine days compared with a lifetime? I'm not going to behave like Tony.

'Good. I can't take you up there myself, I'm afraid, as I've promised to take Lina on the motorbike, and if I back out now I shall never hear the last of it.' He made a routine face. 'But I can see you there and go with you to the orphanage and so on. You might even be able to carry the baby away with you there and then, on the next day, if I can work it right. State orphanages aren't too fussy, I'm afraid, and my cousin knows the director of this one.'

I thought: And this is the man who initially sulked all the way to Borovili, who stood beside the railway line in Mazagon and accused me—

'You seem very keen now,' I said, ungrateful. 'But you weren't in the beginning. Were you?'

His eager face shut. He looked away from me.

'Look,' he said after a moment, in a hurt voice, 'I want to help you. I told you that. Do you want a baby or don't you?' He pronounced it *ay baybee*, since he no longer bothered to try to restrain his accent in my presence; this, too, like Shanti's 'very much of love' I suddenly found unbearably touching. Perhaps it was partly this that made me say:

'Yes. Yes, I do. I really do.'

*　　*　　*

I telephoned Tony. The hotel operator told me afterwards, in wonder, that he had managed to dial straight through to London at the first attempt. It seems slightly indecent, or at any rate contrary to the natural law, to be able these days to telephone so easily from one world to another, one time of day and season to another. I sat on the edge of my bed waiting for the 'phone to ring back, and played with the idea that, with only a slight further technological

195

advance, we will be able to telephone other periods of history. *Hallo ... Bombay 1760? Is that Eliza's house, please?*

Tony, from his—our—London setting sounded more pessimistic than I was about the wisdom of substituting one baby for another at this stage. He seemed generally disgruntled. Perhaps it was too early in the morning there. He wasn't worried on the human level, it seemed, but on the legal one.

'Well, for Christ's sake, be careful. Are you sure whathisname, da Souza, really knows what he's doing?'

'He knows much better than we do, Tony.'

'Well, mind you see that lawyer and check that every single document is still OK. We don't want any sort of balls-up like the Loewes made.'

'There won't be a balls-up... Are you all right, Tony?'

'Of course I'm all right. Are *you* all right? You sound a bit faint and far away.'

'I am far away. It's frightfully hot here.'

'Well, I wish it was here. It's pissing with rain and so cold I had to turn the heating on again yesterday. When are you coming home?'

'Like I told you, I can't fix a date till I've been to Poona on the—the 7th, I think it is. The Saturday anyway. Look—had I better call you again that evening, when I've actually seen this other baby?'

'Half a mo'.' Rustling of the pages of the

196

enormous office diary into which we both write everything: 'Saturday 7th' What time will you ring?'

'Say—nine p.m., here?'

'Nine minus five-and-a-half, that makes around three thirty in the afternoon here. Um ... I'm goin up to Strathclyde on the Friday; Julius and I are going to look over that library extension site again. I'm not sure whether I'll be back Friday night or some time Saturday. Tell you what, I'll ring *you*, that'll be simpler. Where will you be that evening?'

'The Turf Club, Poona.'

'You're joking!'

'No, really. Apparently that's one of the places people stay there. It isn't particularly expensive.'

'You amaze me. I wonder if it's still full of tiffins and punkahs and whatever the other things are.'

'Tiffin is just lunch,' I said dampeningly. 'And punkahs disappeared when electricity was invented.'

'Well, all right, love, we will be, as you say, in touch. "Don't call us, we'll call you"—'

*   *   *

'You'd better stay at the Turf Club,' Nicky said, 'because that's where my cousins are having their wedding reception too, on the

197

lawn, in the evening. You can come to that, it'll amuse you—don't worry, anyone can go to a wedding reception. No, the Turf Club isn't very grand these days. Not what it was, they say, like practically all the old British clubs. If it was, people like my cousins wouldn't be having their party there.'

We had been together to Sion Fort on Sunday afternoon. The traffic was bad: it took longer to get there than Nicky had thought it would. He began to swear at buses and lorries. I didn't mind. I just enjoyed riding there behind him for its own sake, holding on to his belt as we bumped wildly over the bad tarmac. Tony had had a scooter when I had first met him, but it was years since I had ridden around a town like this. It was like being young again. On the back of the motorbike I felt alive; the rest of the time in that torrid, pre-monsoon April heat I felt drained of resolution and competence, as if suffering from some obscure sickness. When I looked at myself in the glass a pale, sweaty face stared back at me, a person almost rubbed out by the strong colours, sounds and odours all round, someone who might fade away entirely and not be missed.

Sometimes I thought of those other pale young woman, perspiring and perspiring inside their tropical corsets, seeing their complexions fade and yellow and their hair lose its lustre, prisoners in that mortal climate for the sake of husband and country. Some of them had indeed become sick unto death and never returned home. Their exiled bones lie in Sewri, or in still older cemeteries, now desecrated and forgotten beneath railway lines or docks or tenements. I felt a helpless pity and identification with them.

Sion Fort was on top of a hill like a miniature mountain, and small and ruinous when we got up there. Nicky looked bathed in sweat, as if he were melting. He never ordinarily took exercise, I suspected.

The empty doorways and roofless rooms had what I could now recognise as a European feel about them, even without the old and new roman-alphabet initials cut all over the stone walls. I imagined homesick Tommies, pinkly damp, chiselling away in a bored fashion under the merciless sky. But Nicky was vague about whether they would all have been red-coated soldiers from long ago or whether the fort had still been in use in recent times.

'I can just remember British soldiers in Bombay,' he said. 'When I was a little kid, before Independence. They used to give us kids sweets. And they whizzed about in jeeps, which I thought was just great. There was hardly any cars in Bombay then—or for most of the time till I was grown up, come to that. You'll hardly credit this, but right into the 1950s traffic cops used to stand at road-junctions and salute every car that came past. They knew them all, you see, because there were so few ... Bombay was a beautiful city then, all clean and lovely—well, the main parts of it were, anyway. Not Mazagon, of course, but the main roads, down near the cathedral and Victoria Terminus. The streets there got washed twice a day! We used to follow the water carts. There weren't people everywhere, spilling out of every corner, building shacks everywhere, in those days.'

'It's hard for me to imagine.'

'It's hard even for me to remember. Sometimes I can't believe I ever really knew that Bombay. It seems to have *gone*.'

'Like the Garden of Eden. You lost it. You had to.'

'What?' he looked bemused.

'Never mind. Just an idea ... Do you think that perhaps you remember it all as clean and lovely partly because you were a child at the time, and children do see things differently from the way grown-ups do?' Somewhere in that pristine city, before the Fall, was a laughing schoolboy whom 'everyone liked'.

'Well, it's possible, I suppose,' he said in a slightly offended tone, and I knew he had missed the point. 'But I know I'm right about those water carts. We used to jump about in the spray.' He thought a bit.

'I couldn't leave Bombay, though,' he said suddenly. 'Even though it has changed so much, I couldn't. When Terry first got married there

200

was a suggestion I might emigrate too: it wasn't hard even for someone like me to get a hospital job in the UK then. There was an idea we might all go—Ma, Lina, the lot of us. It wouldn't have been difficult in the 1960s. But when it came to the point I couldn't. And it wasn't just that the UK is cold and the British are stuck up and cold too, though I pretended to the others it was that. It was that I didn't want to leave here. Not India. I don't give a damn about India. But Bombay itself: it just is my place—I can't really explain. And when I see people neglecting it and ruining it and knocking it down, well, I get angry, but it's still my place. I shall never leave it.'

As we were coming down from the fort, he said in a different tone, as if feeling that Sion had let us down: 'I must have given you the impression there's nowhere nice left around Bombay at all ... It isn't true. There's Juhu beach—though that's getting crowded these days. And there's Bassein! I'd forgotten Bassein.'

'Where's that?'

'It's a ruined Portuguese town—oh, way out beyond Borovili. A walled town, and *really* deserted. All the old churches just standing around in the jungle, and the sea comes up to the walls. Hell, why didn't I think of taking you there? Maybe—' he glanced at his gold watch. 'No, far too late now, of course. It's miles and miles ... *Hell.*'

'Perhaps we could go there another Sunday?' I said.

'What other Sunday? There isn't one, is there?' he retorted discouragingly. 'Next Sunday you and I will be travelling back from Poona, separately. Unless I tell Lina ... But even then Bassein is in the other direction. Oh, it was just an idea. You might not have been interested anyway. *I* like Bassein because I like thinking of all those old Portuguese, but for you Poona probably means more. Anyway, I haven't actually been to Bassein myself for years: that was why I didn't think of it earlier. We used to go there on parties with the church, when I was in my teens. It's probably ruined now, too.'

'But you said it was always ruined.'

'I don't mean like that.' Irritably. 'I mean that it's probably ruined now compared with what it was. Spoilt. Like most things.'

'Perhaps, the next time I come to Bombay—?' I said. But he acted as if he had not heard, stolidly descending the path in front of me, shoulders hunched.

Why would I, indeed, ever return to Bombay, once I had got what I came for?

On the way back into town we stopped for a drink, where there were tables under a matting awning that let splinters of brightness through on to our hands. The proprietor and Nicky seemed to know each other. The man brought

202

tea-cups and a kettle without being asked, and when he poured the liquid from the kettle into the cups it was not tea but cold beer. Beyond the awning there were tiny Indian hens pecking about, and a thin cow. A little boy fetched her some bits of pressed cane from a sugar-cane man who was turning the jangling wheel of his press on the far side of the road. The other children in the street ignored the cow: they were more interested in Nicky's motorbike, standing flashing there in the sun.

'I wonder who she belongs to,' I said, watching the cow, who had finished or trampled on the sugar-cane, and was now trying to snatch some fruit from the basket of a woman seller. The woman fended her off crossly, but did not really drive her away.

'No one.'

'She must, Nicky. A whole *cow* is surely valuable.'

'Only when she's in milk. This one isn't—you can see. Her owners have probably turned her loose to fend for herself.'

'How awful. Poor thing. They ought to kill her if they're not going to feed her.'

'Of course they ought, but they won't. It's forbidden. Don't blame me. I'm not a Hindu, I didn't invent this country. That cow takes her chance along with everyone else here. Some devout family may adopt her. She may even get pregnant again. In a cow, that is desirable.'

A little later, as if the cow, her milk and her situation had reminded him of something, or perhaps given him an opening which he had wanted to find, Nicky said, looking at me sideways: 'That baby . . .'

'*Which* baby?'

'The one at Borovili.'

'Yes?' I did not want to talk about that baby.

'I have a feeling—I don't know, but I just have an idea—that she was a prostitute's child.'

I put down my cup, suddenly feeling exhausted. At once he poured some more beer into it, which frothed over and spilt on the metal table. He's physically clumsy too, I thought masochistically. God knows what he's like at stitching a cut or giving an injection.

Aloud I said: 'Are you telling me this because you think it will make me feel better about—about rejecting her?'

'If you like,' he said equably. 'Do you want to know why I think the mother was a prostitute?'

'Go on.'

'Because the Sisters said the baby seemed used to a bottle when she arrived. As far as she had been fed at all, she had obviously had a bottle. And she had running dysentery too, which would fit with that.'

'So? I don't get it.'

'Most foundlings aren't bottle-babies. You can see it, the Sisters say, in the way they react to the bottle, poor little devils. Poor women in

India nearly always do breast-feed their babies still, even if they are going to abandon them. Well, you remember that girl we saw lying with her baby beside her on the floor of a train that first time when we were coming back from Borovili—'

'I remember her well,' I said. 'But I didn't think you would.'

'Oh? Why?'

'You didn't seem interested in her at the time, and why should you remember afterwards? It was months ago, and surely to you she was just one more derelict you couldn't bother about. You even said that at the time.'

'I remember her perfectly well,' he said. 'I remember everything I have seen with you.' He didn't look at me, so I was not sure how I was intended to take the remark. I was genuinely surprised. He had shown no apparent pleasure on meeting me again when I had returned to Bombay, and I thought he had asked me out for a ride that afternoon mainly because he was sorry for me and for the way things had gone, and wanted to show he could take me on an expedition without either quarrelling or making advances. He had made no attempt to touch me while we had wandered round the fort in spite of the associations the place apparently had for him, and I had concluded that he now regretted his behaviour that evening five months earlier in Mazagon, for more than one reason. Perhaps he had been a bit drunk then. But now, after what he had just said, I did not know whether I was supposed to remember it or not.

After a while, I said: 'But why does the fact that the mother didn't feed the baby herself make you think she was a prostitute?'

'Just a hunch, I may be quite wrong. But they're about the only women who don't, in the lower classes.'

'It would create professional difficulties for them, I suppose,' I said self-consciously, imagining.

'Quite. Also that baby, as I said, was a lot paler than most of the ones orphanages get.'

'You mean—her father might have been just anyone? Not necessarily Indian at all?'

'Yes, that's so. If I'm right, and she come out of Kamathipura—she was found in a church near there, you see—her father could have been, well, from any country in the world. The UK even.'

'Kamathipura?'

'Bombay's red light area. Grant Road, Falkland Road—round there. Unwanted babies must have been coming out of there for a hundred years. Or more. Haven't you been there? A lot of tourists find their way there. It's one of the sights of Bombay. Women in booths, like cages, give the foreigners a thrill... No, I am not going to take you there.'

I sat without speaking, turning over in my

mind ways of getting my own back on him for his awful, gratuitous rudeness. But before I had decided on one, he put his hand out apologetically and said: 'To make up for that I'll take you somewhere else. I'll take you to meet someone who lives round here.'

★   ★   ★

A dingy open doorway between a dry-cleaners and a booth selling spare chrome fittings for cars. Stairs going up inside a house which probably was not really old but which seemed infinitely so: betel-blood on the skirting board, walls encrusted with the unspecific dirt of time. After the glare of the outside it was very dark in that house. Down a corridor, we reached door scarred with the marks of by-gone locks. Nicky rapped a signal on it.

Two dark-skinned women in saris, one old and one quite young. They did not seem to be expecting him, but they were not surprised either. The young one looked faintly embarrassed to have a visitor from England— for so I understood Nicky to introduce me. The old one screwed up her wrinkled face in a smile and patted Nicky's shoulder, calling him *bai*, 'brother'.

Someone else was called out from the kitchen leading off the small main room. A boy of about twelve in ragged shorts. He came out slowly,

207

rubbing his face childishly with his fist, then yawning like a man. His grandmother laughed and made signs to me, and I understood that he'd been sleeping. I felt sorry for him. He was dispatched to fetch us cold drinks, and Nicky said to me in English that I must drink it even if I didn't want it. We sat on the edge of the large bed, and Nicky and the women talked. From its tone, their conversation seemed domestic, inconsequential; I wondered if they were distant relations of his, though it didn't seem likely. Perhaps the old woman had been a maid or a nanny once in the da Souza household.

I sat and stared at a shelf containing a display of nicely cleaned brass pots, and at a little god who danced on the wall with a wreath of fading flowers round his neck and a tiny oil-lamp below. The boy came back with two bottles of fizzy stuff and straws. He turned on a transistor radio which played the usual warbling, inward-turned Indian film music. The younger woman sais something to him, and he turned it down a bit, and then sat cross-legged on the floor and picked at one of his bare feet.

The old woman felt the stuff of the loose cotton blouse I was wearing and asked if it was Indian-made. I told Nicky to say to her that I believed so, and as I said so I remembered buying it from a rather expensive shop in South Kensington at the other end of time.

Soon after that, we left. It had been mildly

interesting for me to see inside such a home, but I was not sure what the point of our visit had been. Perhaps it had not needed a point. They seemed occupationless, these women, though I supposed they did some sort of work during the week. Indian society includes such depths of poverty unequalled elsewhere that you could hardly say the family were poor by Indian standards, but I understood that they were by mine. I did notice that, as we were at the door, Nicky passed something from his pocket into the younger woman's hand. She took it quickly without comment, and tucked it into the front of her blouse. It might have been a folded banknote. Perhaps that, simply, had been the point of the visit.

When we returned to the dusty streets of Mazagon he invited me into his house, as if he were unwilling that this only half-successful day should end.

'Come on,' he said as I hesitated. 'We can have a gin and tonic in peace. Mother'll be at church now, and Lina's off at Juhu with her elderly boyfriend.'

'The Parsee?'

'The same. She's got a new bathing dress she wants him to see her in. Can't think how he stands it.'

'I think you've just got into a habit of being horrid about Lina without thinking about it,' I said. An adolescent habit, perhaps, designed to convey to other girls that they had no rival in Lina but that he was not to be impressed by mere femininity. I was developing a theory that he was actually much attached to his sister.

'Oh, she's not a bad old thing really. We used to have quite good times together as kids. Teresa was younger . . . But she's so *useless* for a woman, I'm not surprised no one wants to take her off our hands. She can't even cook.'

We sat, with the rather strong drinks he had made us, by the open window. The scent of wood smoke rose from the tiny brazier of the peanut seller on the corner; it brought a whiff of the country into the soiled town.

I said disingenuously, wanting not so much to know the real answer as what he would say: 'Why don't you get married yourself, Nicky?'

His happy face shut. 'Who to?'

'Well, there must be lots of girls—women, of your religion and background, who—'

'"Who'd be glad to" is the usual phrase, I believe. Maybe. But I don't find most of them particularly attractive. Too Westernised.' He was evidently paying me out for something, perhaps for asking in the first place. I said nothing, and after a minute he said, in a different voice:

'You see, most of the girls—women—I might fancy, have rather high expectations, materially. That's one of the problems of our community. Like the Parsees. We're trying to support a

Westernised standard of living on Indian incomes. Have you any idea how much I earn from the hospital?' I couldn't guess, so he told me. I had not thought it would be a lot, but I hadn't realised just how little it would be.

'Oh Nicky, I'm sorry, I do see the problem,' I said. A man telling you his earning power is, in my terms, doing something much more intimate than many of the things traditionally considered intimate, though I was to discover afterwards that in India this does not necessarily apply.

'Perhaps you should marry an Indian,' I said. 'I mean, an *Indian* Indian.'

'Who do you suggest?' he said, not challenging, but reasonable and friendly.

'Well—Shanti Desai?'

He groaned, rubbing his face with his hands.

'I can't marry Shanti Desai. Surely you can see that?'

'She's very fond of you,' I said. I had been going to say 'in love with you', but substituted the other phrase at the last moment.

'I know,' he said quietly, as if it was indeed 'in love' I had said. 'But I can't. She's a Hindu. You don't understand, but it goes right against—against everything I've grown up thinking and feeling. For us Christians, marrying a Hindu—it's a sort of defeat.'

'I see . . .' I said. Everything seemed to be infinitely more complicated than I had realised.

'And vice versa, of course,' he said more

211

briskly. 'Shanti's family would be pretty disgusted about her marrying me. They're high-caste and devout, you see. They naturally look down on Christians, especially Roman Catholics. They think we're unclean in our habits, and drink and are immoral. And they may have a point there.'

His mother came home from church, wearing gloves. I thought she looked a little put out to see me there again. She asked Nicky if he were going to the last Mass of the day and, to my surprise, he said he was.

*　　　*　　　*

I saw Nicky only once during the following week. We agreed to meet in Poona on the Saturday afternoon. Till then I was alone, in a way I had hardly ever been before and perhaps, now, will never be again.

I walked about the city. I hated it in a way, but I could not leave it alone. The unthinking, random cruelty of the place, which on my earlier visit I had been able to regard as something alien and essentially unknowable, to be viewed from the outside as a film or a dream, now smote me with a personal pain. Certain things haunted me, lying in wait for me behind my eyelids in the disturbed, fetid heat of the night, for now in April the dark brought no coolness. The crippled beggar children, whose eyes were still

212

bright and hopeful and whose limbs had been deliberately twisted in infancy, I had been told, so that they could follow this calling ... the defeated old, just cloth bundles on the pavement ... the earth-coloured ragged boys who squatted all day, waiting like patient animals for their food, outside a mosque near my hotel ... the countless dogs themselves, balding, infested, lying on pavements, grateful just for a flat surface, a foot or two of shade ... These thronged my brain, a hideous population problem, driving out the image I tried again and again to fix there: a lovely little thing with curly hair, a very happy child, only rather dark-skinned.

'You have the gall to suppose you're rescuing the children from the misfortune of being Indian, when really you're robbing them of their birthright—'

'How can anyone take on the poverty of India? I find one baby a good home with you—that act is sufficient unto itself ... You Westerners understand nothing.'

And yet it was not even the classic street-horrors of urban India that touched me most deeply. What I also retained, what drove me out into those streets again and again, was its fragile happiness, like scent from the flower-sellers' baskets, which seemed to carry even in its dampness and softness a hint of incipient decay. A man turning a hand-crank to propel a set of miniature roundabout chairs slowly round and round against the setting sun; another walking in a dung-strewn lane, pursued by excited children, carrying on his back a glass box full of tiny dabs of candyfloss; a young woman patiently teaching her child to eat from a plate as they both squatted on the pavement outside the main station; an old man washing his squealing naked grandsons at a stand-pipe opposite the Law Courts; office clerks stroking the head of a cow and feeding her leaves as they passed; the memory of Shanti Desai wiping my face with her sari . . . These things filled me with such a yearning love and an irrational desire to identify myself with this land of regrets, that I wondered if I could ever bear to return again through that cold, grey, thickening opacity, down, down into our ordered world once more.

One evening Shanti Desai took me to visit her family out in the suburbs. I expect Nicky had asked her to. The house seemed full of people. Uncles and brothers of all ages came and went, children in white cotton pyjamas pattered about. There were goats in the courtyard and wheeling, crying birds against the sunset sky. Plump mothers, aunties and sisters of varying degrees plied me with things on little saucers and sat nodding and smiling at me while I ate them. The were all so gratuitously and unnecessarily kind to me, I could hardly bear to leave them.

Another evening, one of Tony's contacts who

had heard from Tony that I was in Bombay again invited me to a buffet supper with twenty other people. He kept his driver up to take me home afterwards.

'You will be quite safe with Mendez,' the wife assured me warmly, so that I did not tell her that late the evening before I had walked back from the seafront to the centre of Bombay alone. 'We're so lucky to have Mendez,' she said. 'He's a Goan—a Christian—and they *are* more reliable than the rest.' She was a Parsee herself, a handsome woman with a degree from Girton. 'Servants are getting so difficult now,' she said. 'You wouldn't believe what one has to pay to get a good cook these days.'

Shall I ever again go to parties with rich, successful people? Perhaps not.

I had originally wanted to understand Bombay and its past because I thought it would be our child's past, the place where the sources of its life lay. Now I walked all over it because it was someone else's too. Nicky's. 'I shall never leave it,' he had said.

*   *   *

At last Saturday came. When I arrived at the Poona Turf Club, Nicky was loitering on the verandah talking to a servant. He was far more smartly dressed than I had ever seen him, in a white safari suit. On the green, endlessly

215

watered English lawn servants were setting out chairs, and gardeners were draping fairy lights over the balcony and across the trees, presumably for the reception that night.

'*There* you are,' he said. 'I've been waiting for you.'

'I didn't say I'd be here till now.'

'Well, I hoped you might come before. Let's go.'

'Where?'

He stopped and stared at me. 'To the orphanage of course, where else? There was a lunch party at my cousins'. I left it halfway through to come and meet you.'

'I'm sorry.'

'Doesn't matter. I've got to see them all again this evening. Are you ready then?'

'Can't I even wash? I've been on the train.'

He sighed exaggeratedly, but let the servants lead me up to my room, coming along behind himself. It was a huge room opening on to the first floor balcony, with twin beds, wicker armchairs and oval mirrors. On the dressing table was a china powder bowl. I almost expected to see silver-backed brushes lying there.

'I hope you like it,' he said with a touch of pride, as if he had been responsible for furnishing it.

'I do, but you said it wasn't grand. It is.'

'Not really, any more. It's a left over. I'll be

216

downstairs.'

The blinds were drawn. I gazed into the oval dimness of the looking glass, and generations of pale-faced women gazed back at me, pained, restrained, civilised and subtly censorious.

'... *curly hair and rather dark-skinned* ...'

You've got it all wrong, I said to them. It's all different now—all that's finished.

The past is never finished, they said. It is there for ever, in people's bones and hair, their eyes and gestures, in their words and in what they do, not say.

There were several rickshaws standing under a pipul tree at the corner of the pleasant suburban road. Nicky put his fingers in his mouth like a commissionaire and whistled one over.

'Haven't you got your bike?'

'Left it at my cousins'. I didn't want to get oil on this suit.'

'Is the orphanage far?'

'Several miles—out towards the old Government House at Ganesh Kind. Poona's spread out like that. You'll see.'

Everyone had told me how English a place Poona was and how at home I would feel there. I could see what they meant, as we crossed bleached greens and an unmistakable English church wheeled into view, but the feel of the place to me was Mediteranean rather than English. The luxuriant trees, the flowering shrubs and the hot, dry air, so different from the humidity of the plain, reminded me of holidays in the South of France. I suddenly felt cheerful and optimistic, ready to face the momentous encounter ahead and even to rejoice in it.

But when our rickshaw finally found the orphanage, after several false turns, the guard at the creeper-hung gate was reluctant to let us in. We were not, it seemed, expected. The supervisor was not there today. Eventually his deputy was sent for, and arrived wiping his mouth; a black-skinned young man who spoke even worse English than Nicky's houseman. 'There is mistake,' he kept saying with mild, infuriating persistence, waggling his head. 'Is next day you are coming, I think.'

'Can't we just *see* the baby now,' I said to Nicky. Nicky asked, repeated himself in Hindi. The deputy just smiled and waggled harder.

'I am not knowing which baby you mean, doctor-sir and lady. Here is many baby, isn't it? We are orphanage, you see. You see Mr Dvardkhar yesterday, I think.'

'But yesterday we were neither of us here—' I began frantically.

'He doesn't mean yesterday,' said Nicky to me, and, to the deputy: 'OK. Tomorrow. In the morning. At about ten o'clock. You tell Mr Dvardkhar.'

We trailed back to where Nicky had paid off the rickshaw. Of course it had gone.

'We'll walk a bit and pick one up,' he said quietly. I realised then that he was very angry but was suppressing it. I was struggling to suppress my own painful disappointments also.

'Why did he think we were here yesterday?' I said after a while.

'He didn't. He just got the wrong word. In Hindi, and several other languages, "yesterday" and "tomorrow" are the same word—"the next day".'

'Christ!'

'Exactly. It doesn't help us to be efficient—as you've noticed.' He strode on, his lips pinched together.

'I'm glad you didn't get cross with him,' I said.

'Why?'

'Because I couldn't have stood it.'

He looked at me then, but he just said, 'I never get cross with people of that sort.'

Then, as if to distract both of us, he began talking fast about his cousin's wedding.

★　　★　　★

When the dark had come the lawn beneath my room gradually filled with a well-conducted crowd beneath the fairy lights. Suits, elaborate cocktail dresses, long dresses, saris... The bride arrived in a long white dress and veil, her hair piled high; her young husband was in a dinner jacket. They sat on a dais while guests were ceremonially presented to them in twos and threes. Trays of drinks were carried round. A swing band (also in dinner jackets) played Western music from 1940s and 1950s musicals: *Oklahoma* seemed to be the favourite.

Eventually Nicky came to find me.

'Why are you still up here? Why haven't you come down to join the fun?'

'Nicky, I'm shy, and I don't want to intrude. Won't they all wonder what I'm doing here?'

'I've told you,' he said. 'Weddings are for anyone who's around. You know Indians are hospitable. They won't wonder anything about you, they're all far to busy wondering if Noella is a virgin.

'Isn't she a Catholic?'

'Yes of course, but that's got nothing to do with it. Come on, I'll introduce you to Noella and Francis and their parents and to one or two other people who might be offended if I didn't, and then you needn't bother about anyone else. Oh, except my doctor-cousin, whose name is Mrs Mendez. It was her husband who booked your room—he's a member here. She's the only one, by the way, who knows why you're here, and I told her not to tell anyone else for the moment. Just say, if anyone asks, that you happen to be staying here and you happen to know me.'

It sounded implausible to me. I still hesitated.

'They look very young from here,' I said, for something to say. 'Him, particularly.'

'Francis? He's about—what? Twenty-two I suppose. His father's my first cousin, like I told you. I remember going to his parents' wedding.'

'Does that make you feel old?'

He sat down on the arm of a wickerwork chair, which creaked under his weight and nearly overbalanced. He slid on to the seat.

'Now don't *you* start again,' he said with an exaggerated sigh. 'Ma and Lina are bad enough. Not to mention every other damned female at this sort of occasion. "And when shall we dance at *your* wedding, Nicky?"—nudge, wink.' He slumped down in the chair and tucked in his chin with a fed-up expression. He had been joking when he began this speech, but I saw that genuine annoyance and depression had set in by the end of it. Damn. Oh, damn him.

'I would like a drink, if you don't mind, before I go down,' I said. 'Would you like one?'

'Have you got some up here?' he asked sulkily.

'No, but as I'm staying here I can ring for the bearer and ask him to bring some up. At least, I imagine I can?'

'Oh yes, certainly,' he said hastily, and I remembered that of course he wasn't used to staying in places like this.

The elderly bearer fetched up whiskies and sodas and a chit to sign and then hung around

221

for a tip. I would have given him one, but Nicky waved him impatiently away.

'This is good whisky,' he said when he had tasted it, cheering up.

'It's imported, I imagine.' I had seen the amount of the chit.

'I don't know why we can't make decent whisky in India. We can make nuclear bombs.'

'Decent ones?'

'Huh, maybe ... Oh, I suppose we've just got an inferiority complex about everything the British used to do better than us. Whisky, gardens, drainage, medicine, education, law, government ... We don't really want to be measuring ourselves against the British standard in these things any more. But we're stuck with the ghost of the British Raj.' He seemed to like the phrase, and repeated it. 'Most Indians won't admit that,' he said, 'particularly if they're my age or younger. They'll tell you Britain is irrelevant and that Japan or Canada's where it's all happening now. They're lying. Britain can never be irrelevant to India, unfortunately.'

'I feel haunted here by the Raj myself,' I said slowly.

'Here in Poona? I'm not surprised. I told you it was like this.'

'Yes, but not only here. I have been—all the time. Right from the beginning. I realise that now. You said something like that to me before—'

222

'I know I did. You needn't remind me,' he said. 'I hurt you, I know. I wanted to. I didn't realise then that you understood or cared about—about that sort of thing. I thought you were just trying to grab something from India like the British always have.'

'Perhaps I was.' Am. Was.

'It's funny, you know,' he said, slopping the last of his imported whisky round his glass. 'It's funny because actually, of course, no pucka British family in the old days would ever have adopted an Indian child . . . and certainly not a no-caste orphanage child of all things.' I could see he was grasping at a paradox which was eluding him. He wasn't used to dealing in abstract concepts. Since the same paradox had been occupying my mind during the afternoon, I had by now a clearer view of it.

'I think that's partly *why* we wanted to do it,' I said. I began to walk round the room fingering things, like the bowl on the triple-mirrored dressing table. This is what I do when I am tense: it is the only way I show tension, apart from smoking, and ever since Tony realised this it has infuriated him to see me do it. He is a perennially tense person himself, but he regards manifest tension as if it were some kind of failure, or a slightly discreditable personal habit like picking one's nose. Nicky just sat waiting for me to say more.

'When we first planned this—this enterprise,'

I said carefully, after a while, 'I thought—we both thought—that, as well as other reasons, it was some sort of *gesture* against just the attitude you describe. That by adopting an Indian child of possibly—probably—low-caste origins, we would be somehow not only getting a child but striking a blow at all that sort of *pucka-sahib*, Poona Turf Club racist tradition.'

'"Keep the wogs in their place," it's called.'

'OK—you know what I mean.' I stopped a second, momentarily repelled by this image, now put into words for the first time, of a sanctimonious British pair after something they wanted and after moral kudos at one and the same time. Ashamed, I could only hurry on: 'We saw it almost as a sort of—well, atonement for Britain's sins in the past.' I had not meant to say 'sins' but the second religion-flavoured word had followed on the first. This is his language too, I thought, the *Atonement of Sin*: perhaps he will understand, and not think it too awful of us. Aloud I said: 'It probably sounds idiotic to you.'

'Not idiotic,' he said quietly. 'But—well, what I really think is that you only saw it this way because you were British in the first place.'

'Yes. Yes, I suppose that's so.' Well obviously, I thought in irritation, and then felt confused.

'I mean that you're still involved with us in some way as we are with you. You can't get away from it, either.'

'Nicky,' I said, 'Nicky, what do you *really* feel about my—our—adopting a child here? At first you seemed rather unwilling, even angry. Lately you seemed much keener on the idea.' I had to know.

But I dreaded what the answer might be. To postpone it, I suppose, I walked out on to the balcony and looked over. A few couples, led by the bride and groom, were beginning to dance now on a floor laid over part of the lawn. Far above them and the fairy lights and the trees, in the dark-blue void of the tropical night sky, I suddenly saw the Plough, the only star formation I can readily recognise. It was exactly and disconcertingly like the Plough that hangs over the English countryside, except that it was standing on end. I came back in again.

'I'm keeping you from the party,' I said.

'I'm going down anyway in a minute,' he said, with unkind reasonableness, 'whether you come with me or not. But first I'll answer your question. What do I think of you adopting here? If you really want to know, I think it's crazy.'

I sat down on the slippery cover of one of the beds. 'Crazy. I see. Why on earth didn't you tell me that before?'

'Because you didn't damn-well ask! You just *assumed*, like a white mem-sahib, that the little Indian doctor would run round supplying your needs.'

'Hardly little.' Gross slob.

225

'You know damn well what I mean.'

I suppose I could have said, to this accusation, that his own behaviour had not done much to discourage this attitude. I could have pointed out that he had asked me hardly any questions about myself and had not even asked to meet Tony. I could have mentioned the subject of money. I said nothing.

'I'm sorry,' he said contritely. 'I've done it again. That wasn't fair. I know that now.'

'We seem to keep apologising to each other for this and that,' I said helplessly—and thought, in a distracted way, of a silly slogan for a sillier film that had been advertised on the London Underground a few years back: *Being in love means never having to say you're sorry.*

'Look,' he said, 'all I can tell you is what I would feel about adoption if it were me trying to. It's my opinion—well, not even that, really, just a feeling. You don't have to agree with me.'

'You wouldn't adopt,' I said quietly. Down on the lawn the band had moved on to *The Sound of Music*. More people seemed to be dancing now: I could hear their feet shuffling.

'I wouldn't adopt,' he said.

Somewhere, in another dimension that was either very close to me or as remote as a star, a child whom I had never seen died.

'I wouldn't do it here,' he said carefully, 'if I were in your place. I mean that literally. And in my own case I wouldn't adopt unless I could

226

find a child of my own community. A child from people of my race and kind, I mean, both sides. One I could bring up to see himself as a Goan and to be proud of—of our traditions and heritage. A heritage matters, you know. It can be the best asset a person has. My sister Lina doesn't understand that. That's why I get so angry with her.'

After a long pause he went on: 'I mean the way Lina doesn't value being a Portuguese— well, of Portuguese descent—and a Catholic, like I do, like Daddy and Auntie did. The way she goes around in those horrible short skirts and things, talking about home. Like a—well, there used to be a lot of words for it when I was a kid... But for you the UK *is* home and your British heritage is the real one. How can you treat it as if it were worth nothing? As if being proud of being British and keeping your own traditions were just some old-fashioned sin that today needed apologising for?—

'Look, this is an unfashionable thing to say these days, but I'm hardly a fashionable sort of fellow. I believe in the past, in what was good in it, like I believe in not knocking down old buildings that people like and are used to. And although, as I say, we don't belong to the British tradition ourselves, the British always were a sort of model for us of what is good class. They set certain standards for themselves and stuck to them: that was my father's view, and it's mine.

And, if you really want to know, I *am* shocked, yes I am, by the idea of a British couple like yourselves taking a little dark-skinned kid from nowhere and pretending it's your own. Because that's what it seems to me, a sort of crazy pretence. It isn't *real*. It's against nature. It's the sort of thing that makes Indians—Indians of almost all communities, not just people like me—say that the British today have lost their self-respect and the good judgment for which they used to be famous.'

He stopped, at last.

In the end, because he did not say anything more, I was forced to speak: 'People might say that's our own problem,' I said. 'Not yours.'

'I told you this was just my personal view,' he said promptly. 'You don't have to agree with it. You probably think it's racist. Well, it is. People *should* be proud to belong to their own race.'

'Why should you worry about us—me? Perhaps you should let us make our own mistakes.'

'But I am, aren't I?' he said. 'I'm not stopping you. That's why you're here, through me. And the decision is yours. It always has been. But I'm not quite irresponsibile, whatever you may think. After all, I could have said nothing and just let you take out of the country that other baby, couldn't I, the one that was retarded? Some people in my position would have.'

After a minute I said: 'You've helped other

228

foreign couples to adopt. What about them? Did you feel they were making a mistake too?'

'Germans and Dutch,' he said dismissively. 'It's different for them. At least, I suppose so, and I don't care about them anyway. They haven't your history and traditions. In fact I should think the Germans are only too glad to pretend their own history isn't there. Those couples weren't involved with an idea of India like you are. They were just treating India— quite politely, of course—as a baby-shop. So I made them pay.'

'I see. Quite a lot, perhaps?'

'A lot—perhaps not by your standards, but by mine. I've told you what I earn. Why shouldn't they pay? They're getting a child, after all, their heart's desire, something of a value that's impossible to measure.'

There was a knock on the door. He jumped.

'Damn that servant, what's he want now?'

'The glasses, I expect,' I said. 'He's probably going off duty.' I collected the empty glasses and opened the door.

'Telephone, mem-sahib.'

'Telephone—are you sure? But no one knows I'm here.' Then I remembered Tony's call from London.

*   *   *

When I had finished speaking to Tony in the

stuffy long distance booth near the secretary's office, I came out again on to the verandah. Nicky was waiting for me beside a carved tiger some British officer had presented to the Club in 1923.

'He was calling you from London?'

'Yes.'

'Everything all right?'

'Yes, I think so.' I realised I was trembling, but didn't feel equal to explaining to Nicky that it wasn't Tony himself that had this effect on me. I said it was chilly. Up in the hills the night did have a freshness missing in Bombay at that season. Perhaps that was one of a number of things that had made me more capable of decision.

'You'll get warm dancing,' said Nicky.

To my surprise, he danced well, if in the old-fashioned style I remembered from dancing lessons in boarding-school days. It was, in any case, that sort of music. We did not talk much. It was the kind of perfect night of which in England you only get a handful in a lifetime, and I think that, on one level, I was as happy dancing with Nicky on that club lawn as I ever hope to be. The fact that, on another level, I was miserable and lost and the future I had planned had suddenly ceased to exist only gave the here-and-now happiness greater intensity.

When he pulled me off the floor a minute to introduce me to Mrs Mendez, I muttered:

'Don't say anything to her about babies. Even if she asks.'

'No, I won't,' he said at once.

She was a large, effusive lady in a brocade sari, but she did not ask, perhaps judging it neither the time nor the place. When she had fox-trotted off majestically with her husband, I said: 'Nicky, I don't want to go back to that orphanage tomorrow.'

'I know,' he said.

'Nor ever.'

'I know,' he said again.

We did another half-turn round the floor.

He said, squinting down to look at my face: 'Perhaps I should never have said all that, upstairs? But I felt I had to.'

You didn't have to, but you wanted and needed to, I thought. That's what people always mean when they say they 'had to'. I said: 'You were right. Don't blame yourself.'

'It's as you said: when we first met, last November, I didn't think much of you, so what you were proposing didn't bother me. And then, by and by, I really wanted you to have what you wanted, because I liked you. But then, this time, I got to care for you—much more; I began to worry about whether I was doing right to let you . . . Even if you hadn't asked me, like you did, I was boiling up to saying something. I had to.'

Yes, I expect I wanted you to as well, I

thought. Aloud I said: 'I'm glad you did, but it isn't that, Nicky, not really. I don't think that anyone can ever make up or change anyone's mind about this sort of subject; it's too important for that. And there aren't any *reasons* behind a decision to adopt or not to adopt a child anyway, or not valid ones. I see that now. It's just a feeling. A conviction one way or the other.' I had already said that to Tony, an hour or so before, but he hadn't wanted to hear it.

'Well, I wouldn't like to think that you were influenced by me,' said Nicky, surely untruthfully. He added disarmingly: 'My views aren't considered all that reliable, in my family.'

'I tell you, it isn't that. If anything that you've said to me has had an effect on me, it's something you said when I was here last November. And I expect that only made such an impression with me because it fitted in with something I was already feeling myself, but didn't want to admit I was feeling. And it's taken me till now to recognise it.'

'What was that I said?'

'About not taking away an Indian child's birthright. You know?'

'Yes. I know.' He danced in silence for a minute and then said: 'You shouldn't really take people out of their own places—their own country, their caste. You may take something irreplaceable from them. Shanti would say that to do that is to go against their *karma*—their

232

destiny. She's a great one for destiny.'

'I thought you didn't care for Hinduism. You once said something rude to me about Westerners who come to India to pursue exotic cults.'

'I've said a lot of rude things to you. It doesn't mean I dismiss all . . . But I'll put it in Christian terms if you'd rather. Let us say that if God doesn't intend you and your husband to have a child, then He doesn't. You've tried various treatments, I assume, and it hasn't worked. Your plan about coming here to adopt hasn't gone smoothly either . . . Well, don't force it. Maybe God'd rather you didn't, and maybe He knows best. Being obstinate and trying to push your way through to something against all the signs is called "spiritual pride" in our Church. Shanti calls it going against the *karma*. It's the same thing.'

We moved round the floor another time. It was crowded now. I saw Mrs Mendez dancing with Francis, the bridegroom, and Noella in the arms of her father. Lina, in a bright blue cocktail dress, had got elderly Mr Mendez, and was talking hard to him. The band was playing, of all things, 'Tea for Two'.

'It isn't even God,' I said wearily. 'I'm prepared to believe in Him, now; I do see it's pretty small-minded not to. But it's not that. It's more that I've realised that to do what I came to India to do, you have to be a lot nicer than I am.

And a lot more naïve as well. Angela hinted that
to me. I didn't listen to her. Actually someone
like Angela might be able to do it and make a
success of it. But not me.'

'Angela?'

'A friend in London.'

'What a pity she's in London. I've always
wanted to meet someone called Angela. I would
expect her to have wings.'

I was so disorientated that it took me a full
minute to look into his face and realise that he
was, of course, joking; that he was trying to
cheer me up out of what he assumed must be
unrelieved misery.

When the band stopped for an interval, I said:
'There's no point in my being here after tonight.
I'd better leave first thing in the morning.'
Poona, mocking, British Poona in the bright
morning light, would be, I felt, more than I
could easily bear.

Nicky glanced round. No one was looking at
us; most people had made a dignified but
purposeful bee-line for the bar, set up on the
verandah.

'We can leave now, if you like,' he said.

We looked at each other.

'How?'

'On the bike, of course. I've got it parked in
the compound.' But he didn't look
conspiratorial, or happy as he had while
dancing. He looked pale and rather tense

234

himself, watchful of my reaction.

'What about Lina?' I said at last.

'Lina can go home by train. I'll fix her—tell her I've remembered an urgent case I have to get back for early tomorrow morning. Or tell her I've had a call from the hospital tonight. That'd be better . . . Look, you go upstairs and collect your things together.'

In the hall I paused, and then went back to him. 'What about the room here? Paying for it, I mean: the office will be shut now.'

'I'll have a word with my cousin. You can pay her back later, through me.'

'She'll think I'm ungrateful—'

'Not if I let her think you're staying all night and leaving on the early train.' He hesitated. 'You don't want to do that, do you? . . . You'd rather we went now?'

I nodded.

'I thought so,' he said. 'But I was afraid I might be wrong.'

'You're not wrong,' I said, after another pause.

'I didn't think I was.'

He seemed to have the practicalities worked out. I wondered how long he'd been turning the idea over in his mind. Perhaps half an hour? Or perhaps for far, far longer than that.

★   ★   ★

I don't know how long the ride down from the hills took. Several hours, I think. The road was not very good and, in parts, quite steep.

We stopped once while the moon was still up, at a petrol station. Nicky had to wake up the watchman, who was asleep on a cot beside the pumps, to get the petrol.

We stopped again for a few minutes for him to wrap my shawl more firmly round me and knot it behind. It was cool on the bike, in the hill air. I had never felt chilled in India before. The dawn was coming by then, and I thought how awful it was that, living in the Western world where the nights are so cold and dark and still, I have hardly ever seen the dawn, perhaps only a dozen times properly in my life, if that. I said so to Nicky, and he smiled faintly as if he were remembering another sunrise, another occasion, but he just said: 'You should try being a houseman on call. That's what I remember most, when I see the dawn.'

We were on the edge of a bend, with a river valley not far below us. The pink sky got lighter every minute as I watched. Two women with pots on their heads appeared out of the landscape and walked, one behind the other, to the edge of the river to fill them. I thought, 'I shall never forget this scene, this moment—never.' Of course you do forget, or what you remember turns out not to have been important anyway, but it is still worth it, I think, trying to

fix a moment: nothing can touch it
from time, provided you do not try to
out into something more. The two peop
concerned grow bored and critical and turn
away from one another—the soft-skinned,
nestling baby turns into an ugly, obtuse man
grinning over pornographic pictures; but the
moment of unadulterated love remains.

I think it was either just before or just after
that, that I said to Nicky: 'That family we
visited last Sunday: those two women—'

'At Matunga? Yes?'

'That boy—'

'Yes?'

'He's yours, isn't he? He looks like you.'

Nicky said Yes; yes, that was so, the boy was
his son. He didn't sound upset that I had
guessed, just rather sad. He said, a little
anxiously: 'Is it very obvious he's like me?'

'Not that obvious. It didn't strike me at the
time. Only later.' I did not ask anything more,
or why he had taken me there, but he said:

'I'll tell you about that—sometime. Not now.
But soon.'

By the time we reached the outskirts of
Bombay the light had fully come. As we rode
through the northern suburbs the streets were
almost empty, except for strings of bullock carts
bringing in hay, but around six the factory
sirens sounded even though it was Sunday. The
pavements filled with men, hurrying towards

...ay from it. The mills with their tall chimneys and their wrought-iron gates are like the British past petrified in an eternal present.

Nicky turned into a wide street, then into another and stopped. He chained his bike to some railings and unscrewed the rear mirrors. He also removed the plugs with a plug-spanner and stuffed the holes with bits of rag. 'I don't want to get anything pinched,' he said.

'Where are we?'

'Just off Falkland Road. Kamathipura. It looks quiet and respectable at this hour, doesn't it?'

'It does, in a way.'

He said humbly: 'You see, there's nowhere else I can take you . . .' And then, 'Can you carry your bag? I'll take the rest.'

An hotel sign, a perpetually open doorway, a dark flight of stairs as in Matunga but bigger, older, perhaps more than a hundred years old, marked with the hands and feet of all that time. Upstairs a mosaic floor sloping unevenly away from us. A pungent smell of cooking, mixed with joss, a radio playing music behind a shut door, a glimpse of an inner courtyard with a shaft of bright light across our eyes.

Then darkness again further down the corridor, where a silent man, who had met us at the head of the staircase, led us to that unimaginable shuttered room towards which we had for so long, separately and then together, been journeying.

★   ★   ★

When I returned to London in the middle of April Tony was not there. My return date had always been indefinite; I was not surprised that he was in Strathclyde. I knew he had spent much of the month there: something to do with a new library at the University. He had left a message on the dictaphone that we always use for this, saying he would be back the following evening. Though the message began, as usual, 'Hallo, love,' his voice sounded stilted, slightly hollow, the voice of a man talking to a telephone answering service. There was no particular indication on it of the affronted man who either could not or would not understand what I was saying as I had repeated to him on the 'phone from Poona that the whole adoption idea had been misconceived and wrong, and that a lot of other things he or I had thought were misconceived too . . . There was no indication, either, that he had got over his affront and was looking forward to seeing me.

I began to walk about the house, touching things here and there as if it were a strange place to me. What sort of people would I suppose lived here, I wondered? Rich people, obviously: rich enough not to be either worried about money or concerned to display it; people who took for granted a level of comfort and convenience unknown over a very large part of the earth's surface. Unknown in Mazagon.

The house seemed dead, oddly muffled, like an instrument that is not able to express itself. It wasn't just the absorbent poly-vinyl tiling in the two offices, I thought, or the thick carpets everywhere else, or even the double-glazing that efficiently cut out the noise of the traffic in the square, turning it into a soundless townscape in an architect's design. It was also that, though the house was Tony's and my home as well as our office, the place to which we returned from journeys and where we sometimes gave quite large dinner parties, it now struck me as impersonal and somehow empty. Before, I had always quite liked its businesslike quality, soft-surfaced but bare, with nothing to catch the dust—the result of Tony's secret meanness about spending money on a small scale, and his declared belief that objects like patchwork cushions, Victorian maps of London and indeed alabaster eggs are just as much tat in their way as crinoline ladies or garden gnomes. But now this well-protected, uncommitted, padded void, 'defensible space' in the currently fashionable planning term, struck me as just that: emptiness.

In Bombay, in the few times I had thought of this house, I had supposed in anguished resignation that I should never leave it definitively and had thrust its image from me again. (Anguished resignation is a good Indian state of mind in any case.) But, now that I was actually back in London, it came to me that this place and everything it comprehended would not be impossible to leave after all. Really, there was not so very much here for me.

I avoided the small spare room with the expensive French wallpaper full of birds and leaves. We could, of course, cover that over with coats of paint. Or Tony could.

What do you mean, Tony could?

★   ★   ★

. . . He said he was the happiest he had ever been, with me, those few days we had together. He said it twice, in different ways. Once, he was a little tight, what with some beer we had had and lack of sleep, but the other time he was quite sober, and dressed, and I do think he meant it . . .

He probably did, at the time. It's the sort of thing one says, and feels at the time. But would he have risked saying it if he had thought there was the faintest possibility of your not going home? Face it, my girl, you are too old to believe in fairy stories: Nicky saw his chance and took it, and you both enjoyed it. Why in heaven's name should you expect more?

He needs more. Shanti saying that time, 'there is

241

very much of love in Nicky. It does not find a proper outlet...'

And what do you suppose Shanti knows about these things? What would Shanti think of the way you and he spent a considerable part of that week? She would be disconcerted and disgusted. Shanti, a good Hindu, meant that he needs a wife who will put up with him and understand him and have a child or two to give him back his faith and optimism in life. That is a proper outlet in anyone's terms. If you really care for him, the best thing you can do now is to sever all contact with him. That is probably what he expects anyway. There is no future substance in you and him any more than there was in the Indian baby you thought you could make yours. Both were dreams. They're over.

★ ★ ★

Tony came back from Strathclyde with a speech carefully prepared. I think he must have been planning it on the shuttle-'plane from Glasgow. Perhaps he even made some notes.

The word 'risk' cropped up in it a lot. He kept saying 'of course I quite understand if you've decided the risk is, on balance, too great to take'—and then went on to give another and another reason why adoption might be a good thing all the same.

After a while I became so irritated that I said:

'Tony, what *is* all this about "risk"? What risk? What is your message? I don't think I can be getting this quite clear.' I'm not sure whether he recognised the echo of his own words from our appalling Poona telephone conversation repeated back at him, but he stopped and looked very angry, eyes cold and blue and bulging.

'I mean the risk of taking on a child who is an unknown quantity,' he said primly, as if asked to express in words some crude bodily function. 'You know perfectly well that's what I mean. We discussed all that.'

'Yes, we discussed it all very thoroughly in a most adult way, I do recall—but unfortunately all that now seems to me a bit beside the point. In fact almost entirely so. Look, Tony—' I tried to take his hand, but he snatched it crossly away from me, as I suppose I knew he would. 'Look, in real life people *don't* "weigh the risks" or "discuss the pros and cons" or "decide things on balance". Not things affecting their personal lives, they don't. They may pretend to or talk as if they do, but they don't, not really. That's all flim-flam, a sort of display of democratic process. It's social workers' jargon—a way of dressing up feelings that really have much deeper roots and aren't necessarily justified or sensible or any of those other things.'

Tony listened politely without listening. When I stopped he began talking again about

243

how he would be really sorry if I were to reject now, on an emotional whim, something that might have 'met our needs' so well.

'Look, Tony,' I said again after a bit. 'There aren't Parker-Morris standards in children. It doesn't work like that.'

'I thought we were in agreement about this—'

'Well, I'm not any longer. Sorry.'

'I see,' he said stuffily after a pause. 'So you really are backing out. I didn't think you'd do that.'

He went off to put on his orange tracksuit for his jog. Since he turned thirty-eight he jogs every day almost without fail when he's home. Oh yes, you have to hand it to Tony, he goes through with things.

I suppose I would have felt more contrite towards him if he had seemed sadder. But he was not acting like a man who is disappointed or is mourning something he really wanted: he was a man who is annoyed, and feels he has been made to look a bit of a fool. It was not his heart that was suffering, but his sense of what was fitting, his pride of position.

But that is not to say pride is unimportant; for people like Tony, it is the essence they run on. I did try again to explain, one night, after days of carefully avoiding one another and talking about office things. I don't think I did it very well. I talked in a rambling way about the British Raj.

Tony interrupted me to say scathingly: 'Oh,

for God's sake, you're not joining those hippy breast-beaters, are you?'

'What do you mean?' I had forgotten, after all that had passed, that Tony himself knew anything about India.

'I met this girl in Bangalore,' he said. 'At a British Council party. She was some sort of hanger-on ... grubby, beads, you know—and into meditation and *karma* and all the other rubbish. She bored me stiff about the Opium Wars and Britain's hereditary sins. Someone told me afterwards she was living in the bazaar with a low-caste Indian, and he beat her up, and she was loving it because she felt she was making up to India for the way the Mutiny was suppressed, or some such bullshit.' Since he's been going to New York Tony has begun using words like 'bullshit'. 'She made jewellery or something,' he said. 'She used to sit and sell it on the pavement. She's probably still at it. There's thousands of people like her in India now, I was told. And of course when they run out of money and get sick from all the filthy food, the British Embassy has to bail them out. God, was she a pain.'

I lay there and said nothing for a bit. At last I said, 'I don't know anything about hippies in India. Or meditation. Or Buddhism and all the rest of it—they're welcome to it, as far as I'm concerned. That isn't what India means to me.' In any argument, a French philosopher once

245

said, it is not the thesis one defends: it is oneself.

'Isn't it what India means to you?' he said sharply. He suspected something but didn't know what.

'No, it isn't.' I thought a bit more, and finally said, 'Hippies are irrelevant to India, surely you can see that? They're irrelevant to everywhere: that's why they're there—that's what hippies *are*. India is real, Tony. It isn't just some drugs-and-dreams place for the Seeker, or whatever hippies think they are. It's real in a rent-and-mortgage, have-I-a-clean-shirt, bring-the-silver-teapot-out-for-the-visitor sort of way. That's why I don't want to exploit it, or—or look down on it.'

'No one's looking *down* on it, exactly.'

'Yes, you do. You look down on India like anything. You know you do. That's your fundamental attitude to it.'

There was another long pause. This time it was Tony who was disconcerted and was marshalling his defence.

'"Clean-shirt-and-bring-the-silver-teapot-out-for-visitors",' he said at last. 'What's that supposed to mean? Sounds like the sort of stifling, lower middle class environment that in England you wouldn't think for a moment of living in.'

'Yes. Yes, I expect it is.'

'Just what *is* all this?'

I didn't tell him. For one thing, I didn't

properly know myself.

Tony went away again. I wanted him to go, right up to the last moment. Then I clung to him and was sad and said I was sorry about everything. He kissed me in a slightly aloof way and said, 'Never mind, we'll get over it,' which meant, I knew, that he hadn't yet forgiven me but probably would. He was glad to get away again, I could see, and I didn't blame him.

It was after he had been gone several days that I began to wonder. I have always had rather irregular periods—that was one of the many 'little problems' with which we kept gynaecologists employed for years—so at first I didn't think anything of it. But one morning I suddenly found I didn't want coffee, and it was the same the next morning, and the next, and all the mornings. I didn't want to smoke either, but then that had happened before when I had come back from India, and it had worn off.

The ink in the photocopying machine began to smell very odd. Then one day, when I had missed lunch because I was reorganising a file for the secretary, I felt faint, and was presently sick.

I drank some milk, and went and lay down on the bed in the small spare room. It was very light in the room, with the yellow glow that comes after rain, and the eyes of the birds on the wallpaper seemed to be looking at me. I remembered the raven that morning in Bombay.

247

I remembered other things also.

'. . . *I never asked you if you wanted me to be careful,' he said, long after it was too late to ask. And I said, 'If I'd been able to get pregnant in the first place, I wouldn't have come to Bombay.'*

I remembered too that gynaecologist, the surgeon with lithographs of surreal eggs in his consulting room, who had objected on principle to the world 'fault'—'Well, we don't like to use the word "fault" in these cases, ha, ha! . . . We prefer to talk about a *couple* having a fertility problem. From what Dr Spitz tells me, and my own notes, the problem with you and your husband, as in so many cases, seems to be a cumulative one.'

There was a message there. I didn't listen to it. No doubt, at the time, I did not want to.

★   ★   ★

Now another gynaecologist said to me: 'Do you want a termination? You can have one if you want, you know.'

'Do I want *what*?'

I must have looked or sounded extremely fierce, for she recoiled slightly.

'Well, it was just a suggestion,' she said huffily. 'I mean, you are in your mid-thirties. And the situation, as you have described it, does not sound at all satisfactory to me . . . What does your husband think about it?'

'I haven't told him yet.'

'But you will, I take it? Who the baby's father is, I mean.'

'Well, of course I will.' I might do many things to Tony, but never that. 'I could hardly not.'

'No, I suppose not. An Indian doctor... Dear, dear.'

★　　★　　★

Tony said, after a long silence.

'You say she offered you an abortion?'

'Yes. Silly cow.' I was lying down, and I shut my eyes. I felt sick most of the time now, and bringing myself to tell Tony semed to have made it abruptly worse.

'Well...' he said slowly, not looking at me. 'Well ... I wouldn't dismiss the idea of an abortion out of hand. I mean, it does seem worth discussing—the pros and cons.'

I sat up abruptly and retched. Lying back again, I said flatly: 'Tony, if you think that after all these years and all that trying I'm now going to kill off what is probably the only child I'll ever conceive, just because it doesn't come from the approved source—'

'That's not necessarily true at all,' he said quickly, in a too-reasonable, persuasive voice. 'Didn't one of those quacks we went to say that if only you could get pregnant once you could probably do it again? We could count this one out—and then start again afresh. I could go on those pills again—'

'No, Tony, no. I'm sorry, but no. I've had enough of all that sort of optimistic bromide at fifteen quid a session in the past, and so ought you to have. Tony, these are the sources of *life* we are talking about. We can't just manipulate them as we choose. Some people may be able to, but we can't. You should know that by now.'

'You just won't take the chance, will you? You won't even try it,' he said, in a deliberately fed-up voice.

I sat up again and stared at him.

'Tony, just what do you think you are saying? And who do you think you are saying it to? My good boy, I am expecting another man's child— and you accuse *me* of not being prepared to take a chance. Are you really listening to yourself at all?'

No, perhaps I didn't really say all this. Perhaps I didn't actually use the phrase 'sources of life', though it was what I meant to say, and it is just possible that if I had done Tony would have started listening to himself and everything might have turned out rather differently. I don't know, and now it is too late. But I do know that I used the phrase 'expecting another man's child', for he flinched at the unexpectedly old-fashioned and real words. I could see he was

250

genuinely hurt, and with reason, but I was furious with him by now.

'If it's taking chances we're talking about,' I said, 'why don't you take a chance and see if you can't accept and love this child as your own. Is that too much to ask? After all, you were prepared to accept a completely strange child, unconnected with either of us.'

'That was different,' he said sourly. 'Because an adopted child would have been just that, unconnected as you say with both of us. That would have been fair. This—what you're suggesting, that we should bring up a child that is yours but not mine—it isn't fair . . .'

'"Fair", "Not fair"—for crying out loud, how old are you? Is this the reasonable, mature, adult bit you've always been so keen on?' I knew that it was an unkind thing to say, indeed an awful thing to say to someone whom I had just asked to make what was, after all, a magnanimous and long-lasting gesture. Even as I said it, I knew in the back of my mind that I was being wantonly destructive, that I had now a dark need to smash the whole modernistic structure of our marriage, even if I smashed myself in the process.

If he had just said to me, 'I'm sorry. I don't think I can do it,' for once in his life admitting defeat, failure, something irreparable, might I have respected him, and wept for him and us and for the child? I hope I would have. It was

251

his face-saving wriggling that inflamed me with a reckless desire to destroy.

'If I refuse to bring up this child as my own,' he said narrowly—the language of tradition and truth had caught up with both of us by now—'Just what exactly will you do?'

'I shall go back to India again, I expect.' I felt sick and exhausted and indefinably strange, and no more like facing the heat and smells and sights of India than I felt like flying to the moon, but I wasn't going to tell Tony that, now.

'To Bombay?'

'Yes, of course.'

'And what, may I ask, are you going to use for money?'

I shut my eyes again. I had not known Tony could be like this. Perhaps almost anyone can be like this, if they're pushed enough, but I had led a sheltered life in this respect. Tony and I had always prided ourselves on being rational and decent about money and paying share-by-share according to who had the most: in recent years of course, ever since Tony had been successful and I had begun working in his office, he had been the real source of both our incomes. 'Tony and I'—but that habitual shelter existed no longer, I saw. I had swept it away myself within the last ten minutes and now seemed to be standing on the edge of a gulf.

'I've got some money in my account,' I said shortly.

'Yes, and how long will that last?'

'Please leave me alone, Tony. If you don't want to stand by me—' again, the traditional phrase came to my lips—'then please mind your own business.'

Even then, I think the situation might have been salvageable. Tony really was upset, I could see. He didn't want me to go: perhaps that was why he had brought up the subject of money, in an attempt to recall me to my senses. Tony, quite rightly, takes money very seriously. We were used to each other; we had spent many years together and had often been happy. Had we had children when we first wanted to, we would probably never have thought of separating. Even now, although from my point of view we seemed to have come to the end, I think that if I had surrendered and cried on his shoulder we might have continued together. Tony is not particularly strong on principles; I have always known that. Expediency and presentation are more important to him. If I had cast myself weeping on his better nature, begging him not to desert me, promising him by implication to drop discreet hints to people like Angela and William about how marvellous he was being . . . ? Anyway, I didn't.

Instead I just went on lying there with my eyes shut, traitorous and apparently unmoved, infuriating him, lifting not a finger to save the situation—to save us. It was, I suppose, excusable, however unforgivable, that he should eventually have said what he did.

He said slowly: 'You surely aren't under the impression that this fellow, whatshisname, da Costa—da Souza—will marry you? You can't be. I should think that when he knows what's happened you won't see him for dust. He probably regards fucking foreigners as an OK sport. Why should he care about you?—just another silly, promiscuous white woman. God, you've really made a mess of things, haven't you?'

After that, there was really nothing left for me to do but leave, and eventually, after a good many laborious and painful arrangements, I did.

*   *   *

There is another house, in Mazagon, that shakes continually with the traffic in the streets below. And yet I know that airless, populated house, with its inherited furniture, its silver teapot, its cocktail cabinet and its travel posters that advertise journeys that will never be made, is a more permanent place than any structure Tony and I could build. It haunts me. Unthinkable yet, just possibly, inescapable.

*   *   *

He had said, 'I won't write to you. I can't write

254

letters. But please do try to come back. Try.'

'*It might be a long time,*' I said, trying to speak lightly. '*You might be married—or anything—*'

'*I will be here,*' he said.

People say these things. To say them is the luxury of the moment, the compensation for the pain of imminent parting. They are not to be relied upon.

⋆ ⋆ ⋆

Will that house in Mazagon, in the end, be my place also, my fate, my prison and my resting place, just as a dank Midlands housing estate was Teresa da Souza's?

She's abandoned her context. There's nothing left of her. But perhaps my arrogant judgment had been wrong.

'*You shouldn't really take people out of their own places—their own country ... You may take something irreplaceable from them.*' But Nicky did not allow either for the fact that there can come a point at which life, which is even more irreplaceable, can only continue at all in another setting.

⋆ ⋆ ⋆

So here I lie once again, in the same room or one that seems the same, in the hotel with mothballs and creaking ceiling fans, with all

Bombay beyond this emptiness. I lie here like someone semi-paralysed, held like an insect between past and future in the fan's tepid draught, inert but tensely watchful, sick as if to death with the life I hold within me.

The stewed tea the boy brought me over an hour ago has grown cold on the bedside table: I wanted it, but its metallic, dark brown taste was too much for me. Beside it stands the silent 'phone.

Everything is too much for me, but I continue because I must—because, like most of the world, I, too, now have no option, no control. I have taken my action, pushed out the boat from the dark shore in hope and dread, and now, washed up in this temporary place, I can only wait. And will him to telephone. And wait again.

I am alone and yet not alone, and even if I wait interminably, far beyond hope and reason and self-fabricated excuses, still nothing will have changed. The past and the future will still be there, unalterable, and eventually I shall just have to get up from this bed, and leave this irrelevant room, and go out into those merciless streets and continue. And continue.

In the streets the sky now shines not blue but white, an intolerable glare. The temperature is something over a hundred. Humidity saturates the air, yet the water fails in the stand pipes where the people queue apathetically with their tiny pots: occasionally a quarrel erupts, a sick anger in a sick place. The leaves of the pipul trees droop and curl at the edges; the dogs and the beggars lie as if dead already in the last rags of shadow. It seems the day will never end. The fan above my head has slowed to a stopping point. Perhaps the electricity has been cut off. Perhaps time has stopped too.

They say the monsoon is due any day now. It will break, they say, and everything will be changed.

They say too that some years the monsoon has been known to fail. It just doesn't come. And yet life has to continue.

I lie here and wait for the monsoon.

Suddenly the telephone rings. I jump.

As if jogged, also, the fan begins slowly to move, at first sluggishly then with gathering momentum.

I pick up the receiver.

THE HOUSE BEAUTIFUL

Happy autumn fields ... said a voice inside Jessica's head. *Happy autumn fields* ...

It was, she knew, a quotation, but for the moment she could not place it. She could not place a great many of the quotations which, like moths or elusive birds, fluttered often across her

257

mind, or were rooted there in quiet, shady corners, twining themselves like creepers round her thin, spindly memories. Others again sat there like great pieces of immobile furniture, so that she was always tripping over them, bored with them (in spite of their undoubted beauty and solid value) but unable to dispose of them. She sometimes, rather desperately, envisaged her own brain as a greenhouse, complete with its fauna like the one at Kew, but which had for years doubled as a lumber room for a family who never organised anything or threw anything away. The process of accumulation had begun in childhood (her mother had read aloud to her a great deal), had accelerated at adolescence when an absorption in poetry became her means of ignoring the drabness of boarding school, and had reached a climax at Cambridge. A degree course in English Literature should, she supposed, help to impose some order on the shifting mass of material, teach one to perceive patterns and classify accordingly, but in her case it did not seem to have worked out like that . . . In her imagination a set of grey steel filing cabinets briefly joined the Victorian sideboards and creeper-wreathed mirrors, but they were pushed together drawer-to-drawer and were clearly empty. No doubt that was why she had only got such a very low Second . . . If those cabinets contained anything, she thought, it was her vague and optimistic hopes of becoming an academic herself, which had of necessity been shelved ('filed'?) after the fiasco of her Finals.

Since those days, she supposed, musing fondly but ruefully on her greenhouse, not a great deal really had been added to it. Perhaps there was hardly room for much more, and in any case she felt she didn't read enough proper literature these days. There was definitely something about working for a publisher which put one off books—real books, timeless ones, that didn't have publication dates and prices and marketing problems. Other experiences had added a few more items—a messy heap of Lawrence Durrell, a crystalline deposit of Nabokov—and a plangent poem or two, legacies of passing loves, hovering in corners, but she brushed them aside as she did the memories they represented. Time went by so fast these days. It was terrifying, really. She ought perhaps to be more terrified by it . . .?

Happy autumn fields . . . Yes, it seemed appropriate. It wasn't autumn yet, not yet the end of August, but there was a dustiness among the heavy green trees, and even a tinge of red here and there which presaged—well, yes, fruitfulness. Pushing Keats 'Ode to Autumn' crossly aside—she was always falling over that, it was too heavy and ponderous and really rather vulgar anyway; she was sorry she had acquired it—she concentrated on the meadow ahead sloping upwards toward a picture-blue sky.

Through the long, bleached grasses and daisies the children ran, picture children with the sun on their blond heads, the little one waist-deep staggering after the bigger ones. There were poppies too: Giles, the children's father, had been right; it really was an enchanting place and they had picked a wonderful day for their walk. *In Flanders Fields the poppies blow* . . . How sad. Most of the poetry appropriate to this day and hour seemed to be harking backward . . . *Looking on the happy autumn fields. And thinking of the days that are no more.* A lump came into her throat, but in practice the emotion of the poem was inappropriate. (*Tears, idle tears*, indeed!) It was Tennyson, of course, and Tennyson, like most poets of the fall of the year, suggested a summer past which had been splendid, an emotional peak to which there could now, with the shadows lengthening, be no return. *The bright day is done, and we are for the dark* . . . But this particular summer had not been good, in fact—that was why everything was still so green and lush, with damp mud round the field gates. Today was the finest they had had since early June. And whatever the hidden feelings that possessed her that afternoon, making her secretly tense behind her air of smiling relaxation, imbuing everything for her with an unnatural, luminous intensity, these feelings were concerned less with the past than with a shadowy, possible, momentous future.

Of course there was a past, and it might be lying heavy on Giles' heart at this moment. Very likely he had walked this way before, years and years ago, alone with Anne, and then with the first child in a carrier and then the second one ... But this was not *her* past: she could not share it and did not want to. *Who has not covered his face when the dazzling past leered at him?* Nabokov wrote that, and it had always made her feel a little inferior, for she had no dazzling past. In fact—she realised now, trudging through the grass, with one of those sudden, rare shafts of perception which illuminated her otherwise trivial and self-concealing days—she had no past at all, to speak of. (*What's her history? A blank, my lord.*) Nothing much had ever happened to her and, unlike many of the people for whom this is true, she had not managed to fashion the few events that *had* come her way into any kind of meaningful shape. She was not married, she was not a mother, she was—for the moment— no one's lover, she was not a young girl, she was not yet *not* young, she had a job she quite liked but without passion, she was quite well paid, lived in quite a pleasant flat in West Hampstead; she was mildly interested in quite a lot of things but had no absorbing hobby. She had a lot of friends, who found her intelligent and easy-to-get-along-with. Jessica never threatened anyone; both men and women felt safe with her. But no one would have missed her very keenly

261

had she emigrated to Australia, any more than she would have missed them acutely either. She was not even unhappy. If she feared the future, it was usually just in a generalised, non-specific human way—('I shall be old and ill and the North Sea Gas will have run out and the Chinese will have taken over and there will be nothing to eat').

But this afternoon, for the first time for years, a different emotion had entered the picture. She felt, as they climbed the hill, that the future, instead of being nebulous and hard-to-create, was *there*, and that she was walking towards it. She and Giles and the children. In the heat, she shivered secretly, in fear and excitement and foreboding. And yet she felt too that she was at a play, or a film. Could such a real, challenging, ready-made destiny really be lying in wait for *her*, for nice, dull Jessica? True, she was a good cook and other women's children seemed to like her, but since when have such attributes ever led directly to passion, commitment, a complete change of identity and a solution to everything for ever?

The smallest child, left behind by its longer-legged brother and sisters, wilted, wandering vaguely and sadly among the poppies, grasping with fat hands at their fragile petals, hoping to keep them for ever. She called winningly to it and it turned and came stumbling towards her, holding out its arms to be picked up. She knew that really it regarded her as a taxi or a donkey: like most youngest children it was not fussy about the identity of laps or arms, migrating placidly from one to another. But nevertheless it was with an interior glow of achievement and pride that she swung the toddler up on to her hip. ('He's prepared to look on me as his mother . . .')

★ ★ ★

'Arrh, when shall I come to the top of this same hill?' Giles, in an all-purpose rustic accent, was being John Bunyan: their afternoon walk was taking place in the Bedfordshire landscape where *Pilgrim's Progress* was written. In the same tongue, she replied:

'Why, master, they do call this the Hill of Difficulty,' adding in her normal voice: 'Of course—that must have been the Slough of Despond there down by the gate.'

'All that mud and cow-pats? Undoubtedly. And the tarmaced road there is presumably the Broad Way that leadeth unto Destruction.'

'Isn't it funny,' she said vaguely, 'I'd always supposed that Bunyan had in mind a much more awe-inspiring landscape—sort of Italian, I think, with mountains—not this tame, English, domestic scene. But of course he never actually moved far from this part of the world, did he?'

'I imagine not. But the House Beautiful

(which we are coming to soon so do not despair, dear Sister) really is on a splendid site and must have been a lovely house once too.' He spoke proprietorially: he and Anne had chosen to make their home in this part of England. Carefully, feeling she shouldn't have used the word 'tame', Jessica said:

'There really are a lot of lovely brick buildings round here. I didn't realise.'

'You should have come to stay with us more often. Anne and I have been lazy, I'm afraid . . . Not inviting friends as often as we meant to. You know: you get dug in . . .'

'Oh, I absolutely understand,' she said quickly, after a pause. Giles and Anne had each other, and by and by four children. Why should they go out of their way to nurture other relationships, ties with people who did not fit naturally into their rural context? They had never really needed anyone but each other. (Jessica lingered over this thought, with an unmarried sentiment and admiration: she did not reflect that Giles and Anne's attitude might also be considered self-centred and short-sighted.) The only reason she had become so friendly with Giles, long ago at Cambridge, where they had been 'mates' in the special, non-sexual use of the word, was that Anne by that time had left the town. She had been doing her final year's training—Midwifery—at a hospital in London. She was a little older than Giles, though he seemed to have managed to neutralise this fact, becoming a heavy, balding father-figure by his early thirties. It was after Cambridge, when they were all living in London for a couple of years, that Jessica had got to know them well, and at that time had seen rather more of Anne than she had of Giles. Anne, the calm dispenser of kindness and good sense, smiling, placid Anne, faintly mysterious and private Anne: *One rare, fair woman* ... Then pregnant Anne, and Anne the mother ... Anne the grown-up. Jessica had never felt as much on the same wave-length with her as she did with Giles, but through the years Anne had become a kind of model for her, a prototype for possible future stages in her own life. The fact that these stages seemed to have been indefinitely postponed, in her case, did not alter her view of the other woman: on the contrary, it meant that nothing had occurred to drive her apart from Giles and Anne, nothing to force her down a different path. After all, suppose I had married someone rich and smooth, a stockbroker say, with a house in Chelsea...

Don't be ridiculous.

Perhaps people with elder sisters sometimes felt about them as she did about Anne? She was sorry she had not had a sister, the relationship would have suited her, she thought. A brother was unimaginable and a father nearly as much so—hers had died when she was five—but she had always been close to her mother. And there was an aunt she was fond of, and one or two girls she had been at school with ... There had been boyfriends of course, off and on, and male friends like Giles—she had now become rather good at having male friends—but men somehow weren't quite as real as women. She had finally come round to the idea that, however normal her occasional sexual desires might be, essentially her strongest emotional links were formed with women, not with men. But now, on that hill, under that sky, with Giles beside her, leading Giles' child by the hand, this thought confused her. She shied away from it.

*   *   *

'It really must have been a most beautiful house,' she said a while later. 'I mean, you can see how lovely it must have been even though it's ruined. It's a lovely ruin, even.'

'Isn't it?' Giles spoke with passion. This was evidently one of 'his' special places. He was a possessor, Giles, an inaugurator of anniversaries and traditions, a natural founder of dynasties: no problems about organisation and meaning in *his* mind. 'The site alone is fantastic, of course,' he said. 'Even today, the view—'

'Oh, absolutely.'

'Of course there is the odd dark, Satanic mill down in the valley now.' He gestured in the direction of some tall chimneys.

'I like them,' she said. 'They enhance the beauty of the rest. And it isn't as if Bunyan's landscape was meant to be all fair.'

'Oh quite. And in fact they're not mills but brickworks, and since brickmaking is the traditional industry in these parts presumably there were some of those about even in Bunyan's days ...' He went on for a little about local kilns, in what Jessica thought of as his Principal-of-the-local-Training-College voice, and she felt a little bored by the subject but happy because he was happy to talk to her about it. Anne had a skilful way of deflecting him when he showed signs of getting into a pompous vein, but Jessica was not sure how she did it. Presently she drifted off through the ruined rooms, their fine proportions open to the sky, admiring pillars and window mullions, sitting for a while on the grassy terrace while the children played hide and seek behind her. Giles became anxious that the little one might fall from some fragmented wall or empty window, and called him to sit with Jessica.

'This house is broken, isn't it?' he said seriously. 'Who broke it?'

'I'm—I'm not sure. Daddy might know. We'll ask him in a minute.'

'Whose house is it?'

'Well, no one's now, I suppose. But it must have been someone's once ... Giles? Can you

267

come over here a minute—Sean wants to know whose house this used to be?'

'It was built,' said Giles heavily, 'for a Countess of Pembroke in—oh, sixteen-something.'

'The Countess of Pembroke? Oh! Good heavens—but surely that's the famous one? The "Sidney's sister, Pembroke's mother" one?'

He did not seem to know whom she meant. Delighted that for once some object in her lumber-greenhouse was proving apposite, she recollected for a moment and then repeated:

'Underneath this marble hearse
Lies the subject of all verse:
Sidney's sister, Pembroke's mother—
Death, ere thou hast killed another
Fair and learn'd and good as she,
Time shall throw a dart at thee!'

She was repeating the last line before the full and awful appositeness of the quotation came home. As a gaffe, it went far beyond tactlessness, and one glance at Giles' face showed there was no ignoring it. She covered her own face with her hands.

'Oh gosh,' she muttered. 'Giles, I didn't mean . . . I am most awfully sorry—'

'Oh that's absolutely all right, Jessica,' he said too quickly, in the too frank-and-warm voice of a man who is behaving well. 'Good God, I'm

268

hardly likely to be *offended*. I'm only too pleased that—that you saw the connection so instantly.'

Jessica began to cry. Anne the good lay in a bed in Northampton, pale and quiet, slipping inexorably away from her husband, her children, from life: let Giles think she was crying for Anne; as he said, he would hardly be offended by such a demonstration of emotion. He extracted it, rather, as Anne's due. But even as she formulated the thought her secret mortification increased. For while (of course) she was sorry for Anne, and for Giles and for the children, she wasn't crying for that at all, not really. On the contrary, she was crying scorched, wretched tears for herself, because *she* wasn't fair and learn'd and good as Anne—not as fair or good, certainly, and not even learn'd. You couldn't call a lumber-greenhouse 'learning', and she hadn't any thoughts or feelings of her own. She was just a picker-up of other people's words, she cried inwardly, a—a parasite: now making use of great poetry to express her own puny impulses, now expecting someone else's husband and children to fall as a ready-made family into her own inadequate lap. Like Bunyan's Pilgrim, she wept angrily for her own unworthiness, while Giles, still gravely intent upon bearing his own tragic role with distinction, offered a handkerchief and pats on the shoulder and shepherded the staring children off to a discreet distance.

By and by she was 'herself' again—whatever
that self might be. The small procession made
its way across the turf and the lengthening
shadows toward the road home. *The Way that
leadeth unto Life*, muttered the inexorable,
tasteless curator in Jessica's head, and she
clenched her teeth. She looked back at the
lovely ruin as they reached the gate.

'It really is a beautiful place,' she said in a
social voice. 'Thank you for bringing me here,
Giles.'

She knew he would read a delicate shade of
meaning into this, and he did.

'Ah,' he said screwing up his face, perhaps
against the low, bright light, 'but how pathetic
and ironic that the House Beautiful should be in
ruins. Don't you think so, Jessica?'

'Mightn't someone, one day, rebuild it?' she
said, trembling a little at the audacity of a
remark so patently full of unspoken
significance. As she had half known he would,
he reached down and squeezed her hand.

But she knew now, with another sudden, thin
shaft of private enlightenment among the
rubbish and the twining plants, that she would
not be the one to rebuild the House Beautiful.
Not for Giles, and probably not for anybody.
She just didn't (to be honest, for once in a while)

270

care for the idea enough. In any case, she thought, with an unaccustomed critical asperity, she had never really liked John Bunyan.

WINTER'S TALE

'Well—I'll be off then,' he said after a considerable pause. He picked up the suitcase: it was the small blue one, the one Helen always packed as the first-three-days one when they went on holiday.

'I think everything's there,' she said. 'I put in two pairs of spare socks; that will be enough I should think? Unless you're going to do much walking...'

'I don't know,' he said at length, after the further expectant pause in her voice. 'I shouldn't think so. I don't know.'

'I've put in *both* your check shirts, as you're going to the country, and your lovat pullover... And I haven't forgotten your asthma pills.'

He said ungraciously: 'You know I haven't needed them for *ages*.'

'Well,' she said with a forced smile, 'let's hope you won't. It would be just like life, wouldn't it, if I left them out and then this turned out to be the one trip you needed them?'

'I feel sure you're right,' he said with

271

measured lack of response. The need both to quarrel and not to quarrel with Helen paralysed him. He wanted to quarrel. He wanted to have a really good excuse for leaving her suddenly in the lurch like that (with all those cousins coming to Sunday lunch too) and staying away for days and days. If he parted from her affectionately he would be entrapped into a web of promises—to phone her that evening, to let her know where he was staying, to look up the Hurlstone-Joneses if he went anywhere near Shaftesbury... He wouldn't be tied like that, dammit he wouldn't! But at the same time... Poor Helen... How rottenly he was behaving, he thought, with sad, voluptuous indulgence in the idea.

'Well—have a nice time,' she said, determinedly cheerful. This abrupt decision of his to take part of his holiday now, without her, to go away on his own to an undecided destination for an indefinite number of days—it was so uncharacteristic of him, of their whole way of life. She minded, of course she did. He saw it, and grieved for her.

But at the same time he also saw that she was coping with it very nicely, thank you, having worked out an explanation for it in her own mind as she always did for everything. She didn't try to boss or demand or make scenes (never scenes, with Helen). But she had her own way of gaining the upper hand. Her very helpfulness, her matter-of-fact acceptance of things, her unobtrusive efficiency, she managed to turn into a control system. She was ever ready to understand him: that was her great secret weapon. Probably, he thought, whipping up his resentment further in order to march out of the house, she already, after only two days' notice, had his present behaviour filed neatly in her mind under the heading 'male menopause' or 'mid-life' crisis' or some such patronising claptrap. iled along with all those other neat folders of notes on her Samaritan cases which occupied so much of her time and energy now that the children were grown up. So sensible of her to have found another interest. Bloody hell.

As he walked round to the car he thought: I wonder if burglars or shop-lifters feel like this as they leave the scene of their crime? I bet they do . . . But no, on reflection the analogy did not seem right, for what crime had he committed in the last twenty odd years of their married life? None, really, till now. And what was he carrying covertly away with him? Nothing. Nothing but his suitcase which Helen had made hers by packing it. Even his asthma seemed not his own, since Helen was the one who remembered it, who knew about it. Long ago, in the early years of their marriage, he had occasionally had it quite badly, at night. It would start in sleep, and it would take him a long time to realise and locate the discomfort.

By that time Helen would be gently shaking his shoulder:

'Darling, you've got asthma... Darling, wake up... Shall I get your pills?' And regularly on these occasions, like a recurrent dream, he had been vaguely surprised, as he surfaced into wakefulness gasping for breath to find only Helen and himself. He had been convinced there was someone else in the room, that someone else had asthma, not he.

From Weybridge he drove to Esher, and then on to the Guildford by-pass. He drove without thinking, enjoying the sensation of mindlessness, the suspension of reality. He was well into Hampshire before it occurred to him that what he had been inadvertently doing was following the westward trail of many previous family holidays: Studlands and Lulworth Cove in Dorset in the 1960s when the children had been small, later sailing holidays in Devon... No, no, that wouldn't do: that wasn't what he was looking for at all. He turned abruptly southwards.

But that way too he presently reached the sea. He had forgotten about Portsmouth and Southampton and the blighted coast between them. He had embarked at Southampton in 1941, on troopship. Seasick and twenty, he had lain in a bunk and had been sure that, like a young officer going out to Flanders' mud, he would never see England again. But of course it

274

hadn't turned out like that at all, and three years later he had found himself at a desk job at Catterick, Yorkshire. There he had met Sally . . .

★   ★   ★

Enough of that. There was no sense in brooding on the past—never had been. Indeed by saying that to himself for the last twenty-five years he had virtually extinguished the past: it simply wasn't there to brood over any more because you were no longer the same person. He felt little interest now in that earnest, enthusiastic young man who had walked with Sally on the north Yorkshire moors and stood with her in the rain under the open vault of Rievaulx Abbey. Anyway you never remembered the things you really wanted to remember. They had been married soon after VE day in Leeds Town Hall. He remembered even now the broad stairs up which they had gone and the worn surface of the desk in front of which they had stood. But he could not, by any device, remember what Sally had looked like. When he tried—he had used to try, once, though he had long given that up—instead there had swum into the frame of memory Helen's face on that other wedding day seven years later, large and animated beneath a picture hat against banks of flowers and a marquee in her parents'

275

Surrey garden.

It wasn't just that he couldn't remember what Sally had worn to be married in. He couldn't remember *what she looked like*. Never had been able to. He had no photo of her. He realised there was no good reason for this: it was just that he had never felt the need of photographs of anyone. (It was Helen who kept the ample family albums, spending whole evenings pasting in holiday snaps and school groups and meticulously labelling them.) Oh, of course he knew Sally had fine dark hair and a round face with regular features and grey, short-sighted eyes. He knew she was about five foot five, and slim, and was twenty-two when he married her and twenty-five when she died: he could have given a perfectly convincing description of her to any police force. But he couldn't, in his own mind, *see* her. He had once been told by an opthalmologist that there is one point on the visual field where objects become momentarily invisible before appearing again: something to do with the position of the optic nerve... Ever since then he had the odd feeling, when he thought about it, that he couldn't see Sally because she was standing just at that point.

Not that he had thought about it much, of course, for years. In any case his inability to recognise even people he knew quite well, in an unfamiliar setting, had been something of a joke between Helen and himself for years. She said

276

that she was sure that sometimes when they had arranged to meet in Sainsbury's or in a theatre foyer, he would look straight through her thinking 'Why is that woman smiling at me?' And once, to his shame, he had momentarily failed to recognise their eldest, Andrew, when meeting him at Euston at the end of a school term. The truth was, he realised afterwards, his mind had been elsewhere because he had been looking for someone else. But who?

★   ★   ★

From the outskirts of Southampton he turned inland again. He was looking for something. After a while it dawned on him that the something was probably lunch. It was approaching two; he had been driving for several hours. He stopped at a pub and ate cheese sandwiches sitting in what seemed to be the saloon bar although it was called the Nook. He asked for Best Bitter, and when it came was unable to decide if it was really indifferent and gassy or whether it was his own taste that had changed. He was out of practice, a pint seemed quite enough, whereas long ago he would have thought nothing of drinking five or six pints in an evening. He wondered briefly what his own children drank, now respectively post-graduate at Sussex and undergraduate at Leicester. He was sure their generation didn't drink in pubs much. Pity, really, but when you looked at the disproportionate way beer had gone up in price you could see why. Fish and chips, too. When he had been demobbed and first went into the Company's northern office, his pay had been under twelve pounds a week, and they had lived well on that, even including the rent of their flat! Unbelievable.

Of course when he had married for the second time the picture had been quite different: Helen's family were relatively well-to-do, and in any case he and Helen had been lucky to be house-buying before prices began to go through the roof in the late 1950s. Lucky—yes, they had been lucky all along really. Helen herself would certainly say so. The last thing anyone would call her was a discontented woman, and when he heard what some husbands had to put up with he felt guiltier than ever at his present lack of appreciation.

He had realised quite early in their married life that Helen regarded making the best of things as a duty and being unhappy as a sign of failure, like taking to drink or not having any friends or (perhaps?) not getting married. Though she always maintained the polite fiction that disasters were entirely a matter of chance and that one could only feel 'There, but for the grace of God...', he yet knew that at some level she believed that tragedy only struck the incompetent, or those who were in some way a little eccentric.

Eccentric and incompetent. It was surely both to die in childbirth, of all things, in 1948, the year of the National Health Act, in a large, adequately equipped hospital? An extraordinary thing to happen, everyone had agreed. Their general practitioner had been particularly insistent on that point. But at the same time he had, looking at his notes, remarked that Sally's last ante-natal check-up had been four weeks previously and of course they did like to see mothers more often than that during the last month ... A holiday away from home before the baby came? Staying in a pub in the Lake-District? Mm-hm. Yes. Well, with hindsight one might ... But of course it was hard to say. These things just did sometimes happen. One must be wary of drawing any definite conclusion.

* * *

No conclusion. No end. So, their marriage had not ended. It had simply stopped one day, unexpectedly, like a clock in mid-tick. For months, years even, with some part of his mind he had expected it to resume, but of course it never did. Like a home unvisited, like a letter unopened, like a railway line on which the trains have ceased to run, it remained, merely becoming out of date. As time went by he had more and more other things to think about anyway.

Suddenly, as if that was what he had stopped for in the first place, he asked the landlord if he let rooms. They didn't, it appeared, but the other pub in the village did. He hurried there; it was just on closing time. A woman said Yes, she could give him a room, but would he mind coming back later as it wasn't Done yet: they didn't get many visitors in winter, she said apologetically. He felt glad, now he reflected on it, that he had chosen the dead, dank end of winter for his journey. Being middle-aged was being constantly surprised at the numbers of people crowding the holiday spot you remembered as small and quiet, being middle-aged was still half expecting beer to cost one and nine a pint and a three-course English lunch for seven and six, even though you had been dining clients on an expense account for years. Being middle-aged was not expecting anything new or different or more important to happen any more.

He told the woman he would return, and drove off again. He was looking for—what? Well, for a way to spend the afternoon. The villages seemed deserted, the fields likewise. What did modern farmers do at this time of year? He felt restless, unsatisfied. This classic English landscape, with its tamed, hedged charm, was what Helen liked: it wasn't his sort of thing really. She might imagine that this was what was meant by the beauty of England, but then she had scarcely ever been north of Birmingham.

★   ★   ★

Then, as he was passing through Bishop's Waltham, his eye was caught by a towering grey wall somewhere off to the left beyond a lake. There were ruins here, and of immense size. That was better. He parked the car and made his way round to the entrance, where a board claimed that this was the remains of the palace belonging to the medieval bishops of Winchester. Well, well. He had always liked History at grammar school and had once, encouraged by the Head, vaguely thought of trying for a scholarship to read it at Manchester University, till the war and the army had put an end to his educational ambitions. These days, when they visited a ruin or a stately home, it was Helen rather than he who read the guide book assiduously and often aloud. Architectural or artistic detail bored him anyway: he didn't want to hear about exceptionally fine vaulting or cruciform windows or carvings believed to be by a pupil of Grinling Gibbons. It was the general vague perception of the past which he enjoyed when strolling around these places, and for that it was much better to be alone, as now. He liked, without ever quite expressing it to himself, the half awareness of other realities besides his own, perhaps still maintaining their existence on the same patch of ground but in some different and alternate time-scale: intimations that the past still lived, was not wholly obliterated... But this afternoon, pacing the spongy turf, this feeling eluded him. He looked up at the enormously high but fragmented walls, where birds now sat in a row above cascading ivy, and tried to see the place roofed, with glazed windows catching the light of the sinking sun, but could not.

Then he realised, with a stab of irritation, he wasn't even alone as he had thought. Someone else was inexplicably visiting the site on this chilly, mid-week afternoon in late February. His eye was caught by a red coat round the side of a piece of masonry. It disappeared for some minutes, but then reappeared again right on the far side of the grass, near the reed-choked moat: a figure in a red jacket, trousers and wellingtons was walking slowly in his direction. As it came nearer it resolved itself into a young, dark-haired woman—or was she just a girl? Perhaps, he thought, she was an archaeology student. Afterwards, he didn't know why he had decided that; something in the way she looked at the place must have conveyed the impression that she knew about it, that she wasn't a chance visitor like himself but was here for a purpose.

She stopped a few yards from him and smiled. 'Good afternoon,' she said.

I know this girl. The thought was instantaneous and positive. Yet when he tried to concentrate on this, ranging in his mind over his acquaintances and Helen's, asking himself *who?*—the sense of familiarity lessened and dissipated itself. The girl continued to look at him as if indulgently amused by his evident failure to place her.

'It's getting colder, isn't it?' she said companionably, hands in pockets. 'I don't think I shall stay here much longer.'

'Yes.' He took a deep breath, shelving the problem of identification for the moment. 'It's damp—a damp site, with all that water all round it. Funny place to choose really, for such a building.'

'I think it must have been a *summer* palace,' she said with the gravity of a child parading its particular bit of knowledge. 'In the winter the bishop would have been in Winchester, wouldn't he? It would have been too far to travel in bad weather from one place to the other every day, even on horseback.'

'Yes, I suppose so . . .' They both gazed at the towering flint remains. 'Huge place just for a summer palace,' he said.

'They were *enormously* rich, those medieval princes of the church. Like oil millionaires and politicians rolled into one. I expect this place was partly for the bishop to entertain in.'

'Important overseas clients you mean?' he said, and they both laughed. 'Do you come here often?' he asked, and then, realising that this sounded ridiculous, added hastily: 'I mean— you seem to know something about the place.'

'I've never been here before in my life,' she said, smiling at him again in that odd way she had, as if they were not just friends but old friends who understood one another well.

After a pause, he said: 'We're quite near Winchester here, aren't we? By modern standards, I mean.'

'Oh yes. About ten miles, I think. Something like that. I was there earlier in the day. But I didn't see you there.'

There was something odd about this remark, perhaps she had misunderstood what he had just said. 'I thought of going to Winchester this afternoon,' he said, although the idea had only just occurred to him.

'Have you never been there?' she asked, and he shook his head. 'I don't believe I have, no. It's an awful admission, isn't it? One of the most important towns in England, historically.'

She said, with a resumption of her serious manner: 'I don't like it as much as York. I like that best of all. But Winchester is a very fine place, all the same. Would you like me to show it to you?'

'Why—certainly,' he said, concealing his

surprise. She spoke so matter-of-factly that you couldn't call her behaviour provocative, and yet... Oh, perhaps she had misinterpreted his remark about thinking of going into Winchester next as a tentative invitation, and this was her way of gracefully accepting. Her reference to York and some slight intonation in her voice made him think she must be someone he had once known up north, but then their conversation had not been that of two people meeting by chance after a gap of many years. In any case he had already half made up his mind that she must be one of his children's friends, one of those familiar faces that come and go in your house but whom you never quite bother to put a name to.

They walked together towards his car. He was about to lock it when something occurred to him: 'Where's yours?'

'My what?'

'Your car.'

'I haven't got a car,' she said, smiling as if the very idea were faintly ridiculous.

'But you said ... I mean, you were in Winchester earlier today?'

'Yes. But I haven't got a car.' As if that dealt with the matter she calmly opened the passenger side door and got in. Funny, he thought he had left the car locked all round as usual. Evidently he couldn't have.

Afterwards, although he knew they had

talked all the time on the way to Winchester, he couldn't remember much of what they had said. It had been mostly about history, he thought: it had been nice being with someone who seemed interested in a subject for its own sake for once. Perhaps she had done most of the talking while he listened? But no—he had the impression afterwards of having been more loquacious than he usually was, drawn out by her friendly warmth and apparently calm acceptance of himself and the situation. Well, if she wasn't worried about picking up a strange man and accepting a lift in his car, why should he be? Her manner was without a trace of flirtation. She told him nothing about herself but then he didn't ask, fearing to spoil the relationship that had sprung up between them by appearing inquisitive.

*　　　*　　　*

The centre of Winchester seemed to be buried in a complex modern defence system, a scheme of ring roads. Eventually they parked the car near the top of the hill and walked down again. It was chilly, and twilight was falling. He felt glad to reach the town's heart, where the main street had been barred to traffic. Here in the lamplight the gabled shop-fronts seemed like a stage-set above the unnaturally quiet street with its rubberised paving.

'Nice place to live, I should think,' he said appreciatively.

'Nice to visit anyway,' she said. 'I enjoy being in a strange town, don't you?'

Had someone else said that to him once? He thought someone had but couldn't place it.

Not many people were about, the shops were shutting. He paused to look in a window here or there—at soft, desirable leather things in a saddler's, at a print of sailing ships in Southampton harbour, once at some rather nice tweed jackets in a tailor's. Each time, she stopped placidly alongside him. It was only after a while it occurred to him that she never paused to look into a shop on her own account. Surely that was very unusual in a woman? Helen, habitually alert for a 'good buy', would by now have already earmarked half a dozen things— shoes, a handbag, a silk frock or sweater maybe—to 'come back and look at tomorrow', although when the morrow came she rarely did, being fundamentally prudent about money. Planning in theory what she might buy was simply her way of getting on to terms with a strange place. But this girl didn't seem to feel any need to look into the shops she passed: in spite of her previous remark she walked as if she knew the place well anyway.

'You don't come from hereabouts, do you?' he said suddenly, feeling intrusive even by such a mild question, and she said casually:

287

'Oh no, I've never been here before today.'

She didn't ask in return where he came from, he noticed, and it only occurred to him now that not only had she proffered no information about herself, she had asked him nothing whatsoever either—not about his home or his circumstances or what he was doing in this part of the country. But if she thought, rightly or wrongly, that she knew him, then she didn't need to, did she? He wondered momentarily with uncomfortable amusement if in her eyes he was someone quite other—that she had simply mistaken him for a person well-known to her out there on the ruins? He did not want this to be the explanation: it would be embarrassing for both of them if she were to realise her error, and anyway he was enjoying himself too much. He did not want to believe that the pleasure of her company and the gentleness with which she spoke to him was all just a matter of mistaken identity.

*   *   *

At his suggestion they went into a café. She said she would like a cup of tea, but, feeling festive, he insisted on ordering slices of chocolate cake as well. It was a comfortable, carpeted place with pretensions to being a Continental coffee lounge, but also serving grilled dishes. Although it was only late

288

afternoon several people were eating these, and again he was reminded obscurely of the North of England.

'I rather like these modern places,' he said comfortably. 'Not much individual style to them of course—but they provide a very decent sort of service.'

'I think it's very nice here,' she said warmly. She had already eaten her chocolate cake, though he hadn't noticed her do so. She had unbuttoned her red jacket and he saw she had on a grey sweater over a checked shirt rather like the one he himself was wearing. He found himself wondering what her breasts were like— you couldn't tell under those thick clothes—and then chided himself for being a dirty old man: their afternoon together hadn't been like that at all.

'Once cafés weren't at all like this,' she said thoughtfully. 'I remember... Food used to be very drab once, didn't it?'

'I'll say, specially for a few years after the war. No coffee bars then, no Indian or Chinese of course—just workmen's coffee shops and dingy, ladylike little places that did scones. It was that or fish and chips. But of course you'd hardly remember.'

'Oh, but I do,' she said promptly and with a shade of firmness in her voice, as if even this indirect approach to a question were a little too personal. 'I remember it very well.'

Her face was turned away from him as she spoke, and anyway it wasn't easy in the diffused, apricot lighting to get a good look at her, but he suddenly thought for a moment that he had been mistaken and that she was years and years older than he had at first taken her for. Why, she was a woman of almost Helen's age . . . No, no, he corrected himself at once, that was ridiculous. And out at the ruins in broad daylight he had taken her for a young girl, a teenager almost. But he was no longer sure.

Yet when he had paid and they were out again in the almost dark street, she took his arm companionably and said, looking up at him with the fresh, confiding face of an imaginary daughter or favourite niece—

'Now for the cathedral?'

'Yes,' he said. 'Yes, of course.' How could they visit Winchester and not see the cathedral? Yet as she led him purposefully through an alley or two and out into a wide, grassy space with the huge, floodlit cathedral on the far side of it, he felt a sudden, obscure sense of dread, as if somewhere in that vast, palatial mansion of God lay an answer he did not seek, a revelation of which he was afraid.

For a moment he felt consciously alone and afraid as he had not done for many years. The girl's arm was still through his, and he pressed it close to him for comfort. As if she understood what he was feeling, she gave it a reassuring squeeze.

★   ★   ★

They entered the cathedral by the west door. Night had extinguished the windows, but had brought to the huge nave a fragile quality: filled with its own internal but dim light against the blackness without, the church seemed vulnerable, a shrine perilously surviving in a dark world. They moved, a few feet from one another now, towards the high altar with its towering screen, and then into the vaulted recesses behind it. Their feet rang on the stone. They wandered along, occasionally stopping to read a tombstone or marble plaque aloud to one another. Under great canopied tombs like four-poster beds slept those great and powerful princes of the church whom she had mentioned when they had first met. Now their palace was a roofless shell in a dark field occupied only by the birds.

He wanted to say something about this to her: he turned towards her, but she spoke first, in the very words he might have used:

'Isn't it strange,' she said, 'how some things last and some don't? Some buildings like this one last and last—and some just as big or important are allowed to fall down, or even to disappear completely.'

He swallowed, and said with difficulty, but

the dull weight of his unbelief in anything beyond this life lay heavy on him—'It's churches that last. There must be something in it...'

'Not always, they don't. Think of Rievaulx Abbey. It's all just chance really—time and chance happeneth to all man, like it says. But it happens more quickly to some than to others. Some people are very durable, they go on and on. But others have a much briefer, all-of-a-piece time—and then it's over for them. Finished. Gone.' And as if to belie what she had just said, or to show that the idea did not worry her, she stopped momentarily with her face turned directly towards him in the haze of a light concealed behind a pillar. She smiled at him.

In that moment, like a flame igniting in his mind, he knew who she was. He knew. But he also knew that it could not be true. He stood still, holding his breath, the great church pressing on him.

She moved away and began to walk once more in the direction of the Lady Chapel. He saw her moving among the bishops' tombs and hastened after her, through confusing pools of light and darkness. His feet echoed and he tripped at a low step between one chapel and another and nearly fell.

He had lost her. In panic he quickened his step, hastening right round the curve of the apse. Coming out into the great nave he thought he saw her red coat again momentarily, just as he had first seen it in the palace, moving among the pillars, but realised as soon as he opened his mouth to call to her that the coat was a full-length one belonging to a quite different woman. He called nevertheless.

'Sally! Come back, Sally.'

And a young couple who happened to be passing, in soft shoes and anoraks, looked in wonder at this middle-aged man calling out a woman's name in the middle of an empty cathedral.

★　　★　　★

Outside, it had begun to drizzle. He turned his collar up and made his way slowly back to the car, getting lost a couple of times on the way.

He did not look for her along the wet, empty pavements with their deceptive reflections. He did not believe that he would find her and perhaps he did not want to, for if he did and demanded an explanation and she turned out to be just a living girl after all . . . He would rather keep what he had experienced in the church, even if it was over, even if it would never happen to him again and he was alone for ever. Even if it never had happened anywhere but in his own mind.

Once inside the car, with the windows shut against the rain that was now beating quite heavily on them, he sat and thought for a long time. He had not left his suitcase at the pub where he was supposed to be staying. Well, perhaps, as things had turned out, it was just as well.

He started up the engine, checked the petrol gauge and pulled away from the kerb. Signs beckoned and confused him, the ring roads were choked with the homeward-going cars of office workers, the rain streamed down. But by and by he found himself at the main roundabout south of the town. He hesitated only a moment more—then took the road for London.

He should be home in time for a late supper. Helen would be pleased anyway. She would be relieved that he had recovered so quickly from his little aberration. She was sure to be able to whip him up something out of the freezer.

SAINT MATTHEW PASSION

Old Mr Cooper was a widower now, but he managed very well as everyone said.

He knew that they said this—his neighbours, the local traders he had dealt with for years, the parish council, the governors of the school where he had taught for forty years, the other members of the Local History Society committee. He took an innocent, if sardonic pleasure in their approval of him: he was aware that, with his lithe, stooped form and gnome's ears, his spryness (despite the slight deafness of his eighty years) and his churchwarden's collars which time and chance had rendered almost a dandified dress, he was something of a mascot. It was, he occasionally thought, as if the wheel had come full circle, and he was back in the position that had been his long ago when he had been by far the youngest child in his family. His brother and sisters had been nearly grown-up when his elderly parents had had him as an 'afterthought', in the euphemism of the period.

With the pristine clarity of old age, he remembered walking between his tall sisters to St Matthew's each Sunday, wearing his first breeches-suit, conscious of indulgent eyes upon him, conscious of behaving well. The habit had stuck; all his life he had enjoyed behaving well. To show if you were peeved about something, big or small, seemed to him a self-betrayal: he was always a little scornful, and a little amazed too, at men who let their glumness show, stalking about with black looks like so many heroes out of Lawrence; and as for women who moaned... His own mother, bless her, had never let an ill-bred complaint pass her lips, and his dear wife had never been a complainer either. Had she been, of course, he would never have married her. He had prided himself, rightly, on picking a wife with just his own point of view on things. He had known her for some years before their engagement: she had been a teacher at the Elementary School that was then attached to St Matthew's, when he himself had first gone to teach at the Boys' High School.

It had all been very suitable and, really, he had had a wonderfully happy life, he considered, taking things by and large. No children, of course. A pity, that, perhaps, for her, though she had never complained... But, for himself, he saw all the youngsters he needed to during his working hours. And a family of his own would inevitably have taken up much of the precious time he liked to devote to his numerous interests, history in particular. It had all been very satisfactory, really.

As the other members of the History Society liked telling one another, particularly those of them who were associated with the University and had not been born in the town, Mr Cooper's own roots in the place went back further than anyone's. His great-grandfather had been a draper in Massingham when it had still been a small market town. During the nineteenth century the place had grown sooty and large, and the drapery had prospered. Mr Cooper's father had been able to move his family out of the cramped lanes of the city's centre and into a large brick villa in the Marley Park district, where the huge, scattered houses of the old manufacturing families were then being invaded by newer commercial neighbours. The Coopers—Mr Cooper had traced it all in the records that were now in the public library—had been among the first people to subscribe to a new church up there; and when it was completed, resplendent in pinkish, rough-hewn stone from Derbyshire, Mr Cooper senior became one of the church-wardens. The Mr Cooper of today could remember his father, so dignified in his frock coat and his grey, spade beard, passing up and down the aisles with the collection-plate in his hands. He had seemed as exalted and set apart as a priest in a mysterious ritual, to the little boy in his first breeches who had understood already that the honour would be his one day, if he loved God and his mother and father and avoided doing anything silly or common.

He had avoided that, and for many years as a young man, after his father's death, had carried that plate himself, and had sometimes read the lessons and had helped year after year on choir outings and Sunday School picnics. He had even thought, at one time, of entering the Church—it would have pleased his dear mother greatly, that he knew, and cast a further social lustre on the whole family—but a fundamental distaste for any form of mysticism held him back. In his heart of hearts he had no very strong belief in

God or in Eternity, though he would have been
sincerely upset and annoyed if anyone had said
that to him. He was a practising Christian
because he had always been one, and because
from babyhood the imposing stone church had
been as familiar and homelike to him as the
large, comfortable villa in the next street.
Indeed, with its seats upholstered in thick,
hairy, red cushions, its red and mauve floor tiles
that reflected and echoed the windows, its
serious cast-iron heating pipes, and its bits of
beautiful, polished marble that were like the
slabs of cold brawn and chicken-in-aspic that
they had for Sunday evening tea, it was rather
like the villa. As a child Mr Cooper had thought
it all beautiful, all of it. Later, he modified his
view to 'very fine'.

St Matthew's was Church of England, of
course. (That 'of course', which he always
added in his mind, disguised the fact that both
his grandfathers had been Chapel.) But it was
Low Church—decently and sensibly so, in his
view. The Cooper family did not hold with
incantations and lace vestments, and as for
incense such as some of these Anglo-Catholic
churches used, like St Peter's at the bottom of
the hill... In his mind, Mr Cooper always
classed that sort of thing with an unhealthy
intensity of passion in other fields as well. He
did not waste much time on the subject, but it
vaguely seemed to him that men (and women

too, for that matter) who liked their clergymen decked out and chanting at them and nodding and bowing in front of altars were the sort of men who might commit adultery, or suicide, or take to drink or to low company or to reading books like *Lady Chatterley's Lover*. He did not condemn exactly—he was aware, as a teacher of so many years' experience, that it took all sorts to make a world, and some of his brightest boys had been difficult, moody lads—but he knew such passions were not for him, and he was thankful for it.

After he and his wife had been married in St Matthew's, he left its congregation for the first time, for in the early years of their marriage they made their home out at Caulwell where his wife's mother lived. He used to come to work every day on the tram, which swung down the main road past Marley Park on the penultimate lap of its journey. On a promising winter morning, when a red sun was doing its best to lift the smoke from the factory chimneys, he liked the glimpses he caught of St Matthew's spire rising above the bare trees: it linked the present with the past for him in a satisfactory manner. He was very happy in his marriage, but his childhood had been happy too and he liked to keep in touch with it. Both his dear parents were dead now, pressed under marble in the cemetery near the Midland Station, and his brother had been killed in 1917. (He himself, though old enough by then to fight, had missed the war, owing to a slight and fortunate congestion in one lung in his teens. Anyway, someone had to stay at home and prepare the next generation, didn't they?)

His sisters, neither of whom had married, he had persuaded to move to a smaller house at the foot of the hill—a sad but necessary step, as he had explained to them. What a pity things had to change, and the people he had known as a child could not go on being there for ever! There was a new vicar at St Matthew's now, a man of his own age. Even the drapery business was not the same: a cousin had run it since his brother's unfortunate end at Passchendaele—so violent, so uncharacteristic, so unnecessary—and Mr Cooper had a shrewd suspicion that all might not be entirely well in that quarter. Times were hard, there wasn't much money about in Massingham these days; one or two of the big, famous manufacturers had even gone into liquidation, and their mansions at the top of Marley were being divided up or turned into private schools or nursing homes. It was all very sad really, but Mr Cooper was thankful that he himself had had the wits to get into teaching rather than standing behind a shop counter selling lace collars to a generation of women who no longer wanted to wear them. However bleak things looked for the country financially, people always needed teachers. Anyway, he enjoyed it.

300

When Mr Cooper looked back on his life in old age, the period between the two wars when he had been in his prime was less clear than any other time. It seemed to him that he had been busy, and happy, and that was all. But exactly what, outside school hours, he had been busy and happy *at*, he could no longer properly remember. It hadn't been local history. That had not come till after the second war, when they had moved to the compact, well-built house just off the Caulwell Road which was the summit of their desires, the consolidation of his successful career. At the back, it looked up over Marley Park, and so for the first time in twenty years they found themselves again on the fringe of St Matthew's parish. It was like coming home, to him.

Things had changed, of course. But he told himself that he had been prepared for that. The congregations were nothing like what they had been, but what could you expect with so many of the houses, including the one where he had grown up, flats now, and their gardens being torn up for more modern buildings? Mr Cooper was glad at first to think that these new houses would be occupied by new families who would bring fresh life and vigour to the church's ageing congregation, but it didn't turn out quite like that. Families, by and large, didn't go to church as they once had. But as soon as Mr Cooper understood this, he decided that it was nothing to moan about. It was ridiculous the way some of his colleagues at work complained about the younger generation—and presently 'the post-war generation'—as if they were some strange new breed of monster. There was nothing wrong with people that hadn't always been wrong with them, in his opinion, and religion was neither here nor there. If respectable people, today, chose not to go to church, what was that to him? He had always gone his own way and pleased himself.

So, for the second time in his life, Mr Cooper became a member of the parish council of St Matthew's and by and by church-warden; and if anything he attended evensong and weekday services more assiduously than he had when he was young, for if he didn't who would? He felt sorry for the vicar, who otherwise on these occasions might have been all alone in the capacious, silent building, whose red cushions were darkened and rubbed now with use, and whose Derbyshire stone without was darkened too by three quarters of a century of Massingham smoke.

But it was about this time that Mr Cooper began to fear for the past—not to regret it, exactly, but to feel anxious and protective towards it, realising now how easily, if no one cared, it could be dispersed into nothingness, just smoke and dust on the wind. And, because he was a practical man, accustomed to taking decisions and acting upon them, he set himself to keep a watchful eye on the past of the city in general, which, now he came to look closely at it, was being destroyed before his very eyes. In the mid-1950s the City Council produced some grandiose scheme for a ring road and a new shopping centre, and pulled down the eighteenth-century Corn Exchange and a row of battered seventeenth-century cottages before anyone could stop them. That shocked a number of people, who gradually came together, and among them Mr Cooper made new friends, many of them better-educated and more articulate than his old ones. He enjoyed their company, and his historical interests blossomed.

In the 1960s, when he retired at last from the High School, he was one of the founder members of the History Society, and after that he became a well-known figure in the new, resplendent and overheated library that had replaced the Corn Exchange. Encouraged by the history librarian, who extracted funds for such projects from the temporarily affluent Council, he began to publish little monographs on aspects of the city's past: on the Chartist Riots and the Model Factory movement, and on the churches of course. It was only then that he discovered to his surprise—he had never had much eye for architecture—that St Peter's at the bottom of Marley Park, St Peter's with its dubious, High

Church tradition, was actually a far older building than St Matthew's, and had been there when Marley Park was a wooded hunting preserve for the Earls of Northamptonshire.

He was interested in St Peter's by then, in fact he had to be. For in 1959 when the current vicar of St Matthew's had died, poor man, the church had passed into the care of the St Peter's vicar, and Mr Cooper found himself churchwarden of a joint parish called 'St Peter with St Matthew'. He could have wished the names had been put the other way round, and was in any case deeply shocked in some level of his being which seemed in direct communication with his childhood rather than with the present day. He found himself wondering guiltily—guiltily, at his age, and in his position: ridiculous!—what his parents would think if they were to find out his perfidy. But, with his adaptable, present-day self, he set to work to serve the new parson, who was a decent enough fellow in spite of the silly way he piped the Creed and the Responses, and who even—in deference to the susceptibilities of the handful of worshippers he had inherited from St Matthew—cut out some of the notorious bowing and scraping. He was anxious to offend no one, and was inclined to make remarks about 'all pulling together in this crisis' and other muscular metaphors. He appeared— or affected—to believe that the present lack of mass enthusiasm for church-going was a mere passing phase, a Valley of the Shadow as it were, and that if he, Mr Cooper and the other Faithful Few could get through 'these difficult times' the churches would once again be packed to the doors.

He was fairly young, so Mr Cooper forgave him his misplaced enthusiasm, but thought him a fool and rather vulgar too. On the Sundays when, on waking, Mr Cooper remembered that matins would be held at St Peter's, his heart sank very slightly, while on those mornings when he knew the service was to be back at St Matthew's in the proper place it lifted, like a bird about to take off in flight from one high drain-head to another. Communion concerned him less: he rarely went to Communion. All his life, without him voicing the fact to himself, it had seemed to him very slightly disgusting, all that messing about with wine and biscuits. Unnecessary, anyway.

So his life continued on its even keel, on into the 1970s, past his dear wife's death, into the time when a woman sent by the City Council came regularly to clean his house, and talkative women young enough to be his daughters or granddaughters gushed over him at History Society meetings and he would grow happily loquacious over the sandwiches. Sometimes he still lectured in schools, or to WIs or Working Men's Institutes, and on these occasions his friend the librarian, now Head Librarian to the

City and grown rich and grand, would send a special car for him. He supposed it was on account of these lectures that people he did not know were always greeting him in the street. With a gentle, sardonic amusement he realised that he was becoming a local institution, like the Castle, or the new shopping centre (now stigmatised as one of the worst examples of post-war town planning in Britain) or like the City football team.

He was getting older, but he was hardly aware of it. He felt now that this pleasant, if slightly unreal life, might go on for ever. And nor, in spite of his duties as churchwarden, was he fully aware that St Matthew's was getting older also. He had known and identified with it for so long that he did not really see it at all. To him, it was still a fine and worthy place.

But others did see that it was getting older, among them the Church Commissioners. They saw that there were small holes high up in some of the stained-glass windows, and damp patches low down behind the yellow-varnished pews. They saw that a blocked gutter outside had left a cascade of green slime down the side of one of the buttresses, and that elsewhere on the roof lead flashings were lifting after close on a hundred years of sun and frost, and letting rain seep through to the timbers beneath. They saw the grime on the Derbyshire stone, and the broken and boarded window in the vestry, and

306

the dead leaves and litter and rank grass choking the corners of the church precinct from one year's end to another. The old part-time gardener had died in 1969, and the vicar seemed to concentrate his own muscular efforts on tidying up round St Peter's, which was on view to the main road and had a few eighteenth- and nineteenth-century gravestones to set it off.

But most of all the Church Commissioners saw that here was a church that was simply not needed any more. Its useful life had been brief, for a church, but they saw that it was over. They did not actually state that this was a building erected by a worldly and transient generation for their own satisfaction and that it is thus that the world's pomp has always passed away. Nor did they spell out the fact that to build of durable materials does nothing to insure that the ideas behind the buildings will last. They did not say that, wherever Eternal Life and Truth are to be found, they are not today considered likely to be housed in the sham-baronial style of 1881. But they announced their intention of pulling St Matthew's down and selling the land, all the same.

When he knew the matter was on the agenda for dicussion at the next History Society meeting, Mr Cooper almost looked forward to it. Now, he thought, was an opportunity for them all to show their collective power, to get up a petition, organise an exhibition, write to Sir

John Betjeman... It would be like the Corn Exchange all over again, except that this time they would win, because they had become so much more adroit at fighting ignorant bureaucracies than they had been in the 1950s, and anyway the tide of public opinion was now running with them. People were absolutely sick of demolition and characterless redevelopments. They would have no trouble in getting half Massingham up in arms about St Matthew's fate. As he came to the meeting he was already happily planning the publicity leaflet on the church's interesting history—with a monograph on the long-defunct Cooper draper business—which he and the librarian would produce between them.

But it didn't turn out like that, not like that at all. The matter was duly raised, but as the discussion of it progressed—or rather, failed to progress—he realised with dawning incredulity that, in this instance, no one felt as he did. Not one of them, it seemed, thought it really mattered if St Matthew's *was* pulled down.

He tried, in his best school-teacher's manner, to rally them.

'You say the church is "typical of many others". But—Mr Chairman, excuse me—surely it is precisely this sort of unthinking, piecemeal destruction of typical features of old Massingham that we are here to prevent?'

They still seemed unconvinced. One of the

bright young women even remarked that she didn't think they were really meant to be a conservation society at all, were they?

The Librarian, who was perhaps the only one who realised that Mr Cooper had been both christened and married in St Matthew's, said kindly: 'After all, Mr Cooper, you will admit that it isn't a very distinguished example of its period. If it was by Pugin, now, or Champneys . . . But it isn't.'

'I think it's ghastly, actually!' said another woman. 'All those blood-coloured tiles and that cheap, purplish glass—And at least if they sell the site to a developer they'll be able to use the money to put St Peter's in order. Actually I went and had a look at the proposals for that the other day. They're rather good, I think—' And the conversation, in spite of Mr Cooper, veered inexorably to the subject of the restoration of St Peter's to its Queen Anne wholeness, and stayed there.

After the meeting, the librarian offered as usual to drop Mr Cooper home. But this evening Mr Cooper refused the lift and went off alone, although it was a cold evening and a mist was coming down.

'Poor old boy,' said the librarian in the pub afterwards. 'I'm afraid he's a bit upset about that church. Perhaps we should have realised he would be and offered to make some token protest.'

'Oh, I don't think we should do *that*,' said the chairman firmly. 'After all, we want the Council to go on taking us seriously, don't we, and not treat us as a bunch of people who protest about anything and everything. And since we're concentrating on saving the warehouses by the canal at the moment . . .'

'I feel sure Mr Cooper will pop up again quite spry at the next meeting,' said a woman comfortably. 'You know how full of energy he is for his age, bless him, and how many different irons he has in the fire. Next time he comes he's sure to be on lace-workers or the gas company or the date on the Infirmary being wrong—you know how he is.'

But Mr Cooper did not pop up again quite spry at the next meeting. For one thing, he was hurt and offended with the Society for the moment. And, for another, he had caught rather a bad cold the night he had walked home alone, and could not seem to shake it off.

Or perhaps it would be more accurate to say that he did not try to shake it off. For some years now he had suffered intermittently from bronchitis in the winter—a recurrence, he believed, telescoping time in his mind, of his old lung trouble. He had become adept at going to bed and calling the doctor at the first sign of it, and indeed, since his wife had died, the doctor had taken to putting him into the hospital and keeping him there till the trouble passed,

310

interludes which Mr Cooper had really quite enjoyed. It had vaguely reminded him of being ill with croup as a small boy, with his mother and aunts and sisters all making a fuss of him. But this time he didn't feel like going to hospital. He didn't call the doctor at all.

Days and nights went by in an uncertain sequence. Sometimes he lay awake in his bed, propped up and coughing, and the pain in his chest was sharp, at other times he had dropped off in his chair in the daytime, an old man's habit which he had always despised, and woke feeling ill, and confused about the day or the hour. On the days his home help came in he attempted to smother his cough and to pretend to eat the unappetising food she prepared for him. Fortunately, he thought, she was a stupid woman, and not much given to awkward questions.

One day he felt a little better and ventured out. His feet carried him automatically in the direction of St Matthew's, and when he reached the corner opposite to it he was unprepared for what he saw.

The roof was already half bare, a skeleton of ribbed timbers. And the tower, that interesting amalgam of Norman and Perpendicular to which his father had generously given a peal of bells—that tower was already being dismantled.

'So it's happening already,' he said to himself, with the slow, painful bewilderment of a man who has never really believed that death is true till now. He stood on the corner looking at the ruined building for a long time, and then he turned round and shuffled back to his silent, tidy home.

For the very first time he sincerely missed his wife, but because it was not part of his creed to miss people he kept saying to himself both silently and aloud: 'I'm glad she's not here to see this. I'm glad for her sake that she went before,' though as a matter of fact his wife had never particularly liked St Matthew's. She had thought it gloomy, and had once or twice dared to say so.

A few days later the librarian, becoming anxious about Mr Cooper's unanswered telephone, attempted to call on him. He saw a light on and heard a wireless playing softly, but gained no answer to his knock. After some hesitation, and consultation with a colleague, he called the police and they forced the front door. Mr Cooper, dressed as always in his dark suit and churchwarden's collar, sat almost upright in his wing chair before the gas fire, but he was clearly dead and seemed to have been so for a little while.

Quite a lot of people came to the funeral, of course. It was at the new crematorium out on the Caulwell Road where (since the old cemetery by the station was crowded) the bodies of the City worthies were now most often reduced to smoke and dust with instantaneous ease. The vicar of St Peter's, who conducted the service in his usual erratic, intense style of which Mr Cooper had disapproved, gave an address on the theme 'The Lord giveth and the Lord taketh away'. Some of those present thought that a silly comment on a man who had died at eighty-two, a ripe old age for anyone. But the librarian, whose way home took him past the corner where St Matthew's was now fast disintegrating into an empty, mud-churned site, thought otherwise. He reflected that the text had, after all, been singularly appropriate.

THE OTHER RAILWAY CHILDREN

When I was growing up my mother and I lived on the fringes of Kentish Town in North London, but we called it 'Highgate Rise' because my mother thought it sounded nicer.

This was about 1950, long before such districts had become visible to the kind of people who want to live there now. When mother and I lived on the edge of it, the holes left in the terraces by incidental bombs were still open to the sky, and that sky was still tainted by the smoke of the steam trains that ran over and through and under the district, making it an unattractive one for people who could afford something better.

It was not a *bad* district my mother used to assure the occasional relative-in-law visiting suspiciously from the country: not bad, merely 'a bit slummy in parts', going down rather, not what it had once been of course ... 'not really what I would have wanted for us in ideal circumstances, but—' and here mother always assumed the conscientiously bright and matter-of-fact air considered suitable at the time for war-widows—'After all, we're quite all right up here, a good half-mile from Kentish Town, quite near Parliament Hill really and the air's much cleaner up here. Margie and I don't often go into Kentish Town, actually: just on Saturdays, to go to Daniels or BB Evans...' My mother, by insisting too much, ended up sounding as if she were apologising for something, when, if she were right, no apology was necessary.

The ostensible reasons she and I had moved back to London after the war were, firstly, to be near my grandmother, secondly that my mother might have more choice of jobs (she was a teacher) and thirdly that I might, when I was older, attend the Camden School for Girls, which was said to be 'mixed' socially but 'very sound academically'. However I was years away from the age at which the Camden might accept me, and the real reason for our return to the City from the impeccable air of Wiltshire (where my dead father's family lived, ensconced in a conviction of rural superiority) was that my mother was a Londoner by birth and upbringing and, whatever she pretended, felt most herself there.

She had sisters and cousins scattered all round unattractive, comfortable inner suburbs, and on Saturdays and Sundays or in school holidays we would take one of the Secret Railway trains that ran in hidden loops between these suburbs, describing great arcs through half-perceived hinterlands to link places otherwise unconnected: you could go from Frognal, by leafy Hampstead, to Dalston junction where 'the slums' reputedly were; from Richmond in the sunset west to Barking in the far east. It was even said that you could go to the Isle of Dogs, which I imagined to be a kind of Hesperides.

Even then the several lines concerned, with their unobtrusive chocolate-brown stations situated between shops or under bridges, were known collectively as the Secret Railway. Their real name was and is the North London Railway, I believe; but, omitting to get themselves incorporated into the District or Metropolitan system at some crucial date earlier in the century, the lines had languished, gradually declining in usefulness, known only to local people. They had missed suburban electrification too: small black tank engines of antique design still hauled their few carriages.

Their stations had all the appurtenances of the full-blown Victorian railway—Waiting Rooms, including sometimes a separate one for Ladies, cavernous lavatories, station masters' offices, coal tips, water towers, sidings. And yet their total mileage can only have been a fraction of that covered by the tube lines that had superseded them, and their routes mapped dead social patterns. True, mother found it useful for visiting her sister May in Leytonstone, but who in Frognal, even in my childhood, wished to go to Dalston Junction? Our own station, Kentish Town, was particularly spectral, since the main line north from Euston also ran through it, and its rustic-wooden walls were ornamented with posters advertising the Flying Scot or the air of Carlisle, but the idea that you could actually travel from here to there was almost entirely a fantasy, for hardly any of the main-line trains stopped there.

★   ★   ★

Recently I travelled on the Secret Railway again. I had not been on it for well over twenty years. As in a dream the line was the same and yet not the same, of today and yet of more than one past period also. As in a dream too, chronology seemed to have become confused and compressed; it was as if I was travelling through the memories of more than one generation.

The steam engines were gone, of course, and some of the old stations had been reduced to boxy ciphers of their former selves, little more than bus shelters. But others still spread their sooty brickwork and wooden footbridges enticingly beyond the rain-blurred glass. The wet soaked into the old, decorative boards as it had always done, a hundred years of rain gradually turning the timber back into a natural perishable thing like a forest tree. The waste lands beside the tracks that had fascinated and repelled me as a child were still there, and so were the rain-pocked reservoirs that were like a great eastern sea. ('That's the Lea Valley, Margie.' Oh infinite world!)

The enamel station names were still there, in the colours of a long-extinct company, and even some of the weak gas lights, prisoners with their little chains; but already in my childhood these things had been obsolescent, at variance with what I knew as Now. For even then a ride on the Secret Railway had brought me fleeting whiffs of a London that was past or passing: the train would rattle by tiny backyards ('Are those the slums, Mummy?') where zinc baths hung on nails, or would rush abruptly from tunnels to afford an abrupt, overhead view of a street with trams, stalls with flaring lights, before extinguishing the vision again in further walls of velvet soot.

317

Now, as I sat there as an adult, racked through those same tunnels, over and under those unchanging iron bridges, where buildings wheeled and rose and died, time receded in vertiginous perspective through the unwashed train windows. It was not merely my childhood that met the train, ran alongside it and swung away again, it was my childhood's own half-perceived past, some undated but ancient point beyond the rain where alien people in heavy dark clothes led lives weighted with unreachable meaning. Then the train was out into another landscape, and I had lost their trace again.

★   ★   ★

'Mummy, who are those children out there?' I had been wondering for some time, but had not asked. Now, as the train was drawing into Kentish Town and my mother began gathering up our belongings, with a child's sense of mistiming it occurred to me to put the question. Perhaps I hoped that if I distracted her from what she was doing it wouldn't be Kentish Town next and the journey wouldn't have to end.

'What children? . . . Put your pixie hood on, Margie, it's parky outside.'

I balanced my disliked pixie hood on top of my head, and continued: 'Who are they, Mummy?'

'Who are who?'

'The children. Outside the window. Only they've gone now.' We were drawing into the platform. Their tense, pale faces had been replaced by those of the Bisto Kids, careering archly on a full-sized hoarding, and at once their reality began to fade: I was not sure I had really seen them.

'There aren't any children,' said my mother firmly. 'Put on your hood, I said.'

★   ★   ★

In the daylight, I never saw them. Only in the dark, on the homeward journey from Leytonstone, and only intermittently, bobbing there in space beyond the train windows.

'Mummy, the children are there again... look.'

My mother looked. At that moment we entered a tunnel.

'It's just your reflection,' she said when we came out. 'Look! There's your green jersey and there's your hair ribbon. Did you think it was another child?' Fondly.

I was no longer sure. It was true, I could see my own reflection as Mother spoke. But a moment later the two—or was it three children?—were back instead; one of them, a girl, seemed to be mouthing something at me.

'Look,' I said without conviction. 'There they

319

are again.'

'I've told you,' said my mother with unyielding, teacher's patience. 'That's just your own reflection.' She bent over her knitting.

I stared at the white face framed in untidy hair that seemed to be speaking to me, and it stared back, mute now. Perhaps it *was* me? With a child's uncertain self-image, I was prepared to believe it, since my mother seemed so definite about it. I was even prepared to believe that the other two smaller children— there did seem to be two—appearing uncertainly behind her, were somehow variants on myself as well: it was confusing, with so much thick glass, and the lights from the streets we were now passing throwing counter-shadows. One of the two seemed to be a small boy in a balaclava helmet like Kentish Town children wore. His nose was running. The other appeared very young, a baby really.

Sometimes the children seemed to be crying, mouths gaping soundlessly against the cold, dark air. At other times they seemed to be jeering at me, the untidy little girl especially, as some rough children in Highgate Road once had when I was out buying a loaf of bread for my mother. I developed a phobia about the Railway Children—as I confusedly called them in my mind, having E. Nesbit's book at home—and wouldn't sit by the window on the return journey. And sometimes I didn't see them at all.

320

'They weren't there, they've gone,' I told my mother confidently as we walked hand in hand from the station back up the Highgate Road to gentility and home.

Her reply was non-committal, but the next time we were in Leytonstone for tea I heard her engaging Auntie May in a muttered conversation about 'too lively an imagination' and 'night fears' and having 'managed to deal with it'. And Auntie May—she taught Gym in Chingford—said more loudly that it was much the best thing, to deal with them, and that everyone knew only children tended to be prone to these things.

'It isn't my fault she's an only child, May,' said my mother rather sharply, and I felt sorry for my mother who was usually so cheerful, and cross with Auntie May for making her sound like that.

On the journey home we had reached the open expanse of the reservoirs when I became aware that the faces were, after all, there again in the windy wet dark, soundlessly weaving and jerking with the train's motion. Because they were reflections (but of what, of what—?) they were transparent and patchy like some ill-exposed negative. Many years later I saw a nineteenth-century glass-negative of a family of beggar children rescued by Dr Barnardo, and for a breathless second or two recaptured exactly the impression of those children beside the

321

train, till adult consciousness erased the perception and I found myself dating the children's clothes and noting how poised and stilted the little group looked.

In childhood, however, there can be no such flight into inessentials. I screamed in fear and buried my head in my mother's lap.

'Margie, stop this! There's nothing there. Look—' She reached over to pull down the window by its leather strap. I screamed again, clutching hysterically at her arm. Fortunately South Tottenham station saved us. The children didn't seem to like stations. They were creatures of the railway waste lands: they lived—I was by now convinced—in the narrow strips of sodden, rank grass between the line and the back of the next gardens, scrap yards or allotment; they roamed the cindery wastes of disused sidings, where empty brick buildings raised their blank or broken windows and where, on a few scummy, water-filled bomb craters, pieces of rubbish floated in black, cryptic shapes. And like these forlorn territories of theirs, the children exuded menace but also pain, physical and spiritual. Was that snot or blood that ran continually from the small boy's nose? And why did the girl, who seemed to be the ring-leader, have one hand and arm in bandages—

Mother and I moved our seats, and quite a lot of people got on at South Tottenham. The children were wary of other people. They went away and did not come back, that time.

We did not go to Leytonstone for several weeks after that. Mother said the weather was 'rather bad' and we would wait till the days were longer. I was unfamiliar with this expression, and it puzzled me rather. Meanwhile, till time should thin and elongate itself like a piece of elastic, she bought me a bottle of Parrish's Chemical Food, which I was supposed to drink through a straw because otherwise it would blacken my teeth. It did not, but being (I suppose) largely composed of iron, it made me constipated, so my mother purchased an equally large bottle of Syrup of Figs. Thus, encouraged over the telephone by her sister May, she did her conscientious best to improve my physical and mental state.

My grandmother said I ought to be wearing long stockings. Bare knees in winter weren't right—she's always said so, particularly for a highly-strung child like me.

With my attention thus morbidly directed to my own state of health, I wilted consciously and gave myself airs. I was almost disappointed, when, on the next return from Leytonstone through the dusk of early spring, the children were not there. I actually gazed into the mauve, light-pricked twilight trying to see them.

I did see them again, once, weeks later, but this time I was unprepared.

It was in Kentish Town High Street one

Saturday. Mother and I had been, perhaps, buying fish from Carters, and possibly a new Enid Blyton book for me from Bishop and Hamilton, and now maybe we were buying some narcissi from a barrow by the station when suddenly I saw them. But this time they were real.

The two bigger ones, the girl and the boy, were dragging after a youngish, drab-looking woman who was pushing the baby in a dreadful old pram. The baby was sucking a dummy. The little boy's nose was running as usual, and he seemed to be crying. The girl was crying more loudly and apparently angrily. She beat her hands, both bandaged and unbandaged, against her mother's arms. The woman thrust her aside and pushed the pram on. She seemed not to be looking at Kentish Town at all, but to have her pale eyes set on some dreary inner vista. Her meagre face, with its forlorn mouth and sharp little chin, was like the girl's; it seemed inadequate on an adult, as if she had been precipitated into that category and it was quite beyond her capabilities.

They were far off, and I could not hear what the girl was crying out, but they were my Railway Children.

I did not point them out to my mother. But when we got home I cried and refused my lunch and said I felt sick. Later, to console myself, I purloined and ate quite a lot of sweets.

I overheard my mother saying on the telephone to Auntie Lily, her more sympathetic sister in Brondesbury, 'I'm afraid I really will have to take a firm line with her . . .' Such were the stock phrases of that time. We have others now, but it makes little real difference for the children themselves.

★   ★   ★

As an only child and one avid for further information about the way adults spent their time, I was an inveterate eavesdropper, a reader of anything left lying about. Recently I had begun to read the old-fashioned local newspaper we took, not because I was really interested in most of the petty crime, weddings, whist drives and Council decisions it described, but because I enjoyed the sensation of being given a glimpse into others' obscure lives, as when from a moving train we look momentarily down into a garden or yard or in at a lighted window.

So was it perhaps in a newspaper, local or national, that I read something?—A story that abruptly made sense to me, fusing with my own perceptions to form a pattern of menacing clarity? I have sometimes, as an adult, played with the idea, imagining plausible headlines, trying to convince myself that I once read them—

Children Dead by Railway Line—Mother Sought

Or (in the local paper)—
How Did These Babes Die? North London Line
Mystery
Then, maybe a day or maybe many days later, they said something like—
'I was Desperate,' says Train-Babes Mother
Three Children Flung from Train: 'I did it,'
Mother confesses
Or simply—
Kentish Town Mother Murders Three
(The invention of such banners is, today, my job; the machine runs smoothly.)

It is all quite plausible, and perhaps, even now, if I were to take a train—a modern tube train—to the Newspaper Library in Colindale, and search industriously into the appropriate years, I would come at last to such black confirmatory headlines, familiar as in a repetitive dream, across paper not yellowed as old newspapers are supposed to be, but white from being so long in a shut file, a memory untouched, its content of fear unworn by use and time.

Perhaps. But perhaps not. Really, I do not know if I learnt the story from a newspaper at all. Perhaps I merely gleaned it from some overheard conversation between my mother and grandmother or my mother and a sister. Perhaps, even, I misheard part of a tale and invented the rest from my too-lively imagination (aided by Parrish's Food and Syrup of Figs)

326

and an embryo journalist's need to turn diffuse, uncertain experience into a coherent drama.

But from whence the experience? Why the fear, the obsession, why the children out there, anyway?

Adult reason suggests no answer to this, unless it is the commonsense possibility that in fact I had heard or read of some gruesome local tragedy *before* I embarked upon my private dramas in the train, and that memory has simply rearranged the sequence into a more artistically meaningful pattern.

I know this is the most likely supposition. But I do not *feel* it to be true. Memory may be fallible, invents, suppresses and disguises, but the basic sense of an event or period remains. And imprinted into my memory is the sense of swelling fear and foreboding, of a horror yet to come, some obscenity from that other world of slums and not-nice people from which my mother so resolutely turned her face. And when it came, or when I knew—when I saw or heard or vaguely understood that some alarming event had taken place and was now past, then the fear subsided again. I knew; and it was over.

The human brain, a young neurologist I was interviewing told me once, does not seem as far as we can tell at present, like a machine for creating thought waves. 'It looks,' he said ruminatively, 'more like a sophisticated kind of receiving set . . .'

★   ★   ★

Recently, as I said, I travelled on the Secret Railway again. 'The down-train to childhood', I thought, storing it away as a nice neat phrase to use sometime. I half-hoped, as I sat down (on a new, inferior and bus-like seat) that through some enduring brick arch or from a high embankment with a view over muddy playing fields, I would glimpse again the world as it seemed when I was young, pregnant with strangeness, reverberating with others' destinies. Perhaps a dog, galloping, one ear blown back, across a desolate park—perhaps a dangerous-looking child running madly away from the fence as the train approaches—would catch me up and carry me away with them into another place. Perhaps in a dingy, lighted window as we creaked past, destructively near, the curtain would pull aside, exposing at last to my dazed eyes the truth about other people's lives. As an inexperienced child I had seen death beyond the train's darkened windows. What might I note, now that I knew so infinitely more?

But the train simply trundled in its wide arc across districts without meaning, and I understood at last that there were no mysteries left to be penetrated. All I could learn, I knew.

328

And if there was something more I, personally, would never learn it.

Photoset, printed and bound in Great Britain by REDWOOD BURN LIMITED, Trowbridge, Wiltshire